PETERSBURG

Out of the Trenches

By

James W. Wensyel, Colonel, USA (Ret.)

 BURD STREET PRESS

All photographs courtesy of U.S. Army Military History Institute, Carlisle Barracks, Pennsylvania; photographic reproductions by Dr. Gerald A. Leidy; and maps drawn by Dave Weaver.

This Burd Street Press publication
was printed by
Beidel Printing House, Inc.
63 West Burd Street
Shippensburg, PA 17257-0152 USA

In respect for the scholarship contained herein, the acid-free paper used in this book meets the guidelines for permanence and durability of the Committee on Production Guidelines for Book Longevity of the Council on Library Resources.

For a complete list of available publications
please write
Burd Street Press
Division of White Mane Publishing Company, Inc.
P.O. Box 152
Shippensburg, PA 17257-0152 USA

Library of Congress Cataloging-in-Publication Data

Wensyel, James W., 1928-
      Petersburg : out of the trenches / by James W. Wensyel.
          p.   cm.
      Includes bibliographical references.
      ISBN 1-57249-139-6 (alk. paper)
          1. Petersburg (Va.)--History--Siege, 1864-1865--Fiction.
      2. Virginia--History--Civil War, 1861-1865--Fiction.   I. Title.
      PS3573.E563P4   1998
      813'.54--dc21   98-35166
                                                                                CIP

PRINTED IN THE UNITED STATES OF AMERICA

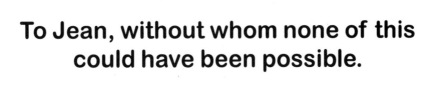

To Jean, without whom none of this could have been possible.

Contents

Illustrations

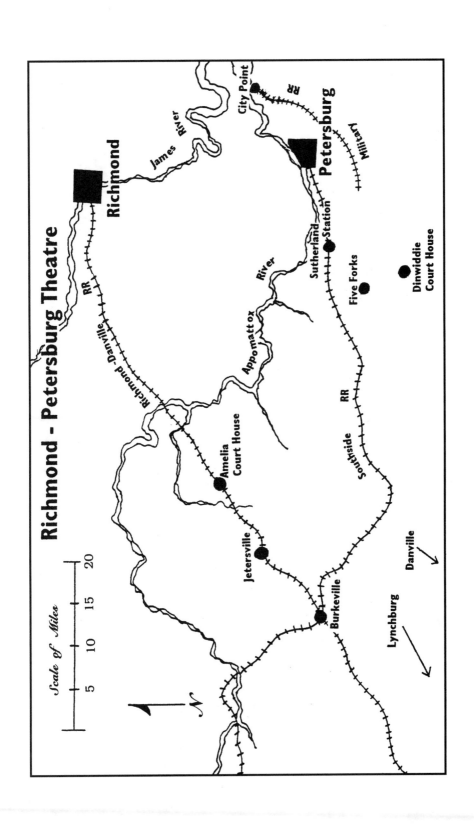

Richmond - Petersburg Theatre

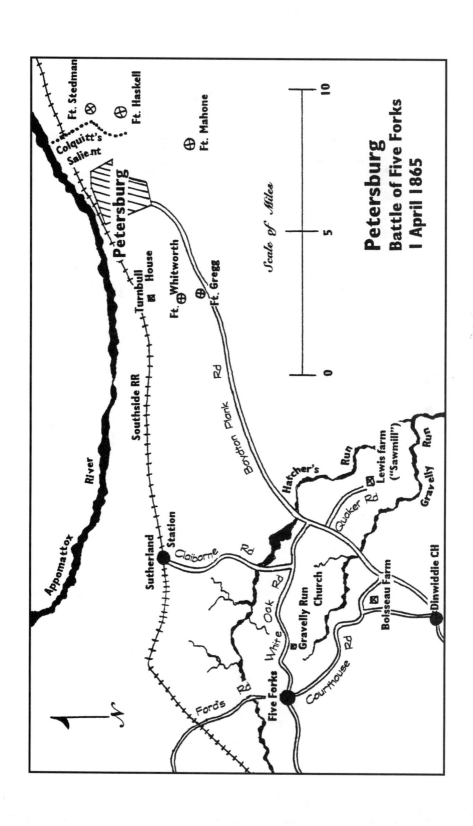

Petersburg
Battle of Five Forks
1 April 1865

Scale of Miles

0   5   10

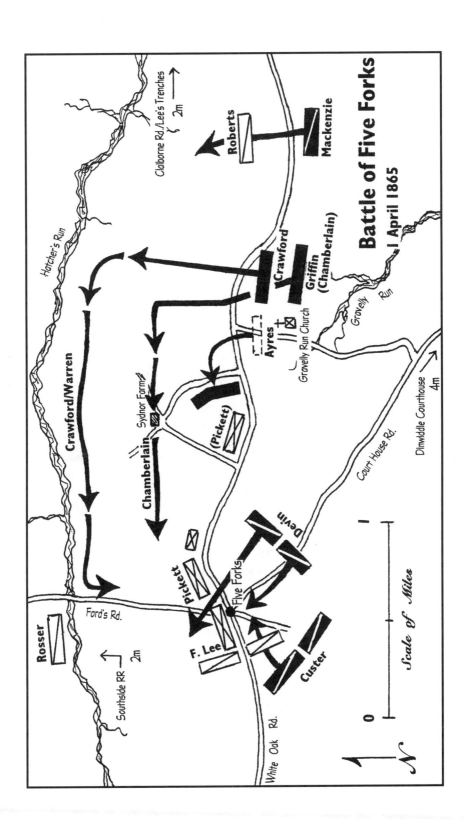

Battle of Five Forks
1 April 1865

Foreword

THE WAR

March 1865. In Washington an overcast sky begins to clear, the temperature inches upward, and the winter officially ends.

It's been a hard winter. Ice still rims the Potomac above the city, and a hundred miles to the south Union and Confederate soldiers shiver in the Richmond-Petersburg trenches or huddle around skimpy dugout fires. There are no trees along the battle lines and, with Petersburg firewood costing five Confederate dollars a stick, hungry, cold, sick Confederate riflemen shiver and have little heart for the war, now nearly four years old.

It has been a terribly costly war. Nearly 1.3 million Americans under arms; $2.5 million drained from the economy each day; more than 600,000 Americans already dead. And the end not yet in sight. The Confederacy still stretches from Virginia to Texas. The tide, however, has turned. The first two years of the war saw one Southern victory after another. After the Union victory at Gettysburg, however, Union generals won battle after battle. Major General George H. Thomas destroyed Confederate Lieutenant General John B. Hood's army at Nashville. Major General William T. Sherman burned a 50-mile swath across the Confederate heartland and now is poised less than 150 miles below Richmond. Major General Philip H. Sheridan decimated Lieutenant General Jubal A. Early's Confederates in the Shenandoah.

Only in northern Virginia have Union armies failed to win a clear-cut victory. There Lieutenant General Ulysses S. Grant, now in his twelfth month commanding all the Union armies, has forced Lieutenant General Robert E. Lee's Confederate Army of Northern Virginia back, back, back to the gates of the Southern capital. That far but no more. For nine months now Grant's armies have been stopped by the Confederate lines stretching from Richmond to Petersburg, some thirty miles to the south. If the war is to be won, Lee's army must be beaten. Otherwise, it will go on fighting. And so will the South. Grant knows that; everyone knows that.

Union and Confederate trenches before Richmond and Petersburg stretch nearly fifty desolate miles; jagged, rugged, bloody crescents cut, as if by a bayonet, across the red clay of Virginia. A caldron of misery and death. Perhaps 42,000 Union soldiers killed, wounded, or taken prisoner in fighting there with little to show for it.

The bitter winter weather slowed the fighting, but now winter has passed. Spring rains wash blood from the rich earth of the Shenandoah. Fruit trees blossom. In Richmond's Hollywood Cemetery, where Major General James E. B. "Jeb" Stuart (shot down at Yellow Tavern in '64) lies among row upon row of other Confederate dead, mourning doves sing a plaintive song, but the cardinals' perky "wet year," "wet year," herald spring. Below the cemetery the James River again flows free and clear past Belle Isle and Libby Prison, both crammed with Union prisoners.

The roads are drying. In both armies blacksmiths are hard at work; cavalry will be active soon, scouting, probing, skirmishing. Then down the long dusty roads and across the fields and wood lots will come the infantry. The hard fighting will begin again. In this the most critical spring in the long war.

In Washington, Abraham Lincoln, two weeks into his second term as President, clears away last minute business, eagerly anticipating visiting Grant's field headquarters at City Point, below Petersburg. It will be a welcome personal break Lincoln badly needs. Although he's very tired, he'll enjoy being with Grant and with Grant's army. Grant and Lincoln respect and like each other. With Grant's predecessors (Major General George B. McClellan, Major General Joseph Hooker, so many more) Lincoln had never felt at ease. Once, tired of prodding McClellan into action, he'd asked, "If you don't plan to use the army, General, might I borrow it for a couple weeks?" Grant needs no prodding; when the fields and woods dry, he'll fight. Lincoln dreads the blood bath sure to come. Perhaps, sitting with Grant, he can offer a suggestion or two for the spring's campaign and set some ground rules for the peace he hopes it will bring. How many springs he'd hoped would be the one to end the war. But this spring, March 1865, victory seems almost certain.

Already the year has seen several peace overtures. In January U.S. Senator Francis P. Blair publicly suggested that the North and South stop fighting each other to meet a perceived common threat, French-supported Emperor Maximilian in Mexico. Nothing came of the idea, but Lincoln allowed Blair to go to Richmond where Blair encouraged Confederate President Jefferson Davis to seek other ways to end the war. Following Blair's suggestion, three Confederate peace commissioners entered Union Major General George E. Meade's lines. As the emissaries' carriage rolled across the bloody ground between the trenches, Blue and Gray soldiers stood on their parapets, ignoring the threat of sharpshooters capable of killing at more than 900 yards, to cheer their mission.

At Grant's urging Lincoln met with the Southern leaders, but the meeting accomplished nothing. Lincoln desperately wishes peace but must insist on two conditions: restoration of the Union and the end of slavery, two conditions the South cannot accept. Following the aborted meeting, Davis denounced its failure, appointed Robert E. Lee General-in-Chief of all Confederate armed forces, and urged preparations to renew the fighting.

Then, in early March, Union Major General Edward O. C. Ord and Confederate Lieutenant General James Longstreet, personal friends, jointly proposed a military commission to work out an armistice, and Lee wrote Grant suggesting that he and Grant meet to discuss such an arrangement. When Grant forwarded Lee's letter to Washington, however, he was officially reminded that he is a soldier, not a diplomat, and may meet with Lee only to accept Lee's surrender. Grant, not surprised at the response, notified Lee and returned to his own plans for the spring campaign.

The soldiers, who must bear the brunt of the fighting, also realize that the war will end only after more fighting, and in their dugouts make their own preparations for the spring campaign.

"All that truck of you'rn," advise the veterans. "If it won't fit in your bed roll, leave it behind. Else you'll drop it 'side the road a few miles up the way."

Informal truces ("We'll not fire on you, Johnny, if you don't fire on us"; "Swap you tobacco for some coffee, Yank") the men have worked out among themselves also soon must end. Until it does, however, commerce between the armies continues. A Union officer calls to his Confederate counterpart, "Nothing doing along my line, Johnny. Anything new with you?"

"Nothing new here, Yank; nothing new here. Reckon it's gotta go on."

RICHMOND

In Richmond, swollen now to more than 100,000 inhabitants, citizens sell personal goods for scarce food, clothing, and medicine. The Confederate economy has slumped steadily for several years. In 1861 a U.S. gold dollar was worth $1.03 Confederate; now it's worth $60 Confederate; by April that will soar to $70.

In backwater areas of the South food still is relatively plentiful and nowhere near as expensive as in Richmond where a pound of coffee (if available) costs $45 Confederate, a pound of tea $100, a pound of butter $25, a barrel of flour $1,250. A plug of tobacco costs $20–$25. As a Confederate private only receives $17, that staple of the Southern diet is issued free to military personnel. Bacon costs $20 a pound, beef $15 a pound, shad $50 a pair, a live hen $50. Substitutes: corncob ashes for soda; sorghum for sugar; wheat, rye, chestnuts, sweet potatoes for coffee, develop as the need arises. Attendants at the Chimborazo military hospital roast rats, insisting that they taste much like young squirrels. Wounded patients are hungry but, having seen rats foraging on the battlefields, aren't hungry enough for that.

In early March, Davis ordered the Confederate government archives purged with the remaining documents sent to safer North Carolina. Heavier stores, reserve guns, and ammunition followed with food, clothing, and ammunition posted along Lee's possible lines of retreat. Anticipating the need to move his family, Davis has been quietly selling his own family's furniture, glass, silver, paintings, and clothing: an old dress, a silk gown, lace, silks, and gloves.

"Starvation Parties," parodies of a social life now long gone, are popular. Men appear in patched, ill-fitting coats; ladies in makeshift gowns. Food isn't available, but James River water "punch" is served in ornate bowls; a Negro fiddler, a drummer, and a piano player provide music; young officers attend for a few hours; and couples dance and for a little while almost forget the war.

THE TRENCHES

Any break from life in the trenches is welcome. Dug deep in the red Virginia clay, the fighting trenches are topped with heavy timbers and lined with firing slits and steps. Behind them are zigzag connecting trenches or timber-covered ways leading to somewhat safer shelters, called "bombproofs." Dug deeper into the ground and buttressed with heavy timbers, sheet iron, and dirt, most of the bombproofs have fireplaces and crude sleeping quarters.

Perhaps 500 yards ahead of Lee's fighting trenches, give or take a bit because of the terrain or the nearness of Grant's lines, are picket posts, a loosely connected series of squad-size strong points to warn of an enemy attack and to give regiments time to rally in the fighting trenches. No fires on the picket lines; not much shelter either. And its soldiers are always exposed to enemy artillery and mortar fire, to snipers, to sudden probing raids.

Time and Union sharpshooters permitting, in front of their picket lines Confederate soldiers have anchored closely spaced, sharp-pointed saplings. Buried in the ground and their points facing the enemy, they're called "abatis." In places the abatis have given way to more formidable "chevaux-de-frise": long timbers, their tips sharpened to points and all bound together with telegraph wire then set on end as a barrier. Separate chevaux-de-frise then may be wired together to form longer breastworks. Here and there creeks also have been diverted to form ponds between the lines.

A couple hundred yards or so beyond the Confederate picket posts is the Union picket line, then a similar series of defenses leading back toward the Union rear. If the opposing lines are close enough, Union and Confederate pickets have established ground rules for this little part of the war that, for better or worse, is theirs. Conditions are bad enough without making it worse by antagonizing those people over there.

The entire line is a desolate, open, shell-churned, winter-frozen or spring-thawed muddy killing ground. There has been little drilling, commanders' cure-all for everything from boredom to sloppy performances. Instead the soldiers concentrate on further strengthening their respective lines.

Life is hard and dangerous in the trenches. Cold, wet, hungry, miserable soldiers man the firing steps. Before them, scattered picket posts; behind them, scattered reserves. At some point along the line there is fighting nearly every day.

A day can be almost pleasant: no fighting, clear weather; and the riflemen, if they've worked out an arrangement with their enemy across the way (officers usually look the other way at such things), might even climb up on the breastworks, look over the situation, enjoy the sun while they strip to pick lice from infected clothing. Two hours later, however, something would upset the delicate balance between life and death in that part of the line. Mortar and artillery shells, their fuzes trailing black smoke and sparks, would arc across the sky to land in some unlucky part of the trench, killing or wounding a half-dozen men. Or an enemy sharpshooter, without warning, would kill anyone who raises his head above a parapet. When that happens, several of the veterans would coax the sharpshooter into firing at some bait—a branch supporting a soldier's cap—then kill him in a hail of Minie bullets. That done, things would quiet again. For awhile.

Nights could be worse. Roving enemy patrols; random artillery or rifle fire; strange sounds, magnified by the night and constant fear into an enemy attack. Sometimes it's just the winter wind playing across the frozen clods of earth. Or rats, scurrying along the parapets and the firing steps. Rats: not harmless but not lethal either, if a man's on his feet or wakes up quick enough. The men hate the rats almost as bad as they hate the sharpshooters. Sometimes it is a trench raid, and there'll be close hand-to-hand fighting until one side or the other prevails. And then it will quiet down for a little while. At dawn, whichever side has lost ground during the night is almost sure to try to retake it.

THE SOLDIERS

Most Northern soldiers are warm, dry, well fed. Confederate soldiers may be barefoot, even through the winter months. Shoes are in short supply in the Southern army, and those on hand are made of green leather which soon separates. Through the winter, the line of march of regiments shuffling back and forth was marked by bloody footprints in the snow.

Lee's army is short of weapons, equipment, uniforms, blankets, and firewood. And it is hungry, always hungry. Southern rations are scant at best. A total of 1,800 calories authorized per day but seldom available. It's not unusual for Confederate soldiers to go three or four days without meat then be issued small portions of rancid bacon or poor, blue beef.

In December Captain Watson D. Williams, 5th Texas Infantry Regiment, wrote his family that he anticipated eating his Christmas dinner from his tin cup and, in place of eggnog, drinking water from a murky well behind his company's breastworks. Perhaps, however, he cheerfully ended his letter, it would be better than he feared. It almost was. As Christmas neared Lee's army was promised a special holiday meal being prepared by the ladies of Richmond. On Christmas day they eagerly waited the feast. Waited. Waited. Waited. Near 3 a.m. on the 26th the 18th Georgia Infantry Regiment finally received its Christmas dinner: one small sandwich of two tiny slices of bread and a thin piece of ham. A bitter disappointment but, when he'd finished, one old veteran lit his pipe and reflected, "Well, God bless our noble women; it was all they could do with what they had."

Confederate morale, sky high early in the war, has plummeted over the winter. Plummeted because of the cold, the hunger, the ordeal of life in the trenches. Plummeted also because Lee's soldiers, returning from Christmas furloughs, tell of the desperate plights of their families at home and of lost confidence in the war.

One March night eleven men deserted their South Carolina regiment. Five soon were captured, court-martialed, and sentenced to death. Four of the five were shot; the last spared because of his youth. Until that night, one of the men executed had been an excellent soldier, three times wounded in battle. He'd simply had enough and meant to go home.

Perhaps 100,000 soldiers on each side are listed as deserters. Grant can scarcely afford that kind of loss; it's disastrous to Lee. Knowing that, Grant offers $8 to any Confederate soldier who'll come over to the Union line and bring his weapons with him.

Both sides now draft soldiers and accept Black enlistments, but no appreciable number of either group have reached the lines.

The Confederate First Corps (Lieutenant General James Longstreet) mans Lee's lines north of the James River; its Second Corps (Major General John B. Gordon) is in the center; and its Third Corps (Lieutenant General Ambrose P. Hill) protects Lee's right, below Petersburg. Confederate soldiers may be spaced ten feet apart in the trenches, with few reserves behind them. Many are in their 60s; more yet are teenagers, as the Confederacy is scraping the bottom of its barrel. Nevertheless, most of Lee's soldiers still believe in their cause and that Lee may yet lead them to victory. "Cut us loose from these damned trenches," they say, "let us march again, and we'll win." So they believe.

On the Union side, Northern trenches are manned by two armies: above the James River, Major General Edward O. C. Ord's Army of the James; below the river, Major General George G. Meade's Army of the Potomac.

After Shiloh and Cold Harbor called a butcher, but dislikes firearms, can't stand red meat or the sight of blood, hates to visit hospitals, is wonderful with horses. Prefers to attack rather than defend but, by a series of feints and sidesteps (rather than frontal assaults) has forced Lee's army back from the Wilderness to the gates of Richmond. Never excited, never displays anger; listens quietly then announces a decision and sticks to it. During battles sets his plan in motion then is apt to sit on a stump, whittling, while his generals do their jobs without his interference. A much more complex man than believed.

Once a heavy drinker, now limits himself to an occasional whiskey toddy at the end of a hard day. In that liberty is closely watched and bedeviled by his friend, confidant, and Chief of Staff, Brigadier General John A. Rawlins.

Has great respect for Abraham Lincoln; no political ambitions for himself. Has memorized a map of the Richmond-Petersburg battlefield and possible lines of retreat for Robert E. Lee. His greatest fear is that he will awaken some morning to find that Lee and his army have slipped away before he can defeat him (and end the war) in the field.

Major General George Gordon Meade. Born in Cadiz, Spain; 49 years old; West Point Class of 1835. With so many of the other senior officers of both armies, served in the Mexican War. On June 28, 1863 was placed in command of the Army of the Potomac and three days later won the Battle of Gettysburg. Not an outstanding field commander there but a competent one and very lucky; given a gold medal by the Congress but reprimanded by Lincoln for not destroying Lee's army. Still commands the Army of the Potomac but has fought for a year in Grant's shadow and constantly defers to him.

Tall, thin, sharp featured, gray bearded, a slight stoop to his gait, subject to various minor illnesses for which he refuses to give up his command but which must limit his effectiveness. A poor rider, known for falling off his horse or for being swept from the saddle by low branches. Calls his troops "my people." Vain, sensitive, quick to find fault with his subordinates then to explode in anger. Wears a slouched hat and thick glasses and has large prominent eyes; for all this is known to his soldiers as "a damned goggle-eyed snapping turtle."

Major General Philip H. Sheridan. Born in New York, raised in Ohio; 34 years old. Suspended for one year from West Point for "a quarrel of a belligerent character with a fellow cadet" but was graduated in 1853. Short, slender, quick, energetic. Face bronzed by sun and wind.

Commanding a division at Chickamauga lost 1,500 of his 4,000 men, including two of his three brigade commanders. Two months later his men scrambled up the heights of Missionary Ridge to seize it from the Confederates. In the spring of '64 Grant brought him east to command the army's cavalry. Seeing him, an observer remarked, "That officer you brought in from the West, General, is rather a little fellow to handle your cavalry." Grant, not missing a puff of his cigar, answered, "Before we're through with him, you'll find that he's big enough." After Sheridan's first battle with the Army of the Potomac, his men boasted that "Little Phil" uses his cavalry sword to climb to his saddle but, once he gets there, he's plenty big enough.

Tough, emotional, always aggressive, Sheridan is a battlefield motivator of the first order.

Devoted to the cavalry, devastated the Shenandoah and destroyed Confederate Major General Jubal Early's army at Waynesboro before joining Grant at City Point. Grant means for Sheridan to be his sword in his campaign to destroy the Army of Northern Virginia.

Brigadier General Joshua Lawrence Chamberlain. Thirty-six years old; former professor of rhetoric at Bowdoin College, Maine, from which he'd taken a sabbatical to study in Paris but joined the army instead.

Tall, slender, handsome, conversant in seven languages, beautiful singing voice. Prefers to be called "Lawrence," possessing a quiet dignity others are quick to recognize and respect. Has left his wife and children to fight a war to free the slaves and to preserve the Union, causes he is willing to die for. And several times he nearly has done just that. Spent a long night at Fredericksburg piling up corpses to shield himself from Confederate rifle fire before Marye's Heights; already five times wounded; will be awarded the Congressional Medal of Honor for valor and leadership at Gettysburg; shot through the hips at Petersburg the year before, so badly wounded that Northern papers published his obituary, but Chamberlain returned early from medical leave to command an infantry brigade in what he hopes will be the final campaign of the war.

Self-taught the soldier's trade, and he's learned his lessons well. Instinctively a very fine troop commander. Proud of his old 20th Maine Infantry Regiment and of his present command, the 1st Brigade, 1st Division, V Corps.

Chamberlain is the solid, dependable field commander generals like to have around. Grant knows that; Meade and Brigadier General John Griffin (his division commander) know that; Sheridan is about to discover it.

Brigadier General George Armstrong Custer. Born in New Rumley, Ohio but largely raised in Monroe, Michigan where he met and married the beautiful daughter (Elizabeth) of prominent Judge Daniel Bacon; 25 years old. In June 1863 promoted from captain to brigadier general and, commanding a brigade of Michigan cavalry, stopped Jeb Stuart's cavalry in its tracks at Gettysburg. Thereafter has fought hard in every cavalry battle of the Army of the Potomac.

Tall, sinewy, very strong, an outstanding rider. Designs his own gaudy uniforms, for which he is accused of looking like a circus rider. Often wears a tight-fitting olive green corduroy jacket and trousers, a scarlet neckerchief with a large gold "CUSTER" pin, and a broad-brimmed blue sombrero. Bright, quick-moving, blue eyes; sharp nose, high cheekbones; always sunburned and freckled. Wears his reddish-gold hair to his shoulders and, like Major General George Pickett of the Southern army, perfumes his hair (hence sometimes called "Cinnamon"). Also called "Fanny" or "Curly." Displays a nervous, snappy, cocksure manner. Unemotional about ordering a charge to the death; heartbroken at the death of a friend.

Graduated last in his class at West Point (June 1861) and even then was detained as punishment when, rather than maintaining order at an imminent fist fight between two junior cadets, he cleared an area that the two combatants might "have a fair fight." Has changed little in the intervening two years. Absolutely without fear; dedicated to drinking to the lees whatever glory might be found on the battlefield; a keen sword for Sheridan to wield in the upcoming campaign.

These commanders fought for the Confederacy.

Jefferson Davis. Born in Kentucky but has spent most of his life in Mississippi; 57 years old; first President of the Confederate States of America. After his graduation from West Point (1829) and service in Mexico (wounded at Buena Vista), resigned from the army and became a major spokesman for Southern planters and slave owners. U.S. Senator from Mississippi ('47–'51) and U.S. Secretary of War ('53–'59). Can't forget his military background and can't resist second guessing his generals and his cabinet; often becomes too involved in the minutia of day by day government affairs.

Above average height, slender, a neat dresser. Blind in one eye. Thin, high-cheekboned face. A very reserved, aloof man never really welcomed into Richmond society and keenly aware of it. Few close confidants. Absolutely devoted to the Confederate cause. After four years' war Union soldiers still sing, "We'll hang Jeff Davis to a sour apple tree," and Davis believes that, if the Confederacy dies, he'll die with it.

Lee has repeatedly warned him that his army (and Richmond) cannot survive a single breakthrough of the Confederate line.

Lieutenant General Robert E. Lee. A Virginian; 59 years old; graduated from West Point in 1829 then fought with distinction in Mexico. Served with the army's engineers; Superintendent of West Point. Considered the finest officer in the Federal army, was offered command of that army but regretfully resigned in August 1861 to command Virginia's newly recruited troops. Commanded the Army of Northern Virginia from May 1862 until March 1865 when he was appointed commander of all Confederate armed forces.

Average height but in the saddle seems to be a much taller man; stocky. Clear, ruddy complexion; bright, steady eyes. Has aged a lot (hair and beard now white) during the war but has aged well. Seems tireless. Always erect, disciplined. Has a temper which he controls well. Does not often share his discouragement with his subordinates but once, following a trip to Richmond, grumbled that the Confederate Congress didn't seem able to do anything more than eat peanuts and chew tobacco while his army starved. An honest, gentle, kind man; a firm Christian; a Virginia aristocrat. Does not drink, curse, chase women.

A tough idol to pull down and to attempt to do so in the South would be sure to provoke a fight. The most respected man in both armies.

Every day Lee rides the Confederate lines on his beloved iron-gray horse, Traveller, wearing a plain gray uniform with the three stars of a Confederate general on his collar but without the buff facings or gold lace worn by most other generals. Adored by his soldiers. Once, on a hot, dusty march, was slowly riding Traveller between two long lines of Confederate soldiers. Lee, wearing a linen duster over his uniform and a straw hat, might well have been a prosperous farmer captured by the soldiers around him. From a Mississipppi regiment an Irish soldier, Billy Day, recognized Lee and called out, "Say there, fellows, where'd you catch that old carpet-bagger? Why he doesn't look like a bad old man. Probably wouldn't hurt a fly. Why don't you just turn him loose?" And Lee, recognizing the teasing, turned in his saddle to doff his hat in salute and smile at the Irish private, a smile the Mississippi men would never forget. The soldiers in the trenches below Petersburg and Richmond are ragged, starving, disheartened but, if necessary, they'll follow "Uncle Robert" to the death.

Lee's problem now, with an army that is hurting in every way it's possible to hurt, is to find a way to defeat Grant's army before Grant can cut his last supply routes and force a Confederate surrender.

Lieutenant General James Longstreet. Lee's senior commander, having served the Confederacy from Bull Run to the present. Born in South Carolina (one of a few Confederate generals who are not Virginians); 44 years old; was graduated from West Point in 1841. Breveted twice for gallantry in Mexico, and one of the most popular officers in the Old Army. Many of his friends from those days still serve the Union army, a few hundred yards beyond Longstreet's lines.

Called "Old Pete" or "the Dutchman" by his contemporaries; "My old war horse" by Robert E. Lee. Has earned Lee's respect and personal friendship. A slow, plodding officer but an excellent field commander and a hard fighter. Lost some favor after Gettysburg when some Confederate officers accused him of being too slow in carrying out Lee's orders. Subsequently brilliant at Chickamauga then critically wounded in the 1864 Wilderness fight. Only recently has returned to active duty with the Army of Northern Virginia.

A large, blue-eyed, full-bearded, slow-talking man. Stubborn, but ahead of his contemporaries in recognizing that advances in technology (e.g., a rifle that will fire three times a minute to 800 yards and a cannon that will range for two miles, three times a minute) must call for changes in tactics. Advocates trench lines, causing one's enemy to stand where he can be destroyed. Like Ulysses S. Grant, a much more complex man than most realize.

Not quite as close to Lee as before but still the officer Lee prefers to counsel with and to have close by in a fight.

Major General John B. Gordon. Attended the University of Georgia but did not graduate. Lawyer turned self-taught military commander who began the war commanding a single Georgia rifle company and now commands a third of Lee's army. Wounded in action eight times. At Antietam, after suffering four serious bullet wounds, was struck in the face by a fifth bullet. As Gordon fell, his head pitched forward into his cap, and he would have drowned in his own blood had not a bullet hole in the cap allowed the blood to drain free.

Above average height, very slender, very erect. Raven black hair; deep bullet scar on his left cheek; fierce, cruel, blue eyes (his men say that one look from Gordon would "put fight in a whupped chicken!").

Like the Union's Joshua Chamberlain, Gordon is a keen, poetic observer of his soldiers and enjoys reminiscing about them. As in Atlanta when Captain Gordon, marching at the head of his brand new rifle company, was asked, "Say there, Cap'n. What's the name of that outfit of yours?" As they'd not even considered naming themselves, Gordon improvised, "The Mountain Rifles." He'd barely said that, however, when a nearby private rejected his suggestion with, "'Mountain Rifles'? Hell, we ain't no 'Mountain Rifles'; we're the 'Racoon Roughs'." Or the prayer meeting when a Confederate rifleman who'd already lost a leg interrupted another's earnest prayer for more manhood, more strength, more courage with, "Now hold on there, Brother Jones. Don't you know you are praying all wrong? We've got more courage now than we have any use for!"

Devoted to his wife and children. His beautiful wife, Fannie, admired throughout the Confederate army for following Gordon on every campaign in an open buggy, several times was unsuccessfully ordered to the rear by Gordon's irascible boss, General Jubal Early. Early also expressed the hope that, "The damned Yankees will capture her and end the matter," but he finally gave up and allowed Fannie Gordon to have her own way. This March she is about to present Gordon with another son.

A solid, unpretentious performer who, like Joshua Chamberlain, believes in his cause and can be relied upon to fight for it to the end.

Preface

PETERSBURG is the story of the fighting that finally breaks Confederate General Robert E. Lee's lines before Petersburg, Virginia; a solid Union victory that forces Lee to abandon Richmond, capital of the Confederate States of America, and begin a desperate march to unite his army with that of Confederate General Joseph E. Johnston in North Carolina. The story of that march, the pursuit by the Union armies of General Ulysses S. Grant, and of the surrender of the Confederate army at Appomattox Courthouse, April 9, 1865, is told in the companion volume *APPOMATTOX*.

PETERSBURG is told from the viewpoints of the presidents, generals, soldiers, and civilians who were there, individuals who, with the exception of Sergeant Thomas McDermott, really existed. I'm sure that there was a "Sergeant McDermott" and that he was invaluable to Brigadier General Joshua Chamberlain; "Sergeant McDermotts" always are.

With that exception, my story is historically correct, and I've included a selected bibliography of other authors who contributed to it. I've condensed some of the action and highlighted certain individuals because I felt their stories more compelling in the overall picture. I've also given those individuals thoughts and words which I can't prove occurred but which seem reasonable to me. And I've changed their manner of speaking at times because men were inclined to speak more formally then, in phrases that might be uncomfortable to you. The character I assign to each of them reflects my own thoughts about that individual; you may agree or disagree as you come to know them better.

Our Civil War is a very important part of our national and personal heritage. The Petersburg and Appomattox campaigns were a critical and poignant part of that war. Thank you for your interest. Enjoy!

Acknowledgements

This has been a work of love, and I'm very grateful for the help others have given me in completing it.

My thanks to Dr. Gerald A. Leidy for his photography; to Lieutenant David Weaver, licensed battlefield guide at Gettysburg, cartographer of my story; to my perceptive editor, Harold Collier, who took the chance; to Chris M. Calkins, park ranger/historian, Petersburg National Battlefield Historic Park, who encouraged my work and whose texts contributed so much to it; to Joe Williams, curator, Appomattox Court House National Historical Park, who answered many questions; to Miss Susan Ravdin, Special Collections staff of the Bowdoin College Library, Brunswick, Maine, for her insights about General Joshua L. Chamberlain; to the Military History Institute, Carlisle Barracks, Pennsylvania, for texts and photographs; to Burke Davis and all the other authors cited in the bibliography, who provided facts to be woven into the story; to Catherine E. Shirk, whose faith helped so much a long time ago; and to my wife, Jean, for her love and support from the beginning, for helping me find the right word, and for walking Fort Gregg, Sayler's Creek, and the hills and woods of Appomattox Court House with me then understanding my shared thoughts and silences.

CHAPTER 1

Fort Stedman   March 4–25, 1865

JOHN GORDON

"General! General Gordon! Wake up, sir! Wake up!" the colonel nudges the slender figure on the canvas cot.

The touch isn't necessary; he's awake at the first calling.

He's had a hard day, riding his entire Confederate Second Corps' line, pausing to chat with his division, brigade, and regimental commanders. Stopping too to talk with younger company officers, sergeants, and soldiers. It's something he does every day, no matter the weather. The men know he's there, and that's important to John Gordon.

He's seen more combat than most of them. They know that. Close-hand combat for nearly four years now, and wounded eight times. They know that too and take perverse pride in it. So he makes it a point to share their lives each day.

Today, at the western end of his lines, he'd chatted with General A. P. Hill, the Third Corps commander, that day returned from medical leave and dismayed at what he'd found.

"A very long line, General," Hill shook his head, "and too few men."

"Yes," Gordon answered. "And they're considerably worn down; but they'll fight, sir. When it's time, they'll fight."

"Soon now, General," Hill shook his head again. "They'll come soon; then we'll know."

Gordon nodded, saluted, "You take care now, General," turned to retrace his line.

Late in the afternoon he'd ridden to his wife in Petersburg. She'd stayed near him on every campaign and waits now in the besieged city, grateful for whatever time he can give her. Especially now with the baby due. Today Gordon had a pleasant surprise for her: a bit of ham a young officer, just returned from furlough, had given him. As they enjoyed the welcome treat, they talked of other places and other times before or hoped to be. She'd been cheerful, but the worry lines around her lips and eyes were undeniable. He'd pretended not to see them but quietly reassured her that he'd always be as near as his duties permitted and that he cared, he really cared.

A long day, and it seemed he'd barely begun to sleep when he'd been awakened.

As Gordon turns on his cot the lantern accentuates his thin, high-cheekboned face with the still-raw bullet scar across his cheek; his coal-black hair; and most of all the dark, hawk-like, killer's eyes, instantly alert.

"It's all right, Colonel. I'm awake. Is there trouble on the lines? Has it finally begun?"

"No, sir. To both questions. The usual shots now and then when the boys get a little jittery or just bored. Nothing more. But Sergeant Tucker just rode in from General Lee's headquarters. Seems he brought the message 'cause he could find us in the dark. General Lee wants you, sir. Soon's you can get to Turnbull House."

Turnbull House. Lee's headquarters. Gordon sits up to study his watch.

"Two in the morning. Seems a might unusual, Colonel, wouldn't you say?"

"Real unusual, sir. General Lee, he doesn't like to fret anyone this time of night lest it's mighty important. I've got some men to go with you. Tucker'll lead them. And your horse'll be ready soon's you are."

"Thank you. Give me a minute, and we'll be on our way. If first light comes and I'm not back, be sure the staff are up and about."

An hour later, cold from the uncomfortable ride, Gordon enters Turnbull House, a large mansion on the western edge of Petersburg; headquarters for General Robert E. Lee's Army of Northern Virginia. Gordon's eyes, accustomed to the darkness, blink as they adjust to the lamp held by Lee's aide.

"Sorry to roust you out so early, General. Thanks for coming."

"It's all right, Colonel Taylor (Colonel Walter Taylor). But it is unusual. Is the General all right?"

"Yes, sir, though he's not getting much sleep these nights. He just said we were to present his compliments and apologies and ask you to come as soon as possible. If you're ready, I'll take you to him."

As Gordon enters the room Lee uses as an office and bedroom, Lee stands alone before a large fireplace. His arm on the mantel, his head resting in his arm, Lee gazes into the coal fire. Obviously deep in thought, he looks old, tired, discouraged. To the army, Lee never shows discouragement, never seems tired. Now his guard is down.

Gordon doesn't stand in awe of more than two or three men, but this is one of them. Four years ago, as a captain, he'd commanded a company of riflemen; now he's a general, commanding nearly a third of Lee's army. But he's not a West Pointer. And, like Longstreet, he's not a Virginian either, as are most of the other Confederate generals. Neither omission seemed to matter to Robert E. Lee; still Gordon feels hesitant before him. Particularly at meeting Lee, alone, in the early morning hours.

Gordon tugs at his uniform, straightens his already erect frame, and salutes, "General Gordon, sir."

Lee jerks erect, all traces of weariness and discouragement gone. The mask has returned.

"Ah, General Gordon," he smiles and returns the salute. "Thank you for coming. I apologize for troubling you so early in the morning, but I couldn't sleep and, before I meet with President Davis tomorrow, I'd like your views on the situation facing this army."

When Gordon nods, Lee continues, "You are thin, General; but you seem well. I hope so. This army needs you. And Mrs. Gordon, I pray she is well. The baby is due soon?"

"We are both well, General. The baby is due any time. Even with the heavy cannonade yesterday, it did not appear. But soon, I am told, it will. And you, sir. You are well?"

Lee smiles, "Tolerable, General; tolerable. But it will do. Thank you for asking."

"Now then," Lee moves to a long table covered with maps, letters, reports, "be seated and let me explain."

"You know the situation within your own corps. Generals Longstreet and Hill face the same problems you face. But read these reports for yourself. When you're finished, I want your thoughts on the options still open to us."

For a long time Gordon reads the reports of his fellow commanders and their staffs, the silence broken only by the ticking of a large mantel clock and Lee's occasionally prodding the fire with an iron poker. He knows the problems in his own command, but he's not prepared for the shortages Lee's army faces all across its line. Food stocks are perilously low. There is little forage for the cavalry. Soldiers desperately need hats, boots, shoes, overcoats, blankets. There is little medicine for ill or wounded soldiers. Many soldiers, always before brave and reliable, now talk back to their officers and sergeants, ignore orders or, worse yet, desert their posts.

Seeing Gordon reading the provost marshal's report on discipline within the army, Lee adds, "General Hill has found it necessary to cut his rations to one-sixth pound of beef a day." Lee sadly shakes his head, "A magnificent army, General, but it's difficult to maintain discipline when men are that hungry."

"Yes, sir; we're down to that too. When we can get it at all."

When Gordon sets aside the reports, sighs, and looks up, Lee turns from his study of the fire to review their tactical situation.

"We're facing about 150,000 Union troops across the lines, General. Thomas has another 30,000 that could come up from Knoxville. Sheridan is expected any day with another 20,0000 from the Valley. Perhaps 200,000 enemy facing us. And Sherman's army is within four days' march. Without help, General Johnston (General Joseph E. Johnston) can only slow his march. We have about 50,000 men in this army, but many can't be considered effective."

Lee silently paces before the fire then turns, "Well, General, what do you think we should do?"

Gordon gathers his thoughts then answers, "Well, sir, it seems to me we're down to three choices, none too good."

When Lee nods, he continues, "First, we should try to make peace with the enemy. As soon as possible, before we have even less a hand to play."

"It that's not possible, we should retreat. Again, as soon as possible. Let Richmond go. It's been a halter around our necks for too long. The men will begin to revive the moment they can march again. March south, link with General Johnston to strike Sherman a fatal blow. Then turn again to face Grant."

"If we can't make an honorable peace," Gordon continues, "and we can't march to join General Johnston, then we should fight. Right here, right now. With all the strength we can muster; while we still can fight. A few more weeks and I'm afraid that option won't be open to us. Force Grant to give up trying to cut our supply lines."

Lee wearily leans back in his chair, nods his head, hesitates for several moments, then picks up the discussion.

"Thank you, General Gordon. Unfortunately, our army can't negotiate for peace. That is for civil authorities, not for us. We are soldiers and must go on fighting until President Davis orders us to stop or we no longer are able to resist."

When Gordon nods, Lee resumes, "I also agree with your second choice. Our men and horses are weak, and the march would be difficult, but we could do it. This army can always march."

"But," he sighs, "until President Davis moves the government to a safer area, we can't retreat."

Lee, his face softened by the firelight but still radiating self-discipline, smiles and confides, "I don't believe we can persuade President Davis to abandon Richmond, General. Not yet. Not yet. And, as you say, we can't wait long."

"Then, sir, we must attack. As quickly as possible."

"Yes. But where and how?" Lee gestures Gordon to the large map covering the table and, tracing the trench line with his hand, discusses Grant and the other Northern generals, their commands, and their entrenchments, mentally probing for a weak link in the enemy line. He seldom glances at the map but, as he speaks, his finger touches the exact spot he is discussing. Gordon is awed at Lee's grasp of the situation facing the Confederate army.

Then the clock strikes the hour, and Lee abruptly ends their meeting.

"General Gordon, I apologize. I appreciate your thoughts, but I've kept you far too long. You must return to your command. We'll speak of this again. Soon. Meanwhile, if we choose to attack before our enemies can attack us, the burden of it must fall upon you. General Longstreet is not yet recovered from his wound; General Hill...," Lee pauses, leaving the thought unspoken.

Then he continues, "If we attack, we must do it in your sector. Say nothing of our conversation but, before we meet again, think carefully of your third choice for I fear it may have to be our first. Where should we attack? What can we hope to gain? What help will you need?"

Two days later Lee again calls Gordon to his headquarters.

"Well, General, I've met with President Davis. I reported the condition of our army and what we can expect from General Grant as soon as the roads and fields are dry. I warned him that, if our line is broken at any point, we can't hope to save Richmond or Petersburg. I again advised him to evacuate his government as quickly as possible, with our army to follow."

Lee smiles grimly, then confides, "I'm afraid, General Gordon, that the President is not yet ready to accept that. Instead, he speaks of remaining here, fighting to the bitter end."

Gordon nods, "Well then, General, what can we do?"

"We must attack. Break their lines; force them to pull back. And as soon as possible."

Moving to the map, Lee again traces the Union line with his hand. "An attack north of the James won't help the situation on our right. If we can break Grant's line below the James, however, it will force him to pull back his left, easing his threat to our Southside Railroad."

"We'll attack in your sector, General," he continues. "You will be responsible. I asked you to be thinking about this. Select the best point for your attack, and come to me with your plan. As soon as possible."

Wednesday, March 22; this time John Gordon stands above the map, tracing the lines with his hand.

"General Lee, I recommend that we strike the Union line here, at Hare's Hill. Meade's IX Corps, General Parke (Major General John G. Parke), is there. This strongpoint," he taps the map, "they call Fort Stedman. It's 300 yards east of our Colquitt's Salient. We'll take Stedman, its supporting redoubts, and three reserve positions I've identified several hundred yards east of Stedman. When we've broken through, we'll expand our penetration then pass through the gap all the infantry and cavalry you can spare. The cavalry can tear up Grant's rear, maybe even get to his headquarters at City Point. It's only eight miles beyond Stedman, and I understand that Lincoln's expected there in a day or so. Perhaps a kind Providence has delivered him to us."

"Perhaps, General, perhaps," Lee nods. "Tell me about their Fort Stedman."

"It will be tough, sir. High, thick earth walls. Besides the infantry, they have a battery of cannon there. Their Battery 10, about 100 yards to the north, can support Stedman with cannon and mortar fire. Their Batteries 11 and 12 to the south can add to that. Cannon in Fort Haskell, also below Stedman," he taps the map, "also could hit us. That is, if they can see us. But I mean to break their lines before they can see what's hit them."

"They have the usual picket posts between our lines," he continues, enthusiastic now. "The ground is crisscrossed with picket posts and trenches, breast-high abatis in likely crossing spots, and chevaux-de-frise before Stedman. But I intend to take out their pickets, slip through their obstacles, and be into them before they know what's happening."

You feel that you can do this?"

"Yes, sir, I can do it. And, if you can spare me the men and horses to follow up our success, I can give you a victory that will do exactly what we hope it can do."

"Very well. Let's review the plan in detail. When can you be ready?"

"Two days, sir. The night of the 24th. If you can get reinforcements to me that quickly. I've found some local men who can guide us, and I've gathered information on the Yankee regiments. We have the names of their officers; that may be helpful."

"Our soldiers," Gordon chuckles, "have gotten to know those people over there pretty well. You know Reverend Jones?"

When Lee nods, Gordon continues, "The other day he was visiting the trenches, and his hat blew over the parapet into the open ground between the lines. One of our soldiers volunteered to recover the hat. Any diversion's a relief to their boredom. Anyway, he slipped over the parapet and was crawling along when a Yank put a bullet clean through his sleeve. Our man got mad and yelled, 'Hey, Yank. You quit that foolishness. I'm not doing any harm here. Just trying to get the chaplain's hat.'"

"Then the Yankee soldier called back, 'Sorry, Johnny. You hurry up now and get that hat 'afore the next relief comes. They're Massachusetts' men; not very neighborly.'"

"The men sense that something is up," Gordon continues, "and many have volunteered without knowing what they're volunteering for. Even Mrs. Gordon is helping. Right now she's busy tearing white cloth into strips to identify the lead groups. Two days, General, with your approval and the extra troops I'll need."

Midnight, March 24; long columns of Confederate soldiers march silently through deserted Petersburg streets. Two brigades of tough, hard-bitten North Carolina and South Carolina veterans. Lean, dirty, long-haired, bearded. They carry blanket rolls over their shoulders, pocketsful of cartridges and caps, canteens and bayonets. Few have food. They don't know where their officers are taking them and really don't care. Anything is better than the trenches.

"Anyways," one reasons, "the Cap'n said Uncle Robert needs us, and that's good enough for me." No one argues with that.

There is little talk. It's cold and dark, and the streets, except for the shadowy figures passing through them, are empty. Little to see and not much to encourage conversation. Now and then a man coughs in the cold night air or softly curses if he trips on the rough cobblestones and knows that the green leather soles of his shoes finally have given away. Then he may try to walk aways, the loose sole flopping with each step, but soon must drop out of the column to bind the sole with twine or just give it up, tossing the shoes aside to walk barefoot.

Sergeants hustle the marching columns along.

"Hurry up, now. Hurry up. Four miles to where we're goin'."

"Where's that, Sarge?"

"Beats me. Some bump in our line called Colquitt's Salient. The Colonel told the Cap'n somethin' big's about to bust loose up there. Reckon we'll be in on it."

Hurry up, hurry up; then probably wait; it's always been that way with infantry. Four more miles to Colquitt's Salient.

General Robert E. Lee and Traveller quietly watch from a small knoll at that bulge in the Confederate line. Lee, as always, seems calm. For four years he's gambled at nearly every turn, and nearly always won. Tonight's attack might be the biggest gamble of all. You'd not know that, however, from looking at him: erect, confident, invincible on the big iron-gray horse. Passing regiments wave their hats in a silent salute; he returns their gesture with a smile and wave of his own hat.

Some 200 yards ahead of Lee, Gordon fretfully waits the last of his brigades. Nervous, facing the most awesome responsiblity he's known in the long war, very much aware that the survival of the entire Confederate army may hinge on the success of the attack he's planned and will lead. A long, long way, he muses, from running mines in north Georgia or even commanding a company of riflemen. A long way.

He mentally reviews his plan. Besides his own corps, perhaps 12,000 men, he'll have nearly 4,000 reinforcements. And Pickett's division with another 6,500 infantry has been delayed but is on its way by train from north of the James. They'll exploit his breakthrough.

"Wish they were here when we start," he mutters to himself, "but I reckon it'll have to do."

For the attack John Gordon commands almost half of Lee's army; not bad for the one-time captain. No time, however, to think of that now; he's set the attack for four o'clock, less than two hours away.

Ahead of him in the dark his men have cleared lanes through Confederate obstacles before their trenches. Then assault teams, handpicked by Gordon, quietly moved through those lanes toward the Union picket posts. Their commanders know Gordon's determination, each one having been told, "I know the courage of your men, Colonel. That's why I've picked them to lead our attack. Remind them that they're not to fire their rifles until they assault the Yanks' main line; meantime, they're to use their bayonets."

Gordon watches as each assault team moves forward. Picked sharpshooters lead the way. Then axemen to hack away enemy obstacles. Close behind the axemen are a hundred infantrymen to assault the enemy strongpoints. When they've taken the strongpoints, more infantrymen will pass through to attack the Union positions Gordon had spotted beyond the front line.

Captain Joseph P. Carson, leading a small detachment of Georgia sharpshooters at the head of one of Gordon's assault teams, is busy checking his men as they step into the cleared lane before the Confederate trenches.

"Fix your bayonet"; "You won't need that blanket roll; drop it over there with the others"; "Close up now; keep a sharp eye on the man ahead of you."

Then he's startled to find that he's picked up an extra man. One whom, even in the darkness, he knows is not one of his sharpshooters. He pulls the dark figure from the column then recognizes him. It's his brother, Bob, assigned to headquarters' duty but now quietly crouching among Carson's infantrymen.

"Bob," he impulsively hugs the younger man, "what are you doing here?"

"I've come to help. Got the General's permission to go with you."

"No," the Captain shakes his head. "I won't have it. You know we're the first ones to go in, and they've had nearly a year over there to get ready for us. Look, Bob, I've got a hunch that I won't make it, and I don't want the family to maybe lose both of us."

"I know," his brother calmly argues, "but I've had the same feeling and, if you fall, I'm not going to leave you out there. I'm here to bring you back, one way or the other."

Faced with his younger brother's determination, Captain Joe Carson gives in, "All right. All right. Stay near me."

Across the dark field some Union officers and men also have premonitions.

Grant has alerted his commanders to anticipate Confederate probing somewhere along the line.

"Post extra pickets, gentlemen. Be sure they're alert. If the enemy get into our lines, seal them off and hold your ground. Come light I'll get more troops in there, and we'll retake the ground."

North of Fort Stedman Captain John C. Hardy, 2nd Michigan Infantry Regiment, accustomed to the pattern of random rifle fire between nervous pickets during the long nights, notices that this night there has been little or no firing. In fact, it's become very quiet. Nervous, he alerts his picket posts.

"Fire a shot or two every couple minutes. Whether anything's out there or not. Just to let the Johnnies know we're about."

When his patrols find nothing, the men laugh at their Captain's nervousness.

At 3 a.m., Lieutenant Charles A. Lochbrunner, 14th New York Heavy Artillery Regiment, hears unusual noises before Fort Stedman. Darkness conceals whatever is out there, however, and the noise soon stops.

"Probably just rats, Lieutenant," his sergeant assures him. "On a cold night like this, when the ground's hard, they can sound like a pack of dogs out there. Can't see a thing."

"Yeah," Lochbrunner answers, "but just to play it safe I'd best tell the Major."

He hesitantly interrupts the poker game going on in the bombproof of Stedman's commander, Major George M. Randall.

Randall, studying his poker hand, half-listens, puffs his cigar, then tells the dealer, "I'll take two cards, Jack." Then, without taking his eyes from the cards in his hand, he answers Lochbrunner, "All right, Lieutenant. Your sergeant's probably right, but keep a sharp eye out. Could be more deserters. We've had a flood of Johnnies out there on the picket line to-night. Reckon they're cold and hungry. And that bonus for their weapons must be working; seems they're bringin' their muskets along. I've told our pickets to hold them out there 'til it's light."

Randall returns to his game, the report already half-forgotten. Then a messenger from Battery 11, below Fort Stedman, again interrupts.

"Major's compliments, sir. Said to tell you we've been hearing noises out to our front the last hour. Sent out a patrol, but all they found was a bunch of Johnnies comin' over, lookin' for a better time. Reckon that's what we heard."

Randall, intent now on the three-of-a-kind hand he's been dealt, noncommitally nods, "All right. Tell Major Richardson it's just a big run of Johnnies. Another hour or so and it'll be light enough to check it out."

Nearly 4 a.m. now. John Gordon and a single rifleman stand on the parapet above the Confederate trenches, straining to see across the dark field.

"Can you see anything out there?" Gordon asks.

"No, sir; black as the bottom of a well. But I've got a feeling this ball's about to begin."

Then the silence is broken. At an opening in the trenches to their left, Gordon's men, clearing overlooked obstacles, drop heavy timbers on the hard ground. The crash echoes across the field.

From the darkness, it seems very near, a harsh voice instantly demands, "Hey, Johnny, what's that noise? Answer quick or I'll shoot."

Blue and Gray pickets have an understanding that neither will fire on the other unless it's necessary; the Yankee picket is weighing that now.

Despite all his combat experience, Gordon's mind freezes, unable to come up with a reply.

The Confederate private beside him, sensing the General's hesitancy, quietly answers, as if to an old acquaintance, "Never mind, Yank. Go on back to sleep. We're just gatherin' a little corn got left over here. You know our rations are mighty short."

A pause then the unseen Union picket decides, "All right, Johnny; go ahead and get your corn. I'll not shoot at a man while he's drawin' his rations."

All again is quiet. Gordon takes his large pocket watch from his coat, holds it close to his eyes, watches the last minute tick away. Four o'clock. Time.

He nods to his companion on the parapet, "All right. Fire your rifle."

The soldier raises his weapon but doesn't pull its trigger.

Gordon again orders, "Fire your weapon, sir! Fire the signal!"

The soldier again hesitates, pondering a matter of conscience; then, his own decision made, he suddenly calls out, "Hey, Yank! Wake up! We're comin'!"

Then, having warned the unseen Yankee who wouldn't fire on a man drawing his rations, and his honor satisfied, he pulls the trigger. The single rifle shot echoes across the field.

Almost immediately, Gordon hears his regiments rushing forward in the darkness: the swish of twine-bound trouser legs, the creak of musket slings, the rattle of canteens, the tramp, tramp, tramp of rough-shod shoes on hard ground suddenly very loud.

Then a crescendo of noise and smoke and flame erupts across the field. Gordon's fight to break the Union line has begun.

The burst of firing, he realizes, is beyond the Federal picket line in their enemies' main trench line.

Union picket posts have been taken without a fight, as when pickets of the 59th Massachusetts Infantry Regiment heard muffled sounds before them and a young Yankee soldier challenged, "Halt! Who goes there? Speak up or we'll shoot!"

From the darkness, a soft voice calmly drawled, "Put up your rifle, Yank. We don't mean no harm. Comin' over; brung our rifles along."

Then eight Confederate deserters, one after another, with their weapons slung upside down in the recognized signal for a man surrendering, walked into the Massachusetts' picket post.

Lulled, their sergeant nonchalantly waved, "Put your weapons over there, Johnny. Then sit down and keep quiet. You'll be out here till mornin'. Reckon we can find some biscuits for you till then."

Then they found their "hospitality" rejected as the dirty, ragged, lean "deserters" suddenly reversed their rifles and the same soft voice drawled, "Sorry, Yank. Don't mean to disconvenience you, but we're not quite ready to lay down these rifles. Now we'd 'preciate it if you Bluebellies would drop your rifles over there. Real quick like. Don't even think about making any noise. Reckon we'll take those biscuits too."

From a nearby post, however, one Union picket escapes a similar fate, shouting, "The Rebels are coming! The Rebels are coming!"

Alerted by the shout and a harsh volley of musket fire near Fort Stedman, a Battery 10 officer orders canister (two-dozen $1\frac{1}{2}$" iron balls) fired into the darkness. Can't see his enemy, but they have to be out there.

His cannon fire two more rounds before dark figures, Confederate infantrymen, swarm over his guns. A hand-to-hand fight follows: clubbed muskets and bayonets against rammer staffs, revolvers, and artillery sabers. A lone, frightened soldier seeing a dark figure loom before them, instinctively thrusts his bayonet, pulls back, thrusts again. This time he feels the shock of the bayonet striking home, hears the scream of a hurt man. His enemy falls, and the soldier can't withdraw his bayonet. As he's been taught, he puts his foot on the man's body, pulls hard, feels the bayonet withdraw. Feels sick, and will be sick when there is time but not now. "Don't think about it," he mutters to himself. "Just pull it out; keep goin'; stay ready to use it again."

The wild, confused melee quickly ends. Union artillerymen, seeing Gray infantrymen pouring in from all sides, throw down their rifles, raise their hands, surrender.

Prisoners are quickly hustled across the field toward the Confederate trenches. In the confusion and darkness some Yankee prisoners drop, unnoticed, from the column to hide in shell holes then return to their own lines.

Meanwhile, in captured artillery revetments, Confederate gunners swing captured cannons to fire at Fort Stedman while more of Gordon's infantrymen swing north and south along the trenches connecting the batteries.

Messengers also hurry back across the field, and soon Gordon knows that Union Batteries 10 and 11, above and below Fort Stedman, have been taken with Confederate infantry closing on the fort itself.

Stedman's gunners also fire canister into the darkness but, before they can fire a dozen shells, Confederate infantrymen are scrambling up the walls of the fort.

Captain Joe Carson's Georgia sharpshooters are among the Southern soldiers huddled before Stedman's walls, tearing aside obstacles while trying to find an entrance to the fort. Union canister passes over them, near enough to sound like a swarm of angry bees and to blow away Confederate hats. The cannons' flames, however, silhouette Yankee gunners above them, and Carson's sharpshooters shoot them down.

Then Carson yells, "Never mind an opening; go over the wall," and they scramble up the sloping earth walls to get at the cannon and their crews. They're not alone; other Confederate infantrymen now are pouring into Stedman from three sides.

Another savage, no holds barred, hand-to-hand fight erupts. Parry and thrust; stab and slash. Union pistols flashing in the darkness. Angry curses and screams of hurt men.

A soldier, very large in the darkness, looms before Carson. No way to recognize his uniform, but the man carries a rammer staff, not a rifle and bayonet. Carson fires his revolver, hears the solid thump of his bullet strike home, sees the Yankee gunner thrown backward by the force of the bullet.

He glances into an abandoned dugout, its lantern still burning, its poker game interrupted; two of its players dead on the dirt floor.

In the confusion the Union commander, Major Randall, has broken free to run toward Fort Haskell. Behind him the fight is vicious but short. Fort Stedman, like its supporting batteries, has fallen.

Joe Carson looks about, counting his losses. He last saw his younger brother with the other men tearing at the Yankee abatis before the fort. Now he can't find him, and there isn't time to look. He orders Stedman's cannon swung about to fire on Yank survivors fleeing east and south and yells to his men, "Come on, come on. Let's find those three positions behind us."

Along the trench line above and below Fort Stedman Union soldiers, fighting hard to confine the Confederate penetration, find the darkness confusing and frightening. Captain John Hardy's Michigan soldiers, holding the trenches above the fort, see a large body of men moving up the trench line toward them. Closer, closer.

Not sure whether the ghostly forms are friendly or enemy, Hardy calls out, "Hold your fire! Hold your fire!"

When they're within ten yards of him, a cannon flashes and he's sure: "They're Rebs! Rebs! Open fire!"

His volley catches Gordon's men full in the face, and a dozen shadowy figures fall across the trench. Then more Confederate infantrymen close with their bayonets, and it becomes another struggle of phantom figures: no one sure until only a few feet separate the fighters whether the dark form before him is friendly or enemy. Shoot, stab, club your musket; and sort it all out later. A hard fight, stubborn Union soldiers not willing to give up the trench line, and Gordon's men trying, with one bayonet assault after another in the early dawn darkness but unable to break through.

Within a half hour of the first alarm, Gordon's men have taken the fort and the batteries above and below it. North of Stedman, however, they've been stopped at Union Battery 9.

Below Fort Stedman Confederate infantrymen have taken Union Batteries 11 and 12 and now focus on Fort Haskell. Take it and they'll have cut a gap nearly 400 yards wide in Parke's line. Enough for Confederate infantry and cavalry to pour through.

Fort Haskell's commander, Major Houghton, lies propped against its earth walls, his thigh shattered by a shell fragment. His fort is being pounded by mortar, artillery, and rifle fire; the dark sky above it laced with the blazing trails of shell fuzes arcing toward their targets; a deadly storm of light that suddenly ends with shattering explosions that hail hot iron fragments. Shell after shell strikes Haskell's walls.

Houghton hears one of his officers, struck by the storm of shell fuzes streaking across the sky, calmly, poetically, likening them to "a flock of blackbirds with blazing tails beating about in a gale." "Blackbirds' blazing tails," beautiful, but the imagery suddenly ended for the young officer when one of the shells blows off his arm.

Wave after wave of Confederate infantry press against Haskell's outer walls but can't breach them. Massachusetts, New York, Pennsylvania soldiers are holding firm while Georgia, North Carolina, and Louisiana infantrymen are beginning to lose heart.

The Confederate attack is stopped in its tracks. Haskell will not be taken.

Gordon's men have broken Parke's line at Fort Stedman, but the northern and southern limits of their success now are marked on the shell-torn trench line. A line heaped with dead and wounded from both sides; the wounded hugging the torn ground, hoping they'll not be hurt more. For them, the fight is over.

East of Stedman Captain Joe Carson's Georgia sharpshooters find other Confederate infantrymen also searching for the final Union strongpoints Gordon had identified. Their guides, confused by the darkness, the maze of Federal trenches and covered ways, and the shell-torn, barren landscape they'd known as peaceful woods and fields, can't find the Union forts. Gray infantrymen, giving up the search, instead attack the camps of Union reserve regiments.

Along the streets of those camps drummer boys of the 29th and 5th Massachusetts Infantry Regiments are beating the Long Roll. Officers and sergeants shout commands, and sleepy soldiers hurry to form battle lines as Gordon's infantrymen pile into them. Northern soldiers, scrambling from pup tents and dugouts as they buckle on equipment and try to find their companies, are cut down by the Confederates.

A lone Confederate rifleman, separated from his squad, sees a Union soldier emerging from a dugout.

"Come out of there, Yank," he yells. "Right now or we'll shoot."

The Massachusetts' soldier lays down his rifle and moves forward. Then another Union soldier appears, lays down his weapon, and joins the first man. Then another, and another, and another. Each laying down his weapon then moving forward, arms upraised. Until more than a dozen enemy stumble from the dugout before the amazed Confederate rifleman.

Undaunted, he waves his bayoneted (but empty) rifle menacingly and herds them together. Then, chuckling to himself, "Wait'll the boys hears 'bout this," hustles them toward the distant Confederate lines.

Private William Klinker, another Massachusetts' man, is a different breed. Backed against a tree, he lashes out with his bayonet, holding his enemy, half a squad of Southern infantrymen, at bay. They pause, not sure what to do about him. Then a hard-bitten North Carolina soldier exclaims, "Ornery cuss!" and calmly shoots him.

A Union officer, wearing only a nightshirt but brandishing a sword, fights hard until he falls below three burly Confederates.

Another Yankee soldier, called to surrender, doggedly shakes his head and shouts, "No! No, dammit! Just can't see it!" and charges nearby Confederates. In the melee he is slashed, choked, struck with a musket butt, his face peppered with powder burns from muskets fired at very close range. He finally falls, and his attackers, seeing his bloody, battered face, turn aside. Long enough for the boy to spring to his feet and, deciding he's done about all he can, run through the Confederate cordon.

Then, with victory in their grasp, Confederate soldiers look about the captured camp and stop.

"Let 'em run, boys; let 'em run," one calls. "There's food here and other truck we need. We don't take it now, we'll sure never see it agin'. Let 'em go; we'll get 'em later."

Gordon's men are cold and hungry. The man makes sense. Let the Yanks run while we fill our bellies and see what's in these dugouts.

By pairs, then squads, then companies they stop to plunder their beaten enemy's camp: shoes here, a pair of socks, an overcoat there; glory be, a blanket. Good wool one too. And food, a lot of food. Good food. Haven't seen anything like this since Cedar Creek. Sugar, tins of dessicated beef (a very poor beef whose name the soldiers have slightly altered). Good enough in a pinch though. Hardtack. Boxes of hardtack. And, glory be, coffee! Real, honest to God coffee! Gordon's men simply lay down their rifles, sit down, and eat.

Captain Joe Carson is there, angrily lashing out at any looters he can reach.

"No, dammit! No! Don't stop now. We can eat later. Push them back. It's getting light; keep going!"

If he can grab a soldier's arm, or hit him with the flat side of his sword, the man will take up his rifle and move ahead. Once he's beyond the captain's grasp, however, he shrugs his shoulders and again stops to plunder.

The point of Gordon's penetration, like its flanks, has been stopped. Stopped by hard-fighting, determined Yankees, by the darkness and the confusion, by the hunger and cold and wet Gordon's soldiers have known for months. Filling one's stomach or finding a decent pair of shoes suddenly is more important to Confederate infantrymen than pressing their beaten enemy. Time enough to get those Yanks later.

Not this time. Parke's soldiers have retreated slowly, sullenly, without panic. This Army of the Potomac is not the army of the early days of the war. It has "seen the elephant," as its soldiers are wont to say, too many

times for panic now. Across the Confederate penetration, Union infantrymen have stopped Gordon's desperate attack and now are gathering to
take back the ground they've lost.

At Colquitt's Salient, John Gordon has been elated by early reports.
Fort Stedman and Union Batteries 10, 11, and 12 have fallen. Haskell is
under heavy attack and may be taken any time. Enough room then for
Pickett's men ("Where are they, Colonel? Any word of Pickett's division?"
"No, sir, nothing yet. We're watchin'"). Confederate casualties, according
to the reports, so far have been light; Union losses heavy. He watches a
steady stream of Union prisoners being marched to the rear.

Among the prisoners is Union Brigadier General Napoleon B.
McLaughlin, captured at Stedman but insisting upon surrendering his sword
to Gordon.

"Bring him here, Captain. I'll be glad to take his sword."

Moments later Gordon formally returns McLaughlin's salute, accepts
the beaten officer's sword, and exchanges handshakes with his former
enemy.

"Now, General," Gordon sympathetically asks, "how'd you happen to
get yourself in such a fix?"

"Well, sir," McLaughlin begins, "my compliments to you. A beautiful
attack. Caught us by surprise. I was sleeping when the first fire awakened
me. Soon's I heard it I alerted my regiments."

Seeing Gordon's approving nod, McLaughlin continues, "Then I rode
to Fort Haskell. Your men hadn't gotten that far yet so I came up the line
toward Battery 12. I ordered an attack there, and our boys soon took Batteries 12 and 11 back."

"Then," he sighs, "I made a mistake. Thought they'd taken back
Stedman too so I rode up there. Hard to see in the dark, General. Black as
a witches'...well, you know what I mean. Anyway, I rode right into Stedman.
I could see a bunch of our boys milling around in the dark there. Seemed
confused. Saw they hadn't swung the cannon back to face your lines over
here so I gave orders to that effect."

Appreciating Gordon's sympathetic silence, McLaughlin continues.
"Well, sir, the men still seemed slow carrying out my orders. So I yelled
again, and they hopped right to it. Well, I still couldn't see what regiment was
there in the dark so I asked their Colonel's name. I didn't recognize it, so I said,
'Well, I never heard of your Colonel. Is this a Massachusetts regiment?'."

"I'm afraid, General Gordon, that did it. They certainly weren't Massachusetts men! North Carolina I believe. Good soldiers," he reflects.

"Embarrassing, General Gordon, right embarrassing; but they took
me fair and square. Well, sir, of course I wasn't about to surrender my
sword to some damned Reb captain. Demanded to be taken straight to
you. And here I am."

"My sympathies for your plight, General," Gordon smiles. "Seems you did the best you could under the circumstances. Now, sir, if you'll accompany my aide, I must move forward."

The generals have met like two ships in the night, exchanged polite greetings, and now separate, each to his own fate.

"Colonel," Gordon orders, "send a courier to General Lee. Tell him what's happening. The attack goes well. Ask him for any word of Pickett's division. I'm going across the field."

In captured Fort Stedman Gordon receives the first discouraging reports. From Lee: the ancient train with Pickett's division has broken down. Pickett's men can't reach him for several hours. On his flanks, the Confederate advance has stalled above and below Fort Stedman. And his local guides haven't yet found the strongpoints he'd identified behind the Federal lines. Enemy resistance is stiffening all along his front. At dawn, soon now, the sun will be in the faces of Gordon's gunners. Not good.

Gordon, keenly aware that his attack must succeed, suddenly feels very tired, frightened. He sends another courier to Lee.

Several miles to the east of Fort Stedman, Major General John G. Parke, commanding the Union IX Corps, orders his reserve, under Brigadier General John F. Hartranft, toward the breach.

Hartranft has been covering the seven-mile corps' front with Massachusetts and Pennsylvania regiments and, awakened by the firing to his front, already had ordered them gathered and moved toward the fight.

At dawn he's retaken the batteries above and below Fort Stedman and stopped Confederate infantry in the Massachusetts' camps. When he's convinced that the break in his lines is sealed, he gallops from regiment to regiment, finding them almost ready with artillery batteries wheeling into position to support his counterattack.

While Hartranft waits for the last of his regiments to form, he storms into the headquarters of Major General Orlando B. Willcox, Parke's 1st Division commander. Willcox's headquarters' wagons, already loaded with the staff's baggage and equipment, wait beside the large farmhouse. Their tents have been struck, and their former occupants are standing about, talking, uncertain; Willcox obviously is prepared to retreat.

Hartranft wastes little time with his superior, "General, this isn't the time to pull back. We've stopped them cold, all along our line. And now we can destroy them. I have two regiments ready to go in now; in a half hour I'll have four more. I'll hit them from the east and the south; if you'll come in from the north, we can retake our line. I'm sure of it."

"Well, General," Willcox hesitates, "if you're willing to take responsibility for the attack."

"Take responsibility!" Hartranft snorts. "Yes, I'll be responsible. Fully responsible. Give me a half hour, General. Then, when you hear my guns, have your regiments attack. They're Gordon's men out there, and they're going to be hurting when we finish with them. Hurting bad. We can retake Stedman, roll up his picket lines; maybe even take part of his trench line. Do it, General; we won't have a chance like this again."

The light is improving fast now as Union regiments swing from defending their ground to attacking their enemy. They retake the lost ground, driving Gordon's men back across the torn field toward Colquitt's Salient.

John Gordon, in fire-swept Fort Stedman, realizes that the fight is lost. The fort is buried under a hail of Union fire. His front and flanks are gone. He has no hope of being reinforced; the cursed, broken down train with Pickett's desperately needed men can never get there in time. All along his line more Yankee infantry and artillery are massing. Bitterly disappointed, he turns now to saving as many of his men as possible.

"All right, Colonel," he orders. "Sound 'Recall'. Get the word to our commanders. Have half their men lay down covering fire; get the rest across that field as fast as they can. Then they can cover us from the other side."

"You're staying here, General?"

"For a time," Gordon growls, "for a time."

As his orders spread, bugles repeat "Recall." Men begin to recross the fire-swept field.

Some Confederate soldiers, however, study the field then simply ignore the order. Private Henry London of Grimes' division is one. He's found some hardtack in a Stedman bombproof. So he shrugs his shoulders and simply sits down to eat. He's not alone. Others choose to enjoy captured Yankee rations while waiting to be taken prisoner.

Most of Gordon's men, however, start back across the field. Running, dodging, dropping to the ground until they can catch their breaths then run again. In the early days they'd worried about turning their backs on the enemy. A terrible disgrace to be shot in the back. That was a long time ago. No time for niceties now, just get across as fast as you can.

Captain R. D. Funkhouser calls for a group of Virginia riflemen to follow him. They've scarcely left Fort Stedman when a shell explodes, knocking Funkhouser to the ground. Barely conscious, the breath driven from him, he hears his soldiers weighing his fate.

"He's dead. Gotta be dead; that shell landed right on him."

"No, he's still alive. We gotta carry him across."

That decided, one man takes his legs, two others his arms, and they begin to run toward the Confederate lines.

They've only gone a few yards, however, when another shell bursts nearby, and they unceremoniously drop him.

Funkhouser, the breath again knocked from him, lies half conscious as they debate the issue again, quickly deciding, "It's no use, boys. This time he's dead for sure. And we can't get across that field. Let's go back and take our chances in the fort."

As his rescuers turn to run back toward Stedman, Funkhouser recovers enough to decide they've made the right choice. He sprints after them and, before they reach the fort, he's passed them by.

In Stedman they all laugh at the captain's miraculous recovery. They're deciding whether to try again when a Federal officer scrambles over the wall and, grinning as he waves his pistol at them, makes the decision for them.

Another Confederate officer, Captain William H. Edwards, 17th South Carolina Infantry, also has tried to lead his men from Stedman, but he's not so lucky as Funkhouser. They've hardly begun when Edwards is shot down. He lies in a shell hole, watching as seventeen of his men fall around him. From across the field he can hear Lee's bugles sounding "Recall"; Edwards and several thousand other Confederates would like to obey but can't.

Nearly eight o'clock and Union General John Hartranft is riding back and forth along his lines, leading, cajoling, cursing, pushing his regiments to retake Fort Stedman, when a messenger from his corps' commander, Parke, reaches him: "General, I've ordered the VI Corps forward to support your attack. Delay your offensive until they arrive."

"No!" an angry aide curses. "Stupid! We can take 'em, General. I know we can take 'em. Right now. With what we have." Then his anger and frustration vented, he sighs, "Well, sir, what do we do?"

"Do?" Hartranft grins, "Why we got this message too late, Captain. Been glad to oblige, but they found us a mite late. All this smoke and all. Get over there now, and hustle those regiments along. Three-day passes for the first regiment into Stedman. Tell them that. I'll be up ahead here."

Captain Joe Carson's few remaining Georgia sharpshooters have fallen back into Stedman. From its now nearly deserted parapets they begin to shoot at their enemy. From their left to their right, as far as they can see, and in lines ten to fifteen deep, Yankee soldiers are nearing the fort. Carson's sharpshooters calmly fire into the Blue mass, a mosquito pestering an elephant, but it's the best they can do.

"Cap'n. Cap'n, sir. Over here," his sergeant calls. He leads him to where they'd scrambled over the battered walls four hours before. Among the dead quietly placed there Joe Carson finds his brother's body.

The sergeant squats to arrange the torn uniform on the still form. Then, forgetting rank (they've been together a long time), he rises and says, "I'm sorry, Joe. I'm real sorry."

Joe Carson, tears streaming down his dirty face, kneels to pat his younger brother's shoulder, smooth his hair. Then he stands, confused, as if a terrible mistake has occurred.

"Bob, Bob, not you. It was supposed to be me. Wrong, all wrong."

He allows that much, then the habit of command takes over, "I know, Jim, I know. Get someone to fetch a blanket and help me. Then start our boys across. Tell 'em to run and keep runnin' 'til they're back in our own lines. Wish 'em luck for me. We'll follow soon's you're all out of here."

"Cap'n," the sergeant shakes his head, "let Jack here help you. The two of you start across now, while we still can cover you. I'll take care of things here then join you in awhile. Do it now, Joe; we don't have lots of time."

Carson nods; it's best that way. They walk across the torn, fire-swept field, carrying the blanket-wrapped body, making no attempt to run or to hide or to dodge. It takes awhile but, in the hail of fire, neither man is touched. Just before they enter the Confederate trenches Captain Joe Carson glances across the field. In the early morning sunlight the Stars and Stripes flies over Fort Stedman.

John Gordon, among the last Confederates to leave Fort Stedman before it falls, receives his ninth wound as he recrosses the field.

Lee is waiting at the Confederate trenches. Bleeding, dirty, tired, very discouraged, Gordon reports his failure. Lee hears him out, nods his understanding, then leans across Traveller to touch the younger general's arm and gently reassure him.

"I know, General. And I know that you did the best you could. Your soldiers were magnificent. Tell them that for me. As for our loss, God has smiled on us in the past. Not today, but perhaps another time. Perhaps another time. Now, see to your men and see to your own wound, sir. I expect those people will follow their success with a heavy attack along our line. We must be ready for them."

The Union attack does continue, seizing Gordon's picket line but not able to break through the Confederate trenches. And still later that day Gordon will counterattack to recover some, but not all, the ground he's lost.

In Petersburg, Confederate surgeon John Claiborne will treat wounded of the Stedman fight then reflect, "Those who participated were cheered and elated with the excitement and the glory of the charge, while I witnessed only the blood and wounds and mutilation and death agony of the brave. I am heartsick, and pray each time that I may see these things no more."

Lee has lost perhaps 4,000 men; Grant about half that number.

Lee reports the failure to Jefferson Davis, warning that he no longer can keep Sherman from joining Grant. Nor can he protect Richmond. He advises an immediate retreat while his army still can break free.

CHAPTER 2

City Point
March 24–30, 1865

THE LINCOLNS

Dusk, Friday, March 24. "Are we nearly there, Father?" she asks without looking up at the tall, dark figure standing beside her at the rail of the *River Queen*. Instead she continues to gaze at the dark river ahead, a river dotted here and there, as far as she can see, with the lights of other boats.

She's really not looking for an answer to her question; only reassurance that he is there. He'd been so deep in thought, studying the darkening shore, that she needed to pull him back.

"Are we nearly there, Father?" she asks again.

He starts, instantly concerned. For many months Mary Lincoln's despondency, anger, and jealousy that erupts without warning and simply must run its course, has been his public embarrassment, his private torment. There are grounds enough for her troubled mind: bad enough to have lost her favorite son, she's also lost three of her five brothers fighting for the South. And she's been the target of vicious Washington slander and laughter. Quick to imagine hurts or slights, especially slights to her position as the wife of the President, perhaps those incidents hurt her most. For whatever reason, she's so visibly worsened in the past six months that he's consulted several physicians.

"It may pass or it could be the onset of severe mental illness, Mr. President," they'd shaken their heads gravely but could only suggest he keep her as calm and as reassured as possible and, when the storms come, try to ease her through them. Abraham Lincoln, beset on all sides by the war, by his political enemies, and by his concern for her, has neither the time nor the ability to soothe all her hurts or to calm all her fears. But he tries, as he does now.

"Soon now, Mother. When Captain Bradford anchored near Fort Monroe to fetch fresh water for me, he told me we should reach City Point before nine o'clock. Soon now."

"Well, it seems such a long trip. The terrible storm last night. Your illness. That dark shoreline." She shudders, "There could be an enemy behind every tree. Why did you insist upon coming?"

"Now, now," he pats her arm, "you recall General Grant's telegram. He said he'd like very much to see me and that he thought the rest would do me good. Mary, he's the only general whose welcomed me, and this campaign is more important than any other we've known. If my being here can help, I'll risk an enemy behind every tree. Besides," he brightens, "the change will be good for us. At least we are away from Washington for a few days."

"Well, I do not expect to enjoy myself here."

"Mother, you insisted upon coming. Perhaps the trip has been too much for you. Rest tomorrow and then return. I'll follow in a few days."

"I shall remain with you; my place is by your side."

"As you wish, Mother. You see the *Bat* ahead of us?" he tries to distract her. "Captain Barnes there is assuring our safe passage. There are many sunken ships in the channel. We must steer clear of the shore yet be careful of obstructions."

"If you're not too tired," he pleads, "watch with me a bit longer. We'll soon see the lights of City Point. You've not yet been there. I'm told that since my visit here last summer it has nearly doubled its size. Do you know that it's considered the fourth busiest port in the world? Imagine that: a little four-street, two-dog Virginia village on a little spit of land where the Appomattox and the James come together, and now the fourth busiest port in the world."

Then he adds, "And, when we end this terrible war, City Point will wither away almost as fast as the soldiers can strike their tents. Amazing! But stand here with me to see the lights, perhaps just around that bend ahead."

A little before nine, as he'd promised, the *River Queen* rounds a bend of the broad river to dock at City Point. Also as he'd promised, their first nighttime view of City Point, Grant's headquarters for all the United States' armies and the supply base for the Union armies besieging Richmond and Petersburg, is spectacular.

The bright red, green, yellow, and blue lanterns of more than a hundred ships anchored in the James or nestled against the long wharf below the bluff light the river and nearby shore. On the bluff above is an installation whose size is only hinted at by the glow of hundreds of additional lamps. Another sign of City Point's importance are the hundreds of laborers who, despite the late hour, work unloading food, clothing, and ammunition onto the half-mile wharf. And everywhere there are Union soldiers.

The busy, colorful scene brightens Mary Lincoln, particularly after their eldest son, Robert, resplendent in his newly commissioned captain's uniform, hurries up the gangplank to greet them.

Not quite sure, as a soldier, how to greet his President-father, Robert Lincoln manages a salute that becomes a hug. Another hug for Mary Lincoln and for his younger brother, Tad.

"General and Mrs. Grant will be along in a moment, Father. It's so good to see you all. In the morning I'm to give you a personal tour of City Point. You can't believe all that is going on here."

"You seem a bit thin, son," an anxious Mary Lincoln again squeezes his arms, as if to confirm her fear.

"Oh, no, Mother. Just getting a lot more exercise than I did at Harvard. I'm really fine."

"Are you enjoying your duties, Robert?" Lincoln smiles at his son's enthusiasm.

"Yes, sir. Very much. Of course I've much to learn. The headquarters' staff tease me a lot," he smiles at the recollection. "The other day the Colonel asked me to go to the Quartermaster and fetch five and a half yards of firing line. And I'd have gone too except I caught the Sergeant Major's wink. He's taken me under his wing."

Lincoln is pleased with his son. He'd asked Grant if there might be a minor position for the boy following his recent graduation from Harvard and had been pleased with Grant's offer of a captaincy on his own staff. Now it seems to be working out well. The boy is happy, and that should ease his mother's concerns. Even now Robert's pointing to the dockworkers and excitedly beginning to tell them about City Point.

As for the scene before them, Abraham Lincoln finds it both reassuring and troubling. The soldiers, the weapons, the unloading of shot and shell and powder and rations, all outlined by the bright lanterns. Wherewithal to do the job that had to be done, but there is another side to it.

"Beautiful," Robert had just described the scene. No, Lincoln weighs the word, not "beautiful." "Ominous." Yes, that's a better word. Ominous. The fourth busiest port in the world, he muses, but the goods being unloaded here aren't for commerce; they're for the war and that just a few miles away.

Turning from his family, he realizes that Ulysses and Julia Grant have arrived.

"General Grant."

"Mr. President. Good to have you here, sir."

"Good to be here, General," and, as the two men warmly, firmly shake hands, Julia Grant appreciates the closeness between them. They're alike in many ways, she decides; the visit will be good for Ulysses too. Then, seeing Lincoln's arm persuasively urging her husband to a more secluded part of the deck, she concentrates on welcoming the President's party.

Mary Lincoln seems tired, tense, drawn. Julia Grant, having seen the older woman's outbursts on several occasions, hopes that the visit may be good for the First Lady too. If not, that at least her presence here might not cause either man more concern. Especially right now. Ulysses shares his plans with no one, certainly not with me, but everyone knows that there will be fighting soon. Lincoln has come; Sherman and Sheridan may be here tomorrow. They'll talk, and then the fighting will begin. He'll need to concentrate on that.

"Good evening, ma'am. Welcome to City Point."

"Thank you, Mrs. Grant. It's been a long, tiring journey. The President was made ill by the storm, and I was concerned that enemy soldiers might be along the river. But he could not refuse General Grant's request, and it is my duty to be with him." Turning to a nearby staff officer, she adds, "Have you met Captain Penrose? He is my officer."

As the two women talk, Grant is quietly reassuring the President that the situation facing his armies before Richmond and Petersburg is much as it has been for the past several months.

"My constant fear, Mr. President, is that I'll wake some morning to find Lee and his army gone. Before that happens, I hope to either turn his right flank or to break his lines once and for all. Either way will force him into the open where I can destroy his army. If he should retreat before I can do that, however, he may be able to join General Johnston. That would cause a costly campaign that could go on most of the summer."

"General," Lincoln nods, "that's also my greatest fear. I know I needn't urge you to move quickly, but I've come to help in any way I can make that possible. Have you heard from General Sherman?"

"He'll arrive tomorrow or the next day. The same with General Sheridan. Sheridan did a fine job in the Valley. Destroyed Early's army."

"I understand," Lincoln smiles, "that some generals and reporters felt that Sheridan might not be a big enough man for the job; I trust that they've come around to your way of thinking."

Then he laughs, "Grant, do you recollect the peace commissioners last month? That long, thick overcoat Alexander Stephens wore?"

"Yes, sir. Quite a coat. Wide shoulders and reaching to the floor. In that coat he looked like a mighty big man."

"A long ear of corn indeed," Lincoln chuckles. "Well, he was wearing that coat when I met with their peace commissioners. From my days in the Congress I didn't recollect his being such a large man. Matter of fact, I remembered him as a dried up little tadpole. Well, when we started talking he insisted on wearing that blessed coat. Wouldn't take it off. Then the cabin began to get warm. Pretty soon Stephens was sweating like a young man courting. Finally he just had to take off that coat. Well, he shuck it like an ear of corn; and when he'd shuck it, there just wasn't much left of him. Blamed if I didn't think 'That's the biggest shuck and the littlest nubbin I ever did see.'"

The two men laugh heartily, and Julia Grant looks toward her husband; not hearing the story but approving of the warmth the men feel for each other.

"I think, General," Lincoln laughs again, "if we take off Sheridan's coat, we'll find he's still big enough to do the job you'll give him. We'll talk about that?"

"Yes, sir. If you'd like, your son can show you around City Point in the morning. Then we'll ride the Military Railroad to Meade's Station where I'll have horses waiting and a carriage for the ladies. Meade's planned a review they might enjoy and, if things are quiet, you may want to see a portion of the lines before we talk about what I hope to do here."

The following morning, Captain Robert Lincoln bounds up the gangplank of the *River Queen* to share breakfast with his family and to report, "There was heavy fighting this morning, Father. Around Fort Stedman below Petersburg."

Lincoln takes a worn, often-folded map from his pocket and, with calloused hands that have known heavy work, spreads it on the table. Robert Lincoln is surprised to see how well his father has marked the Union and Confederate battle lines.

"Fort Stedman is here?"

"Yes, sir. Early this morning the Confederates attacked our lines there. It was touch and go for awhile, but I'm told that things are going much better for our army now."

Lincoln would like to visit the battlefield, but Grant sends back word that he can't allow it until the fighting ends.

Robert Lincoln takes his parents for a tour of Grant's base at City Point. Lincoln is amazed at how it has grown since his June '64 visit.

The river is jammed with hundreds of ships: tugboats, barges, four-masted schooners, troopships, steamers, each waiting to load or unload or to take part in the river's defense. Not too many miles above City Point is Richmond and, between Richmond and City Point, there are at least three Confederate ironclads and seven gunboats under the command of Rear Admiral Raphael Semmes, notorious blockade runner and former captain of the Confederate raider *Alabama*. As they're a constant threat to come down river, Union warships are picketed nearby.

Along the wharf are warehouses, wagons, ambulances. Near one warehouse are hundreds and hundreds of neatly stacked, odd-shaped, wooden boxes: coffins waiting to be used.

Also below the bluff is a spur of the Military Railroad, a rail line without a solid bed but simply rolled out by Grant's engineers across hastily smoothed ground, up and down as the ground chose to lay, for better than fifteen miles. Professional railroad men snicker at the "corrugated washboard" railroad but admit that it works. And twenty-four hours a day the line hauls supplies to the armies then returns with Union and Confederate wounded and Confederate prisoners.

Soldiers, sailors, teamsters, laborers, clerks; everywhere. There is much noise: whistles; rattling chains; rumbling of wagon wheels, artillery carriages, caissons, ambulances; shouts; curses. A man's world and, to Abraham Lincoln, a strange, ominous world.

"We store a month's supply of food and three weeks' forage for the horses," Robert proudly explains. "General Rawlins told me that's better than nine million meals and 12,000 tons of hay and oats."

"Over there, the tents with the yellow flags," he points, "is the depot field hospital. Actually it's seven hospitals all put together. They can handle thousands of patients. More than 1,200 tents, barracks, laundries, dispensaries, bakeries, dining halls."

"Beyond the hospital, over there near the defense line, is our bakery. They turn out 100,000 loaves of bread there every day."

"So much. So much," the President gravely shakes his head. "No wonder the war costs so much each day. But, if it takes this to win the war, no expense is too great."

Then, pointing toward a big, enclosed area near the river below them, he asks, "What's behind that high fence? It's a very large area, and I see guards everywhere. They look about as friendly as fussin' porcupines."

"Oh," seeming almost embarrassed, Robert Lincoln describes something he obviously finds unpleasant, "that's the 'Bull-Ring,' Father."

"Bull-Ring?"

"Yes, sir. The penitentiary for soldiers being court-martialed or serving their sentences. Men convicted of everything from theft to desertion. General Grant likes for his commanders to handle their own problems, and when they send the real hard cases up here he doesn't waste much time on them. They have a dozen or so court-martials a day in there and, if they judge a death sentence, the findings go straight up to General Grant, he approves them, and the men are executed, usually within twenty-four hours. General Grant doesn't waste a lot of time, sir."

Lincoln nods, "Yes, in the past I've been asked to commute many death sentences. A very difficult task for me. But since General Grant took command of the armies, I find the sentences carried out before the pleas ever reach me. Perhaps," he sighs, "it's just as well. The discipline here seems better than I've ever seen in our camps. He must be handling it well."

"Yes, sir," his son grins. "And it's not very pleasant for the prisoners serving sentences behind that fence. Not much shelter; I've seen hundreds of men huddling there in the rain and cold. No fresh water; and the sinks are terrible. I've heard officers say they'd rather spend six months in Libby Prison than one week in the Bull-Ring. I told General Rawlins that, and he said, 'That's fine. If a man's considerin' doing something wrong, it'll make him think twice knowing he might wind up behind that fence.'"

"It 'pears," Lincoln smiles a bit grimly, "that this place could offer a prairie lawyer a pretty lively practice, but I don't think I'd care to open an office here."

Mary Lincoln alters the conversation by probing again, "You look well, son, but I see that you've been out in the sun a lot. Are you finding a soldier's life agreeable."

"Yes, Mother. Of course I've not seen combat but even headquarters' life is a far cry from Harvard Yard. Every day is exciting, and General and Mrs. Grant have been very kind."

"You like Mrs. Grant?"

"Yes; she's very cheerful, friendly, intelligent. I've accompanied her on trips to visit our sick and wounded. She's very good with them, and they like her. She often takes meals with our headquarters' mess. The mess is very pleasant. Officers come and go as their duties require, and there is excellent conversation."

"Conversation with General Grant?" his father smiles.

"He doesn't say much himself, Father, but he encourages the others with a smile or a nod of his head; and he's always aware of what's going on around him. He carries flint and steel in a small silver tinder box, and he'll light up his cigar, lean back in his chair, and enjoy the others. He's always very cheerful and pleasant. You'd never know the concerns he must have. It's especially fun when Mrs. Grant is there because they tease each other a lot. It's amusing to see him relax that way."

"He does have a good sense of humor," his father nods his head.

"Sometimes Mrs. Grant," Robert Lincoln explains, "will pretend to be a newspaper reporter trying to discover his latest battle plans. Then he'll improvise the most fanciful schemes you can imagine."

"Like what, son?"

"Well, General Rawlins tells me he gets most of them from suggestions people write him. Like firing artillery shells filled with sneezing powder into Richmond. Then, while the Rebs are busy sneezing, we'll rush in and capture the city. Or last winter he told her as soon as the James River froze we were going to charge over the ice. And not long ago, anticipating her asking his latest plans, he showed her elaborate drawings he and General Benham (Brigadier General Henry W. Benham), our engineer, had prepared for a scheme to build a wall around Richmond. Then they'd let the James River flow through a hole in the wall and flood the city."

"The Grants are close then?"

"Yes, Mother. I think so. Sometimes she refers to him as 'Mister Grant'; sometimes as 'the Old Man'; but most often as 'the General.' Privately, she calls him 'Ulysses' or 'Victor,' the name a reporter gave him after Vicksburg. I've seen them holding hands in the evening. And once I found him wrestling with his boys and pretending they'd gotten the better of him."

"He's completely tone deaf, Father," Robert Lincoln sees he has their complete attention. "Can't tell one tune from another. You'll find that he prefers to ride Cincinnati or Jeff Davis in parades because he can't keep step."

"Music's altogether a mystery to him," Robert Lincoln chuckles. "For awhile a different regimental band came every night to play while he was dining. Finally he said, 'Rawlins, I've noticed that band always begins its noise just about the time I'm sitting down to dinner and want to talk. Can't we do something about that?' When General Rawlins explained that they were there to entertain him, General Grant apologized for not being more gracious. Then someone told him that one of Admiral Porter's (Rear Admiral David Porter) commodores had ordered, 'Have the instruments and the men of that band thrown overboard,' and he grinned, said he felt better."

"Well, it sounds almost like a frolic," Mrs. Lincoln snaps.

The young captain reflects a moment, glances at his father, then answers, "No, Mother. It's not a frolic. I think those things are his way of living with the rest of his job. Much like Father's stories. And, aside from Father, I know no one who works harder. He knows this army like the back of his hand. He can look at a report or a map and never glance at it again for he has it memorized. When he leaves his desk to find a paper, he doesn't waste time straightening up; just remains crouched until he sits again. And he never ends the day until his desk is clear. No, it's not a frolic. It's hard work, and a lot of worry. We'll be taking the field soon. Everyone says that. And when we do, the army will be ready for whatever he asks them to do."

When the Lincoln party arrives at Meade's headquarters, a smiling Meade hands the President General Parke's telegram reporting the Union victory at Fort Stedman. Lincoln skims it but is more interested in some 11,000 nearby Confederate prisoners being herded back to City Point. They're dirty, brown, lean, athletic; with matted hair and tangled beards; wearing battered, slouched hats and carrying their belongings in their blanket rolls, an astonishing mixture of carpets, horse blankets, and multi-colored shelter halves rolled and slung over their shoulders. Many are barefoot; many wear bloodied bandages; others have open wounds that have not yet been treated.

"Thank you for the report, General Meade," Lincoln returns Parke's telegram, "but there (pointing at the Confederate prisoners) is the best report anyone could show me. For them the war is over; praise God if it could be over for all of us."

Later, as he watches Meade's soldiers pass in review, Lincoln recalls the parades he'd seen early in the war; young soldiers, stiff and uncomfortable in their new uniforms, awkward with their weapons, and not too successful in carrying out the orders of equally young, inexperienced officers. Now, in the 1865 springtime sun, veterans carry their rifles and bayonets, casually, easily, as if they couldn't imagine not having them nearby. Their uniforms: worn and faded but clean and comfortable. Their officers casually calling commands while V Corps' soldiers respond smoothly, naturally, easily.

"They've grown into a fine army," he shares with Grant. "I mind their youth, and I'm pleased to see what they've become. They've walked a long, rocky road, and I believe that they're truly ready now to end the job we began so long ago."

He'd have considered their performance the more remarkable if he'd realized that a few hours ago, while the battle for Fort Stedman was raging a few miles away, these regiments, not needed for the fight, had ignored the distant thunder of cannon fire and the harsh rattle of musket volleys while they calmly shined buttons, buffed musket stocks, cleaned bayonets for the parade. Just as if they were on the Plain at West Point instead of three miles from a desperate fight.

If the enormity of that incident doesn't occur to Lincoln, it does to a Virginian, Captain R. D. Funkhouser, among the prisoners being marched to City Point. Funkhouser stops dead in his tracks to stare at the thousands of well-equipped, well-fed Union soldiers marching from the completed parade while the Lincoln party casually enjoy refreshments beneath brightly decorated tents as a regimental band entertains them with popular songs of the day.

"Dear Lord," Funkhouser, completely whipped, exclaims, "the enormity of it. If I did not know before, I surely know now. This war is over, and we have lost it."

When Lincoln visits the battlefield several officers attempt to explain the military situation. The haggard President, however, sadly smiles, "Enough, gentlemen. I can see for myself what has happened here."

As he watches, a truce is in effect. Stretcher bearers and burial details are hard at work between the lines. Still forms lie everywhere, torn and twisted, sometimes in clumps as they fell but often alone, making clear that war can be a very personal thing. Wounded men, dirty, dazed, not sure just what has happened to them, await their turn with regimental surgeons. The dead who have been collected, separated by their blue and gray uniforms when a color can be distinguished, and neatly aligned, head to toe, head to toe, also wait.

Lincoln sighs and quietly orders Meade, "Do all you can for them, General. The living and the dead. Both sides."

Turning to Grant, he adds, "I've seen enough horror for this day, General. I hope and pray that this may end soon and without another battle. End it as quickly and as humanely as possible. May God help all of us to do that."

The following morning the military pageantry continues as the Lincolns, the Grants, Major General Philip Sheridan (newly arrived at City Point from his victorious campaign in the Shenandoah Valley), Rear Admiral David Porter (the President's escort), and other staff members watch 10,000 of Sheridan's cavalrymen cross a pontoon bridge over the James.

As some cavalrymen lead their horses across the river, others bathe, wash trail-dusty uniforms, or water horses near its far bank. Sheridan's men, their faces, hands, and forearms, bronzed from sun and wind, lean, neatly dressed in tight-fitting uniforms, and waving their fork-tailed scarlet and white guidons, cheer the President's party on the *River Queen*.

The brightness of that moment, however, is spoiled by an ugly incident that afternoon at another parade honoring the President.

The President and Grant have ridden ahead to the headquarters of Major General Edward O. C. Ord's Army of the James while Mary Lincoln, Julia Grant, and Colonel Horace Porter of Grant's staff follow in an army ambulance. The log-corduroyed road is muddy, bumpy, slow-going. Mrs. Lincoln, fearful that the parade will begin without her, orders Colonel Porter to have the driver hurry.

Porter reluctantly relays the command. The corporal driving the ambulance shrugs at such foolishness, spits a long string of tobacco juice onto the muddy road, and snaps his reins. Mud flies in every direction, spattering the ambulance. Then the ladies are thrown against its top, crushing their hats.

"Enough," Mrs. Lincoln angrily insists, "I will walk the rest of the way."

"Ma'am," Colonel Porter pleads, "you musn't do that. The mud is up to the horses' forelocks. You'll be covered with it. Please wait. We'll be there shortly."

Mary Lincoln reluctantly resumes her seat but with each passing moment becomes angrier.

Meanwhile, the President, riding Grant's Cincinnati, has ordered that the parade begin.

In the excitement of the initial burst of music by a dozen regimental bands, the blare of bugles sounding "Assembly," and the shouting of orders to thousands of soldiers, the ambulance bearing Julia Grant and the First Lady reaches the parade ground unnoticed.

When it seems that no one is coming to welcome them, a red-faced, hands on hips' Mary Lincoln appears at the opening of the ambulance's canvas cover.

Across the field, near the reviewing party, she sees a half dozen, colorfully dressed, female riders. Then one of the women, seeing the ambulance, points to it and calls to their obvious leader, Mrs. Ord, wife of the commanding general of the Army of the James.

Mrs. Ord turns and, leading the other female riders, canters toward the ambulance to welcome the First Lady and her party.

Mary Lincoln, however, having seen Mrs. Ord and the other female riders near the President, erupts, singling out Mrs. Ord for all her displeasure.

"What does that woman mean riding by the side of the President?" she demands of Julia Grant. "And ahead of me? Does she suppose that he wants her by his side?"

Julia Grant, having seen Mary Lincoln's tantrums before, tries to head off the storm.

"Oh, no, ma'am. As the wife of General Ord she's expected to be present when he reviews his army. That's all. Please don't be angry with her. And today she and the other ladies are here to honor you. You see they're coming this way now to escort you to the parade."

Refusing to be appeased, Mary Lincoln now turns on Julia Grant.

"Well! You're so well informed! I suppose you think you'll get to the White House yourself, don't you?"

"Oh, no, ma'am. Of course not. I thank God that Ulysses has come this far, but we are quite happy with our present situation."

"Oh? Is that so? Well, if you can get it, you'd best take it. 'Tis very nice."

She's calmed a bit at Julia Grant's explanation, however, and the storm might have passed had not a staff officer then reined beside the ambulance to grin and offer, "Afternoon, ladies. Major Seward. The President's horse is very gallant. See how he insists on riding near Mrs. Ord?"

Red-faced and very angry, Mary Lincoln demands, "And what do you mean by that, sir?"

Seward, realizing his mistake, mumbles a, "Nothing, ma'am, nothing."

"You meant something, sir, or you'd not have said it. Explain yourself."

Seward looks desperately toward Julia Grant then, realizing that he's on his own, suddenly develops a problem with his horse and must attend to it. Elsewhere.

He's not gone a moment before Mrs. Ord arrives at the head of her colorful escort. She waves a saucy salute with her riding crop but has barely gotten beyond, "Good afternoon...," when Mary Lincoln turns on her.

"Explain yourself, madam. What do you mean, daring to ride beside the President? Don't you know that is *my* place, and mine alone? You are nothing but a camp follower."

Then, warming to her task, the First Lady continues to attack the general's wife, firing a volley of barracks' words Julia Grant would hope she'd never heard let alone dare use.

The other mounted ladies, of one accord, turn and flee, leaving Mrs. Ord to face Mary Lincoln's wrath.

Cringing before the barrage, the hapless woman can only stammer, "Mrs. Lincoln, what have I done? What have I done?"

"That you should need an explanation clearly shows me what you are," Mary Lincoln snaps, more angry by the moment.

When Mary Lincoln's anger continues, becoming even more violent, Mrs. Ord simply bows her head, enduring the abuse until, looking up, she sees Julia Grant frantically waving her to ride away.

Wheeling her horse and without a word, she gallops away. Behind her, Mary Lincoln continues to shout, hurling oaths at the slumped figure until Julia Grant and physical exhaustion finally calm her.

The President, if he is aware of the incident, chooses to ignore it, going on with the parade while the ladies who'd come to escort Mrs. Lincoln huddle a safe distance from the reviewing party and the ambulance.

That evening the Lincolns host a dinner honoring the Grants and the general's staff. During the dinner Mary Lincoln complains about General and Mrs. Ord to her dinner companion, Ulysses S. Grant.

Grant listens politely but does not answer. After trying several times, Mary Lincoln decides that complaining to Grant is as profitable as talking to a post. Angry, she ends her discourse, "Well, General, you must agree that General Ord is not fit to command an army...his wife also not capable of meeting her responsibilities."

This time, however, Grant leans toward her and quietly answers, "No, ma'am, I fear you're mistaken. And you must leave this matter to General Ord and to me."

Angry, she turns upon the President, demanding that he explain to all their guests why she'd been required to ride to the parade in an army ambulance.

When Lincoln attempts to calm her with raised hands, gentle head shakes, pleading eyes, and softly repeated, "Now, Mother; now, Mother," she angrily repeats her question.

Their guests carefully study their plates in discreet silence. Silence that only makes Mary Lincoln's angry voice seem louder.

Seeing that nothing will work and unable to bear the humiliation further, Lincoln stands to quietly announce, "General and Mrs. Grant, ladies and gentlemen, I'm sorry that our dinner must be interrupted. Mrs. Lincoln and I have had a very full day; we really must retire. General Grant, I will see you in the morning. Meanwhile, the band is here; please enjoy the evening. Good night."

With Mary Lincoln on his arm, he leaves the room.

SHERMAN

Dusk, Monday, March 27. The *Russia*, a Southern steamer commandeered by the U.S. Navy, ties to the City Point dock. Its gangplank barely touches the wharf when a slender, well-built man; with unruly, rust-colored hair; close-cropped, sandy whiskers; and restless, twinkling eyes; and, despite the two silver stars of a major general on his shoulder straps, wearing a shabby coat, slouched hat, and pants stuffed into his boots like an Ohio farmer, strides ashore. Major General William Tecumseh ("Cump") Sherman, "Uncle Billy" to the men of his Western army.

Waiting on the pier stands Grant: wearing a private's uniform with three silver stars tacked to its make-do shoulder straps and a stiff-brimmed black uniform hat; muddy, well-worn boots. One of his hands is stuffed in his trouser pocket, the other grasps a large cigar.

Beside Grant stands a tall, thin, sharp-featured man with large, bespectacled eyes, a gray beard, a stooped gait. Major General George E. Meade.

Grant speaks first: "How d'ye do, Sherman!"

"How are you, Grant!" Sherman fires back.

Then, with no more formalities, the two generals, old, loyal friends who have seen many rough times but now are at the peaks of their military careers, shake hands then hug each other with genuine pleasure.

During their walk to Grant's T-shaped log cabin headquarters' home atop the bluff, Sherman talks quickly, bringing his commander up to date. As he speaks, Sherman gestures a lot, his eye darting everywhere and missing little of his surroundings.

Later Julia Grant joins them around a campfire where Sherman entertains them with a graphic account of his army's march to Atlanta, then to Savannah, and now north into North Carolina. It's a straightforward, intriguing story, sprinkled with anecdotes Julia Grant finds delightful.

Anecdotes filled with broad, parade ground humor. As Sherman speaks, Julia Grant realizes that he is quietly studying her reaction to his stories. Nothing off-color or ungentlemanly about them, but if a story does not meet her approval he'll end it quickly and there'll be no more like tales.

"Cump" Sherman, she quietly measures him, he's just marched through the heart of the Confederacy, burning a path of death and destruction fifty miles wide so the Southern people might understand the price of the war they'd begun and still continue. Two years ago Northern reporters judged him insane. Sam Grant stood by Sherman then. And when, in the middle of the hell that was Shiloh, Ulysses thought of resigning, it was Cump Sherman who'd talked him out of it. And here he is, wanting to boast of his soldiers yet he'll not do it if I show the least sign of disapproving. She smiles and Sherman, warming to the tale, tells of his skirmishers: "bummers" he calls them.

"The older hands know me pretty well, Grant. On the march they'll call out as I pass. Not a lot of cheering and all that, just calling out. You know, one soldier to another. I enjoy it."

"One fellow," he laughs, "was wading barefoot across a creek, and I called to him, 'That's a stout pair of legs you've got there, my man. On a march like this I wouldn't mind exchanging mine for them, if you don't object.'"

"Well, he sized up my legs there in the water beside him, thought a minute, then decided, 'General, if it's all the same to you, I guess I'd rather not swap.'"

"Another one," Sherman chuckles again, "was up a telegraph pole, hacking away at the wires, when one of Schofield's (Brigadier General John M. Schofield) officers yelled at him, 'What are you doing up there? You're destroying one of our own telegraph lines.' The soldier gave the officer a pretty indignant look and, went right on hacking away at the wires while he answered, 'I'm one of Billy Sherman's bummers. Reckon I'm way ahead of the others, but the last thing Uncle Billy said to us when we started out was to be sure and cut all the telegraph wires we come across, and not to go wastin' time askin' who they belong to.'"

"I've seen this Virginia clay before," Sherman continues. "Know what a heavy rain can do to it. But it's nothing to the rains we had below Savannah. Five straight days of it, heaviest I've ever seen. Everything under water."

"Two of my men," he chuckles, "were trying to fight their way upstream on a flooded country road, sinking over their boots with every step. Finally one got disgusted, stopped, and said to the other fellow, 'Say, Tommy, blamed if I don't think Uncle Billy's struck this river lengthways.'"

Sam Grant hasn't said two words in the last hour Julia Grant realizes, but I've not seen him this relaxed in months. Cump Sherman's good for him.

Finally, Grant interrupts, "Sorry to break this up, Cump. Can't tell you how I've enjoyed it; but the President is aboard the *River Queen*. Suppose we go pay him a visit before dinner."

When the two men return, Julia Grant has tea waiting. First, how-ever, she asks, as a wife might, "And how is Mrs. Lincoln?"

"Oh, no!" her husband hangs his head. "Reckon we should have asked. But we went there on business and didn't even ask if she was aboard."

"Well, you're a pretty pair!" she judges.

Grant glances sheepishly at Sherman, smiles, and replies, "Well, Julia, we're going to pay another visit in the morning, and we'll take care to make amends for our conduct today."

"Now, Cump," Grant turns to Sherman, let's talk about what I hope to do."

———

Grant and Sherman are talking before a large map when Major Gen-eral Philip H. Sheridan, Grant's cavalry chief, arrives to join them.

After a time Sherman abruptly suggests, "Sheridan, why don't you come back with me tomorrow? I'll start my drive north on the 10th. That'll give you time to get the lay of the land down there and a feel for my soldiers. You'll find that the armies are different in lots of ways. But cavalry's cavalry, and they'll serve you well. That country's great for cavalry opera-tions, and you'd be a big help to me. The quicker I can get up here, the quicker Grant can end this business. What do you say?"

Grant puffs his cigar, waits for Sheridan's answer. Three days be-fore he'd announced his orders for his campaign to end the siege of Richmond and Petersburg. Sheridan grinned when he read that he was to move around Lee's right to cut the Southside Railroad, but his dark features flushed a deeper red in anger when he came to the part ordering him then to be prepared either to return to Grant or to march on to join Sherman in North Carolina. Jamming the orders into his tunic, he'd stalked out of the meeting.

Grant smiles, recalling how he'd followed Sheridan outside then, emphasizing his points with jabs from his cigar, explained.

"Now Sheridan, listen to me. This is for you and no one else. Don't get yourself wrapped around the axle about maybe going on to join Sherman. I don't have any intention of that happening. I put that in there because, if you can't turn Lee's right, the newspapers'll second-guess us right into the ground; and I've had enough of that. If you can't take that railroad, we'll tell them that all along your attack was just meant to be a raid. Then I'll pull you back, and we'll try something else. Either way I don't intend to send you off to Sherman."

"We're going to end this business right here," he'd ended his speech to the fiery little general, about as long a speech as Sheridan ever remem-bered Grant's giving, "and you're going to do it for me. You'll have a full corps or more of infantry, plus Crook's (Major General George Crook) cav-alry. And you'll operate independently so Meade won't get in your way. I'll be close by, near as you need me; and we'll take advantage of whatever turns up."

"Meade won't like that," Sheridan answered.

"No, I don't suppose he will," Grant nodded. "You know, the President told me that when reporters criticized him for not giving Sigel (Major General Franz Sigel) a bigger role in the Valley, he told them that, if Siegel couldn't do the skinning himself, he could hold a leg while someone else did the skinning. I don't think that Meade can carry this off, Sheridan. You can. So we'll let Meade hold a leg while you do the skinning."

When Sheridan heard that, Grant remembers with satisfaction, he grinned from ear to ear, lit up like a rocket, and almost ran for his horse.

"Glad to hear it, General," he called over his shoulder, "and we can do it."

Then he'd galloped down the road, as fast as he could, impatient to get things started.

Now Sheridan's reaction to Sherman's invitation is just as strong.

"Thanks, General. But no, hell no. We've fought too long and too hard here, and we're just about to end this thing. There's no way I won't be in on the finish here with Grant."

Grant takes a final puff on his cigar, grins, and adds, "That's it, Cump. Appreciate the suggestion, but I've already filled in Phil's dance card, and the armies are already in motion."

THE WAR COUNCIL

He repeats that decision the next morning when he, Lincoln, Sherman, and Rear Admiral David Porter (commander of the Navy's North Atlantic Squadron) meet aboard the *River Queen.*

Grant begins the conference, standing before a large map and tracing with his broad hand the operations of all the armies under his command. Then Sherman discusses his campaign into North Carolina. On April 10 he'll march north toward Richmond.

"Is it still possible, General Sherman, for General Johnston's army to escape?" Lincoln asks. "So many times in the past we've thought we had a Confederate fox cornered and then he escaped."

"Not this time, Mr. President, not this time," Sherman grimly answers. "I'm pressing him too hard. Besides, his army's too badly used up to march far, and I've destroyed his railroads."

Grant suggests, "Tell the President what's to prevent their repairing the rails, General."

"Well, sir, my bummers don't do things by halves. Every rail for miles and miles is heated over a hot fire until it's red hot. Then the men bend them around telegraph poles until they're as crooked as a ram's horn." Smiling, he adds, "They call them 'Sherman's neckties.' No, sir, they won't be laid again."

Grant then turns to the Richmond-Petersburg front.

"I'll try to move around Lee's right," he explains, "cutting him off from Johnston. If he retreats before I can do that, I'll push him hard, but my hope is to turn his right flank or, if I can't do that, to force him to stretch his line so thin that I can break it somewhere else."

Sherman interrupts to add, "If Lee moves toward North Carolina, sir, my army can hold him and Johnston back until Grant can arrive."

"Now," Grant runs a stubby finger along the map then stabs it, "here. Five Forks. That'll be Sheridan's job. Sheridan reinforced with one or two corps of infantry. Take Five Forks and I turn Lee's right flank. And from there Sheridan can drive north, here, to cut the Southside Railroad. Then Lee has to abandon Richmond and Petersburg. And once we've drawn him from his trenches, we can finish him off."

Lincoln has listened quietly, nodding his understanding and agreement. Then he asks, "When will this begin, General?"

"I issued the necessary orders on the 24th. Sheridan's cavalry started across the James this morning. Three of Ord's infantry divisions and one division of cavalry will follow. They'll replace Humphreys' (Major General Andrew A. Humphreys) II Corps and Warren's (Major General Gouverneur K. Warren) V Corps in the lines so Humphreys and Warren can move southwest, this way, to support Sheridan. What's left of Ord's men, under General Weitzel (Major General Godfrey Weitzel), will hold north of the James. And down here, just below the river," he touches the map again, "Parke's and Wright's (Major General Horatio G. Wright) corps of Meade's army will attack Lee's Petersburg trenches the minute Lee pulls troops from his lines to counter Sheridan. Once we've begun, we'll push hard to end this as quickly as possible."

Lincoln nods again. Then the melancholy returns to his face as he shares, "There has been so much suffering. So many lives lost. Can this end without another terrible battle?"

Sherman starts to speak then looks toward Grant; it's for him to answer.

"Mr. President," Grant replies, "we'll continue to hope so, but that's up to Lee. I believe that he'll fight so long as he is capable of fighting. And, if he fights, we'll have to fight too."

Lincoln then shares his plans should the war end suddenly. "I expect the elected officials in each of the seceded states to continue to represent those states until others can be elected. We'll assure those states that their rights will be preserved, as if this terrible war had not been fought. I simply want them all to lay down their arms and return to the Union. I've given a great deal of thought to that wonderful time when we are one country again, and I feel that we can handle it well."

Sherman then asks what will happen to Jefferson Davis if the South surrenders.

"Well, General, there was a man who'd taken a pledge of abstinence. Offered a glass of brandy, he declined, citing the pledge as his authority. Offered a lemonade, he accepted. His host then suggested that the lemonade would taste better with a little drop of the brandy, that is if his guest wouldn't mind the addition. 'No,' the gentleman responded, 'if you can add it without my knowledge.' Well, the truth is, like our temperance man, if Jefferson Davis flees the country without our having to hold the door open for him, it would solve a difficult problem very nicely. Reckon we'll just have to decide what to do about Mr. Davis if and when the problem comes up."

"Mr. President," Sherman then asks, "it's likely that either Grant or I, perhaps both of us, will have to dictate the terms of surrender to the armies opposing us. We may have to do that with little warning, in the field. Have you any guidance for us?"

Lincoln smiles, "General Sherman, I won't presume to tell either of you how to do your jobs. You've already demonstrated your capabilities there. I'd only suggest that you let 'em up easy; let 'em up easy."

―――――――――――

Grant and Lincoln walk Sherman to the *Bat* which will return Sherman to his army.

As they walk the pier Lincoln confides, "General Sherman, do you know why I've taken such a shine to the two of you?"

"No, sir. You've been very kind, but I do not know why."

"It's because neither of you ever criticized me."

A few minutes later the *Bat* slips away from the City Point wharf. Sherman, watching the tall, sad figure waving to him, will always remember Abraham Lincoln as a great and good man.

THE PRESIDENT

Mary Lincoln has returned to Washington, and the President begins to enjoy his visit to City Point. The miles prevent his doing anything about the concerns he has for her or the other matters that fill his every day in Washington. He and Tad take advantage of each day, wandering freely about City Point, talking with soldiers, sailors, laborers, doing what they feel like doing at the moment.

They settle aboard Admiral Porter's flagship, the *Malvern*, Lincoln selecting a stateroom about the size of a closet. His host objects, "Sir, there isn't enough room in there to swing a full-grown cat. Please take my cabin."

Lincoln won't hear of it, "No, no, Porter. I'll be fine."

That night, pressed for space, he leaves his boots and socks outside the cabin. Porter finds them there and, noticing holes in the President's socks, has a sailor darn them and shine the boots.

At breakfast Lincoln looks a bit tired but is in good spirits.

"A miracle happened to me last night, Admiral Porter," he explains. "When I went to bed I had two large holes in my socks. This morning the holes are gone. That never happened to me before. Grant told me you'd performed military miracles for him; now I believe it."

Porter chuckles then asks, "You do look a bit tired, sir. How did you sleep?"

"Toler'ble, Admiral; toler'ble. Reckon you were right. There really isn't room in there for a middlin' cat. You know, when I was at Gettysburg the town fathers misjudged my height. Reckon some Democrat told 'em I was a little man, and they took the report literally. Brought a tadpole of a horse for me to ride to the cemetery. I got aboard him, but it wasn't a great success. I told them that you just can't put a long blade in a short scabbard. I was a little too long for that horse; reckon I'm too long for that berth. Well, tonight, I'll curl up a bit more."

Porter has another solution. While Lincoln is ashore he summons ships' carpenters to the *Malvern*. By afternoon they've stretched the President's berth from six feet to eight and one-half feet and to a width of four feet. Then sailmakers provide new bedding. When Lincoln returns, he's not told of the changes.

The next morning he greets Porter with a broad smile.

"Admiral Porter, a greater miracle than ever happened last night. I shrank six inches in length and twice that sideways. I also got somebody else's pillow. All in all I slept in a better bed than I had on the *River Queen*."

There is no way, however, for him to completely escape his cares in Washington. Each day brings telegrams from cabinet members, each certain that the President can't manage without his help.

The Secretary of State, William S. Seward, wires, "Shall I come and join you?"

"What shall I tell him, Mr. President?" asks Porter.

"Admiral," Lincoln is emphatic, "I don't want him here. He'll only quote some Prussian marshal to prove how poorly I'm doing my job. This war's going to be over in a week or so, Porter, and I just don't want to hear any more about all the things I'm doing wrong. Tell Mr. Seward that the berths are too small; that you haven't room for a single more passenger. And the next wire you get will be from Mr. Stanton. I'd be much obliged if you'd tell him the same."

The next wire is from Secretary of War Edwin Stanton, scolding Lincoln for visiting the Stedman battlefield: "I hope that you will remember General Harrison's advice to his men at Tippecanoe that they can see as well a little farther off."

Lincoln smiles, "Thank him for his advice, Admiral. Tell him I promise to be careful. But, Porter, I do intend to get close to things so you'd best come along. With all these miracles I'm seeing on the *Malvern*, you're all the protection I'll need."

Abraham Lincoln explores City Point or joins Grant's afternoon rides. His favorite spot is Grant's telegraph office where he enjoys a well broken-in rocker before a warm woodstove while studying commanders' reports and updating his well-worn map. He and Tad Lincoln also enjoy playing in the warm office with three tiny kittens the telegraphers have adopted.

"How'd you come by them, Captain Beckwith (Captain Samuel Beckwith)?"

"One of my telegraphers found them, sir. The mother had died, and there they were. So we took them in. If they pester you...."

"Land sake's no. They're like windup toys for Tad and me. You know, a body just can't be unhappy around a kitten, let alone three of them. Poor little critters," he strokes their fur then daubs the eyes of one with his handkerchief, "there, there, don't you cry no more. You'll be taken good care of."

Turning to Grant's aide, "Colonel Bowers (Lieutenant Colonel Theodore S. Bowers), I hope that you'll see that these motherless waifs are given plenty of milk and treated kindly."

Bowers promises, "I'll see to it, Mr. President. I'll have the cook of our headquarter's mess take them in hand. He'll give them plenty to eat."

"Thank you. But leave them here during the day if you will," he fondles one. "Tad's taken quite a shine to 'em."

With the war council ended; Sherman gone to rejoin his army; Sheridan's cavalry and Meade's and Ord's armies shifting toward Lee's right, Grant announces that it's time for him to move his headquarters to the field.

Lincoln is on hand at Grant's cabin headquarters to see him off, waiting patiently as Grant says goodbye to his family then joining Grant for the walk to the Military Railroad. The headquarters' staff, their horses, and their equipment already are aboard the train.

"Well, General," Lincoln walks beside Grant, "I'm told that you get about as much advice on how to do our job as I do to do mine. Most of it pretty fanciful, I suspect."

"Yes, sir, I do," Grant smiles. "Had one just the other day. The writer proposed a solution so simple that he was amazed that we'd not thought of it sooner. Seems that all we need do to win this war is to equip our men with bayonets one foot longer than the enemies'. Then all we have to do is stand back and dispatch them while we're still out of range."

"Well," Lincoln laughs, "there's a good deal of terror in cold steel. I tested it myself once, when I was a young man on a back street in Louisville, about midnight. A really tough-looking citizen sprang from the shadows, brandishing a Bowie knife; I 'spect it was about three feet long. Waved that thing to see how close he could come to my nose without cutting it off. Sure got my attention in a hurry. Then he held the knife to my throat and asked, 'Stranger, will you lend me $5 on this?'"

"Well, General, you never saw a man reach for his purse any faster than I did that night. I handed him a note and said, 'Here's $10, neighbor; now put up your scythe.'"

Grant climbs to the train's rear platform; Lincoln waits beneath it, his deep-lined face and tired eyes looking up. When Grant and his officers wave their hats in a last salute, Lincoln doffs his own and reminds them, "Goodbye and good luck, gentlemen. God bless you all. Remember, your success is my own."

Grant stands on the rear platform until Lincoln has passed from sight. Then, taking a seat in the coach, he lights a cigar, reflects, then shares, "The President is one of the few visitors I ever had who never tries to squeeze out of me every one of my plans, though he's the only one with a right to know them."

Smoke wreathes his broad face, then Grant continues his reflection, "He'll be waiting at City Point, the most anxious man in the country to hear from us. His heart's so wrapped up in ending this war. Well, I think we can send him good news in a day or two."

Grant's campaign to end the war in the East has begun. Perhaps it's just as well that he doesn't know that Lincoln sleeps badly that night. In the morning the President shares with his secretary, Ward Lamon, a terrible dream he'd had during the night. In his dream he'd awakened in the White House to a deathlike stillness. Then he heard subdued sobs, as if from many mourners. Rising, he'd searched the upstairs halls. Nothing. Then he'd gone downstairs. The glow of many candles lit the lower rooms and the sobbing continued, but he could see no one there. Then, coming to the East Room, he saw a bier bearing a corpse; soldiers guarding it with fixed bayonets. Many people, mute but crying, gazing at the corpse.

Lincoln then asked one of the soldiers, "Who is dead in the White House?"

"Why, the President," the soldier whispered. "He was killed by an assassin!"

"Then, Lamon," Lincoln concludes his story, "a loud burst of grief awakened me."

When Lincoln has shared his frightening experience with his secretary, he sighs then concludes, "Well, Lamon, maybe it's as well we can't see too far up the road. We'll just have to take it a step at a time, same as all our soldiers. Reckon that's my role in it."

CHAPTER 3

Soldiers in the Rain   March 29–30, 1865

GRANT

As his train sways and bounces across the fields below Petersburg, Grant sits quietly alone in a corner of its single coach, thoughtfully smoking his cigar and reviewing his plans.

Ord has about 15,000 men south of the James, he counts off his units. Humphreys' II Corps and Warren's V Corps are slipping southwest in case Sheridan needs them. Sheridan might get to Five Forks today.

By now Lee will know that we're moving; too many men and horses and artillery and supply wagons to avoid that. All right; if he moves to counter Sheridan, Parke's IX Corps and Wright's VI Corps can break his line.

Sheridan, he's key to the whole business. If he can take Five Forks then cut the railroad, we'll have a solid line around them. And the river at Lee's back. Then I'll draw the net tight.

Sheridan, Grant studies the passing fields as if he can see the cavalryman in action out there, will be pushing them hard; right now. Aching for a fight.

I just wish this rain would stop.

Seems to be getting stronger all the time, and he stares at the driving rain, trying to picture the roads ahead of them: the Boydton Plank Road, running southwest from Petersburg, below the Appomattox, for about a dozen miles to Dinwiddie Court House. Dinwiddie Court House: three miles below Five Forks and six below the Southside Railroad. The Boydton Plank Road cut by the White Oak Road and, below that, by Gravelly Run.

Warren will start near Gravelly Run and strike up the Quaker Road, a few miles east of Five Forks, to cut the White Oak Road. If he can do that, it'll make it tough for Lee to get more infantry over there to block Sheridan.

Major Young's (Major Henry Young) scouts say the Rebs have a lot of infantry up the Quaker Road. Well, Warren'll keep 'em busy while Sheridan turns their flank at Five Forks. Take Five Forks and they'll have to pull back; give up the railroad; their backs to the Appomattox. Then we've got them. But Sheridan must hit hard; it all depends on him.

Through the dirty, rain-streaked window, he pictures the ground his soldiers must cross. Flat land or low, rolling hills; pine woods with scattered houses; clearings marked with abandoned sawmills. Creeks cutting through the sand and clay. Creeks, he gauges the heavy rain again, that have to be running mighty high about now. They'll have burned all the bridges, and they'll have trees down across the roads. And this rain; bad news. The roads will be like quicksand. Hard for men to move; harder yet for the artillery and for the supply wagons.

His train rattles past hundreds of blackened, crude, stone and wood, mud-daubed chimneys, starkly standing above the barren landscape like headstones in a vast cemetery. Soldiers' abandoned camps. Many of the chimneys are made from the wood of boxes that once held hardtack or beef or ammunition. They've taken down the shelter halves they used for roofs, Grant notes, but left the walls standing; in case they have to come back. If Lee stops us again, or if this turns out to be another "Mud March," the men figure to come back here and reclaim their huts. It's always been that way.

"Well, by gum," he muses aloud, "it's not going to be that way this time. Not this time."

The wind and rain lash the train even harder, causing it to sway on the uneven tracks. Its oil lanterns, swinging wildly, cast odd shadows across his staff officers hunched over their card game ahead of him. Up ahead, where Sheridan marches, Grant can see whole roads, little more than dirt traces in the best of times, disappearing in the flood. Those remaining will be pitted with Virginia quicksand. Grant's seen a span of mules slowly sink deeper and deeper into that quicksand until soldiers must pull them free.

As if he's reading the General's mind, Grant's chief quartermaster, Colonel Rufus Ingalls, busy dealing cards, thoughtfully puffs his own cigar, glances out the window, and shares with the other poker players around their makeshift table.

"I've marched with the United States Army across Mexico, up the California coast, from Leavenworth to Salt Lake, and now across Virginia. Seen it all, tryin' to keep Grant's 'Cracker Line' open; but I've never seen a worse marchin' day than this. It's gotta be bad out there, bad. Now, how many cards did you say, Captain?"

That night, a worried Rufus Ingalls will come back to the topic, reporting that a 600-wagon train, helped by a thousand engineers' felling trees to corduroy the road, had moved only fifty-five miles in fifty-six hours.

In his mind, through the rain-washed windows, Grant can see long infantry columns somewhere ahead. Tired, hungry men, marching hard;

not singing now as they'd done that morning. Just putting one tired foot ahead of another. All through the cold, wet, muddy day.

At last his train reaches the end of the tracks. When they've taken their horses from the extra cars, Grant leads the way to a cornfield near Dabney's Mill below Gravelly Run; a half dozen miles east of Sheridan at Dinwiddie Court House. He'll make his headquarters there.

As they ride toward Dabney's Mill they pass horses and soldiers struggling to break wagons free. Soldiers who still have their sense of humor.

"Hey, General," one calls, "when's the gunboats comin' up?" Another, to whom Grant had nodded, spits a long string of tobacco juice into the mud, reflects on the water dripping from his nose, then grins, "Wal, sir, one thing's for certain. If ever anybody asks if we've been through Virginia, reckon we can say, 'Yes, sir! Matter of fact, in a number of places!'"

CHAMBERLAIN

Sheridan's cavalry will have little contact with the enemy this 29th day of March. Warren's V Corps, however, along the north-south Quaker Road, won't have it so easy.

They'd started out at dawn, over 17,000 of them, each rifleman carrying three days' rations in his pack and 70 rounds of ammunition on his belt, with another nine days' rations and ammunition in the corps' supply train. Advancing off to their right is Humphreys' (Major General Andrew A. Humphreys) II Corps; to their left, somewhere off in the woods, Sheridan's cavalry. Warren's orders: move north on the Quaker Road until you take the railroad or are stopped.

Leading Warren's advance are the nearly 2,000 men of the 1st Brigade of the 1st Division, commanded by Brigadier General Joshua L. Chamberlain. Chamberlain, many long, dusty marches and hard-fought battles ago, professor of rhetoric and romance languages at Maine's Bowdoin College. Chamberlain, a poet, seems a most unlikely infantry commander. Yet he's one of Grant's hardest fighting officers; magnificent at Gettysburg; already five times wounded in the war.

Chamberlain rides his chestnut-colored horse, Charlemagne; man and horse only partially recovered from their most recent wounds. Chamberlain, slender, erect in his saddle, alert, wearing a dusty, faded blouse with none of the trappings affected by most generals; his rank suggested only by the handful of nearby aides and messengers and his bright headquarters' flag.

He knows that Confederate breastworks have been seen above them. Even without the scouts' reports, however, he'd expect resistance. Lee must know we're coming, and the railroad a scant three miles beyond. So he anticipates a fight.

"Rebs ahead, General," a messenger gallops up. "Gravelly Runs's pretty flooded; the bridge is down; and there's a heap of Johnnies on the far bank. Orders, sir?"

"Not yet, Sergeant. Tell Major Glenn to spread out a bit and see if he can find their flanks. I want to look around before we go in."

When he's looked for himself Chamberlain calls for his officers.

"All right, gentlemen. General Sickel (Brigadier General Horatio G. Sickel), put eight companies of your 198th Pennsylvania on line to the right of the road; the remaining six will be with Major Glenn (Major Edwin A. Glenn). Colonel Sniper (Colonel Gustave Sniper), your 185th New York will be on the left. General Sickel, when I signal make a lot of noise over there on our right. When you have the Rebs' attention, Major Glenn with your other six companies will charge across the run above the bridge. It'll be deep and cold, but we can make it. Colonel Sniper, have your regiments support us with fire while we're crossing the creek, and I'll bring up an artillery battery to help if need be. I'll be with Glenn's men. Questions?"

There are none, and the regiments quickly shift into position. Soldiers drop their packs, fix bayonets, check their rifles. Sergeants eye those they know are prone to hang back; those who've drawn the sergeants' attention understand their silent messages. It doesn't take long for Chamberlain's regiments to get ready; they've all done this many times before.

When Chamberlain signals, Sickel's regiments to the right of Quaker Road rush forward, yelling, and firing a heavy volley at Confederate infantry in the willows across the creek.

From the far bank Confederate soldiers return the fire. Chamberlain watches, waits; then, when the volume of enemy fire sharply increases, he raises his arm.

"All right, Major Glenn. It sounds as if Sickel has their attention over there; let's push them back."

Urging his horse into the water beside Glenn's, he helps hurry the infantrymen across the deep, swollen creek, calling again and again, "All right, let's go!; hold your weapons and ammunition high!; hurry up, before they can get set!"

He's caught his enemy by surprise, but they recover quickly, and it becomes a sharp fight.

As Glenn's skirmishers reach the center of the chest-deep creek, the scattered rifle fire from the far bank quickly grows. Union soldiers stagger, throw up their rifles, sink into the dark, cold water. Then Glenn's first line reach the far bank and push their way through the willows. Confederate skirmishers slowly, stubbornly begin to fall back.

With his regiments across Gravelly Run, Chamberlain quickly reorganizes his lines then waves them forward. Confederate skirmishers continue to fall back, slowly, sullenly, exchanging rifle fire with their advancing enemy. Back for nearly a mile into a thousand yard-wide clearing centered by the Quaker Road.

Dominating the clearing is the Lewis farmhouse and its barns. Beyond the house, at the far woodline, Chamberlain sees Confederate breastworks. At their center, a large pile of sawdust marking where a sawmill once stood. Confederate infantrymen of Brigadier General Henry A. Wise's brigade have anchored their line on that sawdust pile.

Stuttering Confederate fire suddenly becomes a solid, scorching volley striking Chamberlain's skirmishers. More Union regiments rush forward, their soldiers leaning into the hail of fire as into a gale. As men fall, ranks close on center; officers and sergeants shout orders; soldiers call to one another. Regimental color bearers, always the target of enemy fire, fall. When flags fall, other soldiers quickly take them up, wave them, and soldiers cheer as their lines again move forward.

Confederate fire, however, sharply increases, and Chamberlain sees his lines again stutter, stop, begin to give way. And from the woods more and more Confederates are hurrying to reinforce those already manning their breastworks. Whatever Chamberlain chooses to do, he must do it quickly.

"General Sickel, take the right; Colonel Sniper, the left. Everybody on line. That sawdust pile in the center; if we can take it, the field's ours."

Waving his sword, Chamberlain leads their charge. Charlemagne, his blood up, thunders ahead of the infantrymen, and Chamberlain, recognizing the danger, tries to curb the excited horse. Confused, Charlemagne rears.

At that moment a bullet, fired at close range, tears through the stallion's upraised neck to strike Chamberlain's left wrist, ripping a jagged hole in his coat sleeve and furrowing a bloody path up the arm to Chamberlain's elbow before it hits like a hammer just below his heart.

Chamberlain, the breath knocked from him, knows he's been hit, hit hard; feels himself losing consciousness; desperately clutches at Charlemagne's mane to keep from falling.

The heavy Minie ball, capable of penetrating a six-inch board at 600 yards, is deflected by a leather-bound notebook filled with field orders and by a brass-backed pocket mirror in Chamberlain's breast pocket, deflected to richochet around Chamberlain's ribs then tear its way through the back of his coat to knock a nearby aide, Lieutenant Vogel, from his horse.

Charlemagne, no longer feeling Chamberlain's touch at his reins, stops, bleeding hard; the unconscious Chamberlain's fingers knotted in his mane.

Chamberlain hears someone calling, "Lawrence, Lawrence," and struggles back to consciousness. It's his division commander, Brigadier General Charles Griffin, reaching from his horse to steady him and crying out, "My dear General, you are gone."

Dazed, confused, knowing he's been wounded but not sure how badly, Chamberlain thinks the "*you* are gone" refers to his *brigade* and that his men are losing the fight. As his vision clears, he sees his regiments *are* reeling, hard pressed by soldiers in butternut uniforms.

Struggling to sit erect in his saddle, he answers, "Yes, General, I know." Then someone recovers his sword and hands it to him.

Instinctively waving the sword and calling out to his men, he turns to gallop down his wavering line.

Chamberlain, hatless, his coat badly torn, covered with blood, shouts to rally his men. Behind him, Sergeant Thomas McDermott, who'd attached himself as Chamberlain's orderly after the previous orderly was killed at Gettysburg, waves Chamberlain's brigade's flag and tries to stay near the galloping general.

In the confusion, it occurs to Chamberlain that he's being cheered by soldiers on both sides of the fight. Can't understand that; have to figure it out later.

At the right of his line he finds two of his officers: Major Charles Maceuen and General Horatio Sickel, trying to rally their men. As Chamberlain nears them, both officers fall. Calling to the men around him, and having Sergeant McDermott wave the brigade's flag until regimental color bearers follow McDermott's lead, he rallies Sickel's regiments.

No time to check Sickel or Maceuen. Satisfied, however, that his right, for the moment at least, is safe, Chamberlain gallops back to the center of his line. Then his horse, its neck and shoulders covered with blood, staggers, unable to continue. Dismounting, Chamberlain pats the black stallion, hands Charlemagne's reins to Sergeant McDermott, who'd been struggling to catch up, and tells him, "Keep an eye on him, Sergeant Mac; and keep waving that flag. I'm going with Major Glenn."

Then he hurries forward, on foot, to join Glenn's Pennsylvanians attacking that huge sawdust pile, key to the Confederates' defense.

In the smoke and confusion he can't tell one uniform from another. Can't find Glenn either. So he pushes ahead. Too far ahead; right into the sawdust pile and a squad of Confederate infantrymen.

Chamberlain doesn't know that he's outrun his own men until he's suddenly challenged by a dirty, tired, tough-looking sergeant in brown standing before him, bayonet ready.

"All right, Yank. You drop that sword real quick like or you're a dead man."

The spectre of death or Libby Prison before him, Chamberlain instead reacts instinctively, counting on his dirty, bloody face and faded coat, and the smoke and confusion around them, to confuse the enemy sergeant.

As if he can't understand what the sergeant is talking about, he adopts a bold face and a Southern accent as he turns to point his sword at Sergeant McDermott, waving Chamberlain's brigade's flag some twenty yards away, and shouts back.

"Surrender? Surrender? What's the matter with you? Don't you see those Yanks? Come on, let's break 'em."

Matching his words with action, he waves his sword again and charges toward the Union lines.

The confused sergeant hesitates, and Chamberlain yells again, "Come on! Come on! Don't let 'em get away!"

Convinced, the Southerners cheer and follow Chamberlain into the Union lines where Glenn's grinning soldiers quickly capture them.

Then Chamberlain takes a moment to pat the enemy sergeant on the shoulder, grin, and console him, "It's all right. Things are a mite confusing everywhere today. And you're better off out of this. Good luck."

His former enemy nods then smiles, "Reckon you were a little too quick for me that time, General. Like to have had you on our side."

"General Chamberlain? General Chamberlain?" someone grasps his arm. He tries to sort the voice from the firing, the shouts and curses, the screams about him.

"Are you all right, sir? You sure don't look all right?"

It's Major Ellis Spear, like Sergeant Thomas McDermott, another old friend from the 20th Maine Infantry Regiment who always seems to turn up near Chamberlain in the hottest fights.

"Sir, take a swallow," Spear shoves a canteen into Chamberlain's hand. "It's good stuff. I've been saving it, but you look like you could use it right now."

Chamberlain, his head clearing, grins then turns a "swallow" into a deep, satisfying drink. As he hands the canteen back to his friend, Chamberlain's vision also has cleared enough that he'll always remember the martyred look on Spear's face as the young man hefts the considerably lighter canteen.

Despite the pain in his chest and the hard fight still going on around him, Chamberlain smiles, "It went to a good cause, Ellis; it went to a good cause," and pats Spear's shoulder.

The heavy firing on the left swells to a roar again; someone produces a pale, muddy horse; and they're helping him into its saddle. Galloping toward the heavy firing, Chamberlain finds Confederate infantry pressing Colonel Sniper's regiments hard.

Griffin, their division commander, somehow is there too, shouting to him, "Lawrence, if you can hold them ten minutes, I can get a battery of artillery up here."

Chamberlain nods, dismounts, and runs to join Sniper. The colonel has just lost his third color bearer and is waving the 185th New York's flag himself.

"Come on! Come on!" Chamberlain yells. "Pass the word. Use your bayonets! Drive them back! Fight hard for ten minutes, and we're out of it!"

Sniper's men, finding it hard to resist a thoroughly aroused general, on foot, covered with blood, in the very front of the fight, rally.

More and more Confederate soldiers are appearing in the woods ahead, however, and Chamberlain, knowing he'll need help, desperately looks back down the Quaker Road, praying for the promised guns.

Finally he sees them coming. Battery B, 4th Regulars, charging head-long; horses and men, cannon and limbers thundering up the muddy road then swinging into the field to wheel into action front. Magnificent, smooth-bore, 12-pounder Napoleons. Accurate within a mile, deadly with canister at a hundred yards.

Lieutenant John Mitchell, the battery commander, is very fond of Joshua Chamberlain. Mitchell: regular army; eleven years with the guns; knows his cannon and how to use them. Grim and tough but, as he reins his horse to a stop, he can't help but smile at the ragged, bloody, dirty, one-time professor before him.

"General Chamberlain! And how is your day going, sir?"

Chamberlain has to return the grin. "It's going to be a lot better, John, if you can put some fire into those woods. Can you do that without hurting my men?"

"Yes, sir. If you'll hold them where they are."

"Watch for my signal; then give it to them."

Mitchell's four Napoleons belch fire and smoke, and Union shells begin to burst over the wood lot. Confederate sharpshooters, hiding in the trees, fall beneath the rain of hot iron fragments and, for the moment, Rebel yells are drowned out by the deeper hurrahs of Chamberlain's men.

Confederate infantry launch another counterattack from the woods. Chamberlain commits his last reserves; Mitchell falls, badly wounded, as his gunners fire canister at point-blank range.

Battered by canister and by volleys of rifle fire, the Confederate charge sputters then stops. Southern soldiers fall back into the woods, giving up the fight.

As the firing ebbs, Chamberlain reorganizes his men to hold the ground they've won and notifies Griffin that the fight, for that day, has ended.

Later, Chamberlain's corps commander, Warren, interrupts his work. "General Chamberlain, you were splendid today. Splendid! I'm notifying General Meade; you'll hear from it."

That may matter later, but not now. The exhausted Chamberlain mumbles a polite, "Thank you, General," but hardly hears what Warren has said.

Too many other things on his mind. More than 400 of his brigade are dead or wounded. Some of his best officers, sergeants, and soldiers. As Chamberlain slowly rides across the torn field, searching for faces he can recognize, his borrowed horse instinctively shies from the still forms, gives way to stretcher bearers struggling with their heavy loads, and moves around the burial parties.

Beside the road a blue-uniformed soldier-father is searching too. Searching until he finds the body of his son among others beside a bloody fence line; then kneeling to smooth the boy's torn uniform and to cry. Chamberlain dismounts to pat the man's shoulder.

The soldier, unaware that it's his commanding general who is there, continues to arrange his son's uniform then, without looking up, speaks, as if to himself, "You tell the Lieutenant I'll be along directly; soon's I take care of things here."

"It's all right," Chamberlain answers. "Take all the time you need; I'll see that he gets the word."

Then he leaves him with his grief.

The light is failing quickly now, the last rays of the sun hidden by still lingering smoke from the battle and by evening mist already rising from the rain-soaked ground.

Chamberlain, hatless, dirty, torn and bloody, stops and looks around the battlefield. At that moment he sees the smoke and mist rising from the bloody ground as the tortured spirits of fallen soldiers free now to rise above what has happened to them.

Anguished, the poet-professor, once marked by his mother to be a minister, looks up at the darkening sky and mutters to himself, "Lord God in heaven, I've been responsible for more than 1,500 men, and now more than 400 of them are dead or their bodies torn. Men made in your image, slain or scarred by our hands. And how many from the other side? And who knows which of us is right? Did we fight by your command? Did they? Or should both sides ask your forgiveness?"

No answer. He really didn't expect one. Then, the habit of command taking over, he takes a deep breath, mops his forehead with a ragged sleeve, and nudges his horse forward.

Near the woodline he kneels beside the body of Major Charles Maceuen. He'd promised Maceuen's father, a Philadelphia surgeon, that he'd look after his son. He'd not been able to keep that promise.

Nearby, propped against a bullet-scarred tree, is General Horatio Sickel, the older man calm and cheerful despite a mangled arm the surgeon already has told him must be amputated.

"All right, doctor," Sickel had shrugged, "it's God's will. But see that all these men are cared for. I can wait until that's been done."

Now Sickel, recognizing the younger Chamberlain's despair, smiles gently, kindly, and tries to console him, "General, you have the soul of a lion and the heart of a woman."

Chamberlain spends a moment with Sickel, knowing that his responsibility now is to those still living. Then he sends word for the surgeon to see to Sickel's arm as quickly as possible.

That done, he continues on, stopping often to encourage frightened, hurt, exhausted men.

At last, critical duties attended to, he takes time to see that his wounded horse, Charlemagne, is being treated. Then he walks toward the Lewis farmhouse.

Regimental surgeons are hard at work there, their lanterns' light harsh in the darkness; a constant stream of stretcher bearers around the house and barn. He kneels to encourage a 20th Maine soldier, shot in both legs and waiting his turn with the surgeon.

Dark now; heavy rain washes the field as Chamberlain, very tired and with his fresh wounds still untreated, limps to the porch.

Sergeant Thomas McDermott, never far from the Maine general, comes to him there, a cup of coffee in one hand, a surgeon in tow.

"General, darlin', you're a hard man to keep up with. Now be a good lad and drink this coffee while the doctor here sees to that latest hurt you've got."

After the surgeon has finished, McDermott orders Chamberlain: "Now, sir, I've put the General's bedroll in the kitchen here. Set a bit while I fetch some supper. Then you must rest. I swear you'll be the death of me."

"In a bit, Sergeant Mac. In a bit. One more thing to be done. Then I'll rest."

He finds room in a corner of the kitchen for the ammunition box he'll use as a desk, a candle for light. Then he bows his head in thought and begins to write, "My dear Doctor Maceuen."

SHERIDAN

A half dozen miles to the west, as Chamberlain's fight at the Lewis farm is ending, one of Sheridan's cavalry divisions, under Brigadier

General Wesley Merritt, nears Five Forks, six miles above Dinwiddie Court House.

Five Forks: the junction of five roads, the most important of them Courthouse Road, running southeast to Dinwiddie Court House; Ford's Road, leading north three miles to the critical Southside Railroad; and White Oak Road, running west to east toward the western end of Lee's trenches at the Claiborne-White Oak Roads junction. Five Forks: a rural setting with scattered plantations and farmsteads. No houses at Five Forks itself, just a clearing surrounded by piney woods and open fields. Of little value, real estate-wise. But where these nondescript dirt roads meet is about to become one of the most critical road junctions of the entire war. And Five Forks, like many other woods clearings, will be bought in battle and paid for in blood in the next forty-eight hours.

Merritt's troopers draw fire from Confederate Major General Fitzhugh ("Fitz") Lee's cavalry pickets, and Merritt, in the fading light and torrents of rain, decides to pull back to Dinwiddie Court House. Tomorrow, if it stops raining, he decides, will be time enough.

Sheridan growls his frustration at Merritt's report but reluctantly agrees. He'll put his own headquarters at Dinwiddie Court House: a half-dozen ramshackle houses, a dingy jail, a small once-white sided church, a post office, a weather-beaten tavern whose faded walls are propped with pine poles, and the nondescript remains of the red brick courthouse that gave the crossroads its name.

"Put our headquarters there, gentlemen," he points to the tavern. "Get the word out to the command."

As they dismount the storm again breaks over them. Thunder, lightning, and heavy rain lash the desolate crossroads. Light is failing fast.

"Tell 'em to get their pickets out," Sheridan continues. "You heard that artillery over east of us awhile back. I don't expect any fighting here tonight 'lest it's with the bayonet. Much more of this rain and we'll need a couple days to dry our powder."

Inside the tavern are several ladies of the night who cheerfully inform their Yankee guests that they've followed Lee's soldiers from Petersburg to Dinwiddie Court House and that about now it looks as if they've come to about the end of *that* road.

"You gentlemen don't mean to fight right here, do you?" one asks. "*Our* gentlemen were on picket right here until just afore you rode up, and they told us they'd not allow any bloodshed in our presence. Can't we expect the same of you Northern gentlemen?"

Another is more practical, "You Yanks got any coffee? Any food? We sure could use some."

Sheridan finds a not too dirty feather tick upstairs, in a corner room that doesn't leak too badly. As he retires, his staff officers build a fire, boil coffee, pull hardtack and beef from saddlebags, and invite the ladies to join them.

Soon they've resurrected a dusty, old piano from a dark corner of the tavern and, as Sheridan drops off to sleep, he smiles at its discordant but tinkling notes and the singing of his younger officers and their new acquaintances.

LEE

A scant dozen miles to their northeast Robert E. Lee knows that Grant again is shifting the Union army to try to turn the Confederate right flank. He can't prevent that movement, but he hopes to counter it.

He takes time to report Grant's maneuvering to Jefferson Davis. When its purpose and extent become clear, Lee will strike with whatever strength he can muster. Meanwhile, however, President Davis must be prepared to abandon Richmond on short notice.

Lee also takes time for his nearly daily note to Mary Lee, crippled with rheumatism in Richmond. "What will *you* do," he asks again, "if I must abandon our positions? Will you remain or leave the city? You must decide...." On a more cheerful note, now more a husband than a general, he concludes, "I have received your note with a bag of socks. I return the bag and receipt. The count is all right this time."

Then he alerts Major General George E. Pickett to move his infantry division to Five Forks to unite with Fitz Lee's cavalry. Lee will try to meet Pickett along the Southside Railroad but, should that meeting not be possible, he alerts Pickett to expect Grant to attack at any time and that Pickett, at all costs, must protect the railroad. The army's life, he tells him, depends on that.

CHAPTER 4

Dinwiddie Court House   March 31, 1965

CUSTER

At dawn an angry, impatient Sheridan looks about from the ramshackle tavern's porch. Before him his headquarters' flag, still wet from the rain, hangs limply on its staff. Across the road the red-bricked courthouse, like the rest of the village, is deserted. Only his soldiers are in view, and they're busy boiling coffee and drying clothes over fires of fence rails and wood siding.

It had rained all night, at times the rain turning to snow; and the cavalrymen, left on their own, had found shelter wherever they could. From private to general they're hoping that today the sky will clear. Meanwhile, swamps have overflowed, sandy roads flooded, and the one thing that they're sure of is that it will be another hard day moving men, horses, and supplies forward.

An hour before he'd told Merritt to send his brigades back to Five Forks. Brigadier General George A. Custer, Merritt's hardest fighting cavalryman, won't be with them. Instead, Merritt puts Custer's division to work corduroying the roads they'll need to bring up supplies. He'd had him doing that the day before and watched with satisfaction as Custer rode up and down the long line of supply wagons axle deep in the mud: shouting, cursing, cajoling, his long blond hair and crimson scarf standing out among the soaked, sweating soldiers; the straining horses and mules; the mud-spattered wagons.

Sheridan, not too happy at not having Custer near the front, scowls then accepts it, "All right, Merritt. Your call, but keep him handy."

Custer, as Merritt anticipated, isn't too happy either, not with having to corduroy flooded roads while the rest of the command may be fighting.

"Now, Custer," Merritt consoles him, "I've got your division corduroying roads again because that's the job that needs to be done, and you'll get it done. Don't fret. There'll be no fighting today. Maybe tomorrow, when this ground dries out, but not today. Besides, if you set your men to cutting trees another day, they'll be ready to fight Devin's (Federal Brigadier General Thomas C. Devin) men if you say so. Meanwhile, Devin's been over the ground up there; we'll let him go back for another look."

Then, before Custer can take up the argument again, Merritt smiles disarmingly, "I see your orderly's carrying a new guidon so Rosser (Major General Thomas L. Rosser, a friend of Custer's from West Point days) and every other damned Rebel within a dozen miles of here will know that's Custer over there. Where'd you get it?"

His shot hits the mark as Custer grins with delight, his argument about corduroying roads forgotten.

"I was sleeping under a wagon last night, General. On some barn boards laid across a couple fence rails, barely keeping me out of the water. Hungry, nothing to eat since daylight. Rain and mud everywhere. Not too happy about having to corduroy roads with the best troopers you've got. Then my aide, Lieutenant Boehm, rode in with that guidon. Libby'd (Elizabeth Custer) made it with her own pretty hands then trusted him to get it through the Reb lines. He'd ridden all day and most of the night. Almost got shot by a Reb patrol. That guidon's already got one bullet hole in it; a bullet meant for him. I figure that's a good sign. Well, Boehm made it; and that flag's going to fly today or tomorrow, whenever you turn me loose to fight."

"Tomorrow, Custer," Merritt ends the argument. "Tomorrow. You won't miss anything; there'll be no fighting until tomorrow."

SHERIDAN

"'Scuse me, General," Brigadier General James Forsyth, Sheridan's chief of staff, interrupts the restless general's thoughts. "Rider just came in with a message from Grant."

Sheridan scowls, takes the paper, reads it quickly then slowly, thoughtfully again.

"The heavy rain of today will make it impossible for us to do much until it dries up a little.... You may, therefore, leave what cavalry...necessary to protect the left, and send the remainder back...."

"Damn! He's wavering," Sheridan snorts and pounds the paper with his fist. "Never saw him do that before, but he's doing it now. Have someone fetch Breckenridge. I'm going to Grant's headquarters."

At Grant's headquarters, a small cluster of tents crowded across a slight hummock of corn near flooded Gravelly Run, the buoyance and optimism they'd all felt only two days before has vanished. Huddled around their campfires, Grant's staff officers reveal short tempers, argue among themselves. Some, not known for using profanity, are finding a curse or two helpful this morning.

Brigadier General John Rawlins, Grant's chief of staff, is the most vocal prophet of doom.

"This whole movement has been premature, Grant. We can't get out of this mudsty we've fallen into until the damned roads and fields are dry. And somewhere up ahead of us Lee knows what we're up to, and he's moving to stop us. And," he wags his finger, "if we stay here very long, unprotected by trenches, Joe Johnston (Confederate Lieutenant General Joseph E. Johnston, opposing Sherman's army in North Carolina) just might come up on our rear. Then," he concludes, "there'll be hell to pay."

Grant takes the unlit, well-chewed cigar from his mouth, looks at Rawlins, and snorts, "'Moving to stop us?' Rawlins, if we can't move, the Rebs can't move either. And, if Joe Johnston can find a way to move fast enough to get away from Sherman and get to us in weather like this, he'll be sorry he did it because I'll turn on him and crush him. Then I'll come back and get Lee. No; if we just wait a bit, this rain will stop and, once we can move again, the men will do fine. They always have."

Having said that, about as long a speech as the staff can ever remember his giving, Grant turns to reenter his tent. Rawlins, still not ready to give up the fight, follows him inside.

Despite the optimism he'd just shown his staff, Grant too is discouraged at the prospects. It's the weather, he'd reasoned with himself, not Lee, that's stopping us. But the newspapers won't say anything about the weather; just that we failed. And the country's not ready for another failure. Better to play it safe. So he'd alerted Sheridan to begin pulling back.

As Grant and Rawlins continue their argument, Sheridan arrives, takes in at a glance the sight of Grant's staff huddled on ammunition box walks before their tents. If Sheridan's taken back by their woebegone appearance, they're astonished at his: the general mud-spattered and rain-soaked from his ride, and Breckenridge plunging in mud to his knees with each step.

"General Grant's with General Rawlins, sir," Colonel Horace Porter reports. "Be free pretty soon. How are things where you are?"

"Why they're fine, just fine," Sheridan dismounts to warm his hands at the fire. "Not a care in the world. When I catch up with them, I can drive in the Reb cavalry with one hand. And if Grant'll give me some infantry, I'll hit Lee's flank so hard he'll have to weaken his center to face us. Then Meade can walk right through the rest of his line and into Petersburg."

As he talks, Sheridan paces back and forth, waving his arms and becoming so excited he almost shouts.

"How're you fixed for beans and hay, General?" General Rufus Ingalls asks. "Can you feed your men and horses?"

"Of course; nothing to it," Sheridan snorts again. "I've got Custer's whole division corduroying roads and, if I have to, I'll put every officer and man I've got to work at it. I tell you," his gloved fist pounds his left hand for emphasis, and his voice again carries across his eager audience, "I'm ready to go smashing things."

"Well, General," Porter grins, "that's the kind of talk we need this morning. Rawlins and Grant are in there," he points to the tent, "arguing about the state of things. Why don't you go in and tell them that?"

"Well, I don't want to break in on him; he's with Rawlins you say?"

Porter nods then slips away to interrupt Grant's and Rawlins' continuing argument, "Sir, General Sheridan's out there. He'd like to talk with you."

"Bring him in," Grant answers and, turning back to Rawlins, wryly grins, "Well, Rawlins, in the interest of doing this right, I expect you'd better take command."

When Sheridan doesn't appear, Grant goes to find him warming himself in Ingall's tent.

"Sheridan."

"Grant."

"You got my message; that's why you're here?"

"Yes, sir. General, please let me go on. I know I can do it."

"I'd like to, Sheridan," Grant chews the cigar as he talks, "but you see these roads. Ask Ingalls here. We can't bring up our supplies; the infantry are all bogged down..." his voice trails off.

Sheridan, red-faced and impatient, shakes his head and pleads, "General, turn me loose. My men are already moving on Five Forks. I'm getting our supplies up, and my flanks are covered. The Rebs are hurting more than we are. You know that. And, if we turn back now, the reporters'll crucify us."

"I want to go on, Sheridan," Grant nods. "My instincts tell me it's the thing to do. But the staff and Meade, up the road there, all find reasons to stop. They say the wagons are up to their beds in quicksand; cannon out of sight; ammunition soaked; the men and horses all worn out."

"Still," he stops, lights his cigar, squints at Sheridan through the smoke as he weighs the risk, "I want to go ahead if it can be done."

"We can do it, Grant. I'm sure of it. Why," Sheridan grins, "we've got 'em right where we want 'em."

Grant smiles, grips Sheridan's hand, and decides, "All right then, Sheridan; we'll go on. We'll go on."

LEE

Lee, aware of Grant's movement almost as Union troops began their rainy march, has done what he can to counter it.

At dawn a courier arrives with a message from his nephew, General Fitzhugh ("Fitz") Lee, reporting that late the day before he'd pushed Devin's brigade of Merritt's cavalry back from Five Forks. No sign of the rest of Sheridan's cavalry or of Union infantry. Pickett's five brigades of Confederate infantry have reached Five Forks. Pickett, however, decided that it was too late for the Confederates to continue their attack toward Dinwiddie Court House that day.

Lee frowns.

"Well, Colonel Taylor, perhaps it's too late to attack, but I pray he's moved south to be ready to strike Sheridan at first light. I hope he's not waited too long."

Lee decides to ride to the right of his Petersburg trenches, where the Claiborne and White Oak Roads meet, some five miles east of Five Forks, to judge the situation there for himself.

At mid-morning he hears the first harsh rattle of Spencer repeating rifles to the southwest, later than he'd hoped but an encouraging sign that Pickett and Fitz Lee must be fighting Sheridan.

He listens again, then shares with Confederate Lieutenant General Richard Anderson, his corps commander there, "Still scattered fire, General; Sheridan's not in strength there. Not yet. General Pickett must be in position to stop them."

"Now," he looks to the south, "what is happening to your front?"

Well, sir," Anderson reports, "my scouts tell me that the Yanks are down there a few hundred yards. They're drawing ammunition and rations and, once this rain stops, I expect they'll come on strong."

"Shall I take my division in before they can entrench?" Major General Harry Heth suggests. "If Pickett can cover my right flank, I can push them back."

"No, not yet," Lee responds calmly. "General Pickett has enough to do today. And we're not yet sure where their main attack will come. We'll wait a bit longer. It appears they're not yet ready to attack; we still can move first."

Seeing a captured Union officer, Lee questions him.

The young prisoner, confident, friendly, not too worried about the prospects of a long stay in Libby Prison, responds to Lee's quiet questioning.

"What were you doing at Five Forks, Captain?"

"Reconnaissance, General. We're fixin' to turn your right flank. Been trying to do that for more'n a year now," he smiles grimly, "and now we're gonna do it."

"You're with General Sheridan?"

"Yes, sir, 1st Michigan; Colonel Stagg's (Colonel Peter Stagg) brigade."

"Sheridan's entire command is below Five Forks?"

"Yes, sir," the Union captain grins again. "His own plus a lot of Ord's cavalry; maybe 15,000 men."

A listening staff officer whistles his astonishment. Ignoring the distraction, Lee continues his quiet questioning.

"A strong force, Captain, but he'll need infantry," he suggests.

"We were told there's at least a corps coming to Dinwiddie to join Sheridan. When this rain lets up, General, they'll be coming."

As if on cue, Lee again hears the faint rattle of repeating rifles to the southwest.

"Colonel Taylor, please send a courier to hurry General Pickett. He must strike Sheridan's force before it can be reinforced. Remind him that the life of this army is in his hands."

He extends his hand to the young Federal officer, "Thank you, Captain, and good luck."

"Thank you, General Lee. I don't expect to be your guest for long."

"Perhaps not," Lee smiles, "perhaps not. We shall see."

"General Lee," Anderson reminds him, "my scouts report that Warren's Union V Corps and Humphreys' II Corps still are waiting below White Oak Road."

"Warren's left flank's wide open, General. With four or five good brigades I can roll them up," he again suggests.

"No more word from General Pickett?"

"No, sir. The last was early this morning. He and Fitz Lee planned to strike for Dinwiddie at first light."

"I hope that he hasn't waited too long. As for those people before us, General, your brigades are good ones, but they're not very big."

"We've never been very big, sir," Anderson reasons, "but we can push them back."

Lee weighs the risk then quietly nods, "All right. Send your regiments forward; and may a kind Providence go with them."

CHAMBERLAIN

As the rain stops, several hundred yards below the White Oak Road, Warren, the V Corps' commander, believing his divisions can take the road without much of a fight, finally orders them forward; Brigadier General Romeyn B. Ayers' 2nd Division leads, followed at 500 yards by Brigadier General Samuel W. Crawford's 3rd Division. Griffin's 1st Division, fought out two days before on the Quaker Road, waits in reserve below Gravelly Run.

Griffin finds Joshua Chamberlain resting his accumulated wounds on a heap of straw Sergeant McDermott had taken from an abandoned barn.

"Warren's moving up this morning, Lawrence; Ayers, then Crawford, then us. You'll be my reserve but, if we get into trouble, I may need you forward before this is over. Do you feel up to it?"

"Of course."

As the spring sun burns away the morning's mist, Ayres' infantrymen, bayonets at the ready, cautiously approach White Oak Road. Skirmishers wonder why their enemy, who'd fought so hard before on Quaker Road, are strangely absent.

"Maybe," younger soldiers suggest, "Johnny's skedaddled. Maybe we won't have to fight."

"Not likely," older veterans mutter grimly. "Keep your eyes open; they're up there somewheres."

Through breaks in the woods ahead they see the sandy strip that is White Oak Road. Like every other country road they've known in Virginia, it's more a narrow, sandy-bottomed lane working its way through masses of thickets and undergrowth than a road. The veterans note that the thickets on this side of the road have been freshly cut down or thinned out. No mistaking the cleared lanes of fire; lanes they'll have to cross. Some roads are friendly; not this one. Gripping their rifles more tightly, and moving slower now, they close on it.

When they're within twenty yards of White Oak Road a solid sheet of Confederate rifle fire rips into them. Union soldiers scream in pain, twist, turn, fall. Hidden batteries of Southern cannon, firing canister with fuzes cut to the quick, add to the horrible fire, the iron balls thudding into Ayres' riflemen at very close range. Men are torn apart. The noise is deafening; the smoke is thicker by the moment. Ayres' men, leaning into the leaden hail of bullets, try to find their enemies in the gray-black, acrid smoke. On their left, the fire is heavier, and dozens of soldiers fall.

Through the thick smoke they see lean, dirty, hard-faced, screaming Confederate infantrymen in the thickets across the road while other butternut riflemen are sweeping around their left flank. All while fire from the hidden artillery batteries adds to the devastation.

As the fire fight worsens, squads of Union soldiers, unable to see their enemies, kneel to fire belt buckle-high volleys into the smoke. They can't see their enemies out there but maybe, the sergeants reason, the volleys will cause the Johnnies to pull their heads down long enough for us to get into them with our bayonets.

Ayres' squads and companies suddenly have become confused. A soldier can't see more than a few yards in any direction and, his squad vanished in the smoke, he feels very much alone; not sure whether the enemy fire is coming from his front, or his side, or his rear. Sure only that all around him men are falling. Worst of all, a figure looming before him will be very close before he can be seen and only a bayonet's length away before he's pretty sure whether that's a faded blue or gray uniform he's facing. In the confusion mistakes are made and men are killed.

Ayres' officers, sergeants, and soldiers are falling everywhere. The confusion worsens. Yankee riflemen have reached White Oak Road, but they can't cross it.

The frightened, confused, mauled Union regiments break. At first individual riflemen stop, pause, then begin to fall back; then squads, then entire companies. Walking, then half-running to the rear. Some stopping again and again to shake their fists or shout defiance at their enemies in the awful smoke or fire a hastily aimed shot. Then hurrying to the rear.

When Ayres' lead ranks tumble back through his reserve regiments, more soldiers join the rush to the rear. Here and there squads and whole rifle companies are isolated then cut down or surrendered. Some veterans try to make a stand, but they are few and most are quickly shot down.

Officers strike at retreating men with their swords while sergeants use their fists on anyone they can reach. Then, seeing there's no way they can stop the flood, they allow themselves to be washed back with it.

The panic spreads as Ayres' entire division turn their backs on those high-pitched, hair-raising Rebel yells and hurry to the rear. Half-walking, half-running, they collide with Crawford's division advancing behind them.

Crawford's soldiers, seeing the panic and not knowing what has happened ahead of them, break even faster than Ayres' regiments, joining the headlong retreat to Gravelly Run. Gravelly Run, normally so small a man could jump across it but now flooded chest deep and nearly sixty feet across. A formidable obstacle, but Ayres' and Crawford's men, hardly slowing, splash across into the waiting lines of the V Corps' reserve, Griffin's division.

Four small Confederate brigades have broken two divisions of Warren's corps, pushing them all the way back to Gravelly Run. Only Griffin's division remains intact.

Griffin's men are resting, eating, cleaning weapons, drying rain-soaked blankets when the tremendous uproar breaks upon them. Drummer boys, veterans despite their youth, sound the Long Roll; sergeants bark orders; and soldiers grab rifles and bayonets then run to form battle lines along the south bank of the creek.

Griffin, seeing Ayres' and Crawford's beaten men struggling across Gravelly Run, shouts commands.

"Let them through! Let them through! Then close your ranks. Get some cannon on that rise behind us. Sergeant Major, get our bands playing. Right up there behind our men. Tell them to play hard and loud; play until I tell them to stop."

To soldiers tasting combat for the first time, it's a scene from Hell itself. To Griffin's veterans, however, it's just another "right sharp fight," and they steady the youngsters.

Ayres' and Crawford's survivors stagger through Griffin's waiting ranks then, seeing the waiting bayonets of regiments Griffin has formed across his rear to block their retreat, stop. Then, embarrassed and amused at their panic, they turn to search out their regiments.

Pursuing Confederates stop at the thickets on Gravelly Run's far bank. Rifle fire thunders across the stream. Then, as soldiers on both sides realize that their enemy can't get at them, the firing slowly ebbs. Riflemen take time to select individual targets while their officers consider what they should do next.

Assured that his line is holding, Griffin, accompanied by Warren, gallops to Chamberlain's brigade, waiting several hundred yards below the stream.

Confused, angry, and out of breath Griffin goes straight to Chamberlain.

"General Chamberlain, this corps is eternally damned!"

Not sure of what has happened, Chamberlain calmly smiles, "Well, I hope not, General; not yet anyway."

Griffin rushes on, "I've told Warren that you can turn this disgrace around."

Warren: tight-lipped, nervous, his voice uncertain, interrupts, "Ayres' and Crawford's divisions have broken, General. Disgraceful! We've stopped the enemy at Gravelly Run, but we've got to retake the ground we lost. Can your brigade do it?"

Chamberlain glances about his camp, weighing the losses he'd suffered on Quaker Road and the tiredness of his men.

"We can try, General; we can try. But are we the best you've got? I have the smallest brigade, and we're fought out from Quaker Road. Can't you use General Bartlett (Brigadier General Joseph J. Bartlett)? His brigade's a lot bigger than mine, and it's hardly been engaged."

"Chamberlain," Warren shakes his head, "we've come to you; you know what that means. We want you to lead the attack."

"We can try, General," Chamberlain says again, "but if we can push them back let us keep going until we've done all we can."

Warren misses Chamberlain's plea for the generals' support behind him while he's fighting Confederates in front of him. Instead, relieved at a solution to his problem, his mind already has turned to an engineer's concern: getting Chamberlain's brigade across Gravelly Run. Bridges, roads, trenches, communications—physical things. He's always been more comfortable dealing with physical things than with persuading men to follow him into harm's way.

"I can get a bridge across Gravelly Run in about an hour. Have your brigade ready."

"General," Chamberlain shakes his head, "we don't have time for that. And we don't need a bridge. If they waded across, we can go back the same way. The Rebs' attack has stopped, and they'll be as confused and uncertain about their next step as we are. I should hit them right now. Give me fifteen minutes, and I'll take my men straight through."

He turns to give orders then pauses. Having seen the three generals talking and anticipating what that means, his men already are forming their ranks as sergeants count men, check weapons, distribute ammunition.

"Sound 'Officers Call', Sergeant Mac," he grins. "We have a job to do."

Soon Sickel's 198th Pennsylvania Regiment, now on Chamberlain's right under Major Edward Glenn, begins to wade swollen, soft-bottomed Gravelly Run. Glenn's infantrymen, chest deep in the cold water, and carrying their weapons and cartridge boxes high to keep them dry, quickly draw the Confederates' attention. Rifle fire from the far bank, at first scattered, random, individual shots, grows as more and more Confederate infantrymen rush to Glenn's crossing site.

When the enemy have focused on his right, Chamberlain hurries the rest of his brigade across downstream. Reaching the far bank, he gathers his regiments, forms a skirmish line across his brigade front, then waves them forward.

More Union brigades now move up on Chamberlain's left and right, and Confederate infantrymen, seeing their overwhelming numbers, begin to fall back; retreating slowly. Losing the ground they'd taken an hour before.

Below White Oak Road they scramble into the crude breastworks Ayres' men had held before their advance. Then, facing about, Confederate sergants ready them to fire into Chamberlain's advancing skirmishers.

Chamberlain, seeing their line, moves artillery forward, spreads his infantry, and is about to attack when a messenger from Warren reaches him.

"General Chamberlain, General Warren says you're to hold up here until he's had time to come forward and see for himself."

"Captain," Chamberlain is angry, "this isn't the time to stop. Go back and tell the General that. If we can just take that line ahead of us, now before they have time to get set, we'll be able to take White Oak Road. It's only a couple hundred yards ahead of us, and right now we have them on the run."

"Sir," the courier shakes his head, "the General says to stop here."

"Very well," Chamberlain sighs. "Bugler, sound 'Recall'," and to his couriers, "Pass the word, gentlemen. We'll hold where we are. But tell everyone to be ready to move out when I get back."

Several hundred yards behind his brigade he finds Warren and Griffin.

"General Warren," he wastes no time, "if we keep going, we can take White Oak Road. That road's mighty important to Grant's plans. Besides, I'll lose as many men pulling back across that open field behind us as I will by going ahead. Move Gregory's (Colonel Edgar M. Gregory) 2nd Brigade up on my right; he can keep them busy while we go in on the left. We can do it; but we have to do it now."

Warren, still hesitant but trusting Chamberlain's experience, and thankful for a solution to his problem, orders Gregory forward. When the firing on Chamberlain's right indicates that Gregory's heavily engaged, Chamberlain's Pennsylvanians and New Yorkers yell at the top of their lungs and charge forward. Cannon fire and harsh-crackling rifle volleys strike the Blue ranks and more men stop in mid-stride, twist, turn, throw up their rifles, fall. Heavier fire as Union infantrymen near the Confederate line, but not enough to stop them. Then they're up and over the Confederate breastworks, a human flood.

Chamberlain, again riding Charlemagne, is in the thick of it, firing his revolver, calling to his men. The fight for the Confederate breastworks is short, hard, vicious—with clubbed muskets, revolvers, sabers, rammer staffs, and bayonets.

In the confused, hand-to-hand fighting Chamberlain sees a young Union soldier wrestling with a Confederate color bearer. Then the Southern soldier falls, and the Yankee infantryman takes up the fallen enemy flag. Curious, he spreads its folds across his arms, takes a moment to examine it then, seeing Joshua Chamberlain, grins and offers it to him.

"It's the 56th Virginia, General. Sure never thought I'd capture a Rebel flag. Thought about how it'd be, but I never thought I'd do it. Reckon you'd better take it, sir."

Without taking the flag, Chamberlain returns the grin. "I expect that a lot of us are doing things we never thought we could do. What's your name?"

"Gus Zeiber, General." Then, remembering the way Sergeant Martin had told his squad to do if a general spoke to them, he pulls himself erect on the smoking, torn field, takes a tug at his dirty, wrinkled blouse, and corrects himself, "Private Augustus Zeiber, Company D, 198th Pennsylvania Regiment, sir."

Having remembered it all, he grins and once more offers the flag. Chamberlain smiles his thanks but nods his head.

"No. You took it; you keep it for now. When things get quiet, you come see me. Bring your flag with you. Now, go find your squad. Tell your sergeant to keep going; we've got them on the run."

Then, as Private Gus Zeiber, rifle in one hand, captured flag in the other, hurries to find his squad, Chamberlain calls after him.

"Zeiber?"

The boy stops, turns, and calls back, "Yes, sir?"

"Tell your sergeant that the General's just promoted you to corporal. When you bring the flag, have the stripes on your arm."

Later, Chamberlain will send brand new Corporal Gus Zeiber to Griffin's headquarters with the captured flag. Still later Zeiber will wear the general's corporal stripes beside his Medal of Honor.

As the sun sets, Chamberlain's brigade has pushed several hundred yards across White Oak Road, cutting Lee's last direct link with Pickett's men at Five Forks, and is poised on the right flank of Lee's Petersburg trenches.

When darkness has forced an end to the fighting, and he's settled his regiments for the night, Chamberlain quietly pats Charlemagne while thoughtfully listening to cannon and musket fire to the southwest.

Warren and Griffin arrive, and they too listen as the heavy firing continues.

"It sounds as if Sheridan may need help," suggests Warren, "and we're out of touch with Meade. General Chamberlain, what do you think we should do?"

"Well, sir, we fought hard to win that road. And as soon as it's light we can roll up Lee's right flank. I don't think we should give up the advantage we've won. Meade can hear that firing. If he thinks Sheridan needs help, he has the II Corps to send. We need every man we've got right here."

Then he sighs, "But we're closest, General, and from the sound of that firing, I'm afraid you'll be blamed if you don't send Sheridan some help."

"Well, will you go?"

"Certainly, sir, if you want. But my brigade's pretty worn out, and we're eye-to-eye with Anderson's corps a couple hundred yards ahead of us. You don't want me to pull back and give up White Oak Road, and with light failing it's not a good time to be shifting anyone around more than necessary. Why not send General Bartlett? His brigade's bigger and fresher than mine, and they're not engaged. They could get on the road faster than Gregory or me."

Griffin agrees.

When his commanders have gone, Chamberlain and Sergant Thomas McDermott crawl forward to listen to Lee's soldiers talking in the dusk. There's a lot of infantry there, he decides; and cannon in trenches with heavy log breastworks. A tough position to take, but he expects that at dawn he'll be ordered to do just that.

He walks his brigade's picket line. Then he orders his commanders, "Stay alert, but see that the men get whatever rest they can, gentlemen. They'll need it in the morning. We'll all need it."

He'll push himself, however, several times crawling forward during the night to look for any signs of a mounting counterattack.

SHERIDAN

Sheridan, following his early morning meeting with Grant, rides to Warren's headquarters. Grant has offered him Warren's V Corps for the attack on Five Forks, but Grant and Sheridan share concerns about Major General Gouverneur Kemble Warren. So Sheridan comes to judge Warren for himself.

Warren, already wounded several times and awarded a gold medal at Gettysburg, has been criticized as a troop commander for being too slow and for not being aggressive enough, either charge the kiss of death in Sheridan's eyes. Still, Grant had said that Warren's corps is all he can spare.

At Warren's headquarters he finds Warren, not yet involved in the later fighting for White Oak Road, still sleeping.

Sheridan stands thoughtfully silent before Warren's drawn tent then turns to Colonel Frederick T. Locke, Warren's adjutant general.

"No, don't wake him, Colonel. He'll need all the strength he has if this corps is attached to my command today. All of you will. Just tell him," Sheridan's smile is as grim as his voice, "that I was here but didn't want to disturb his rest."

Then Warren, hearing Sheridan's raised voice, emerges from his tent.

The two generals walk apart, talking, for some moments. Warren: tall, slender, aristocratic; at that moment tight-mouthed, tense, saying little. Sheridan: short, muscular, bandy-legged, mud-spattered to his hips, wearing a field-faded blue uniform and a funny little peaked hat; studying Warren through angry, black eyes; talking loudly, vigorously, emphasizing his points by pounding his fist into his gauntleted left hand.

After their brief conversation ends, Sheridan spins on his heels and, in his haste to mount Rienzi, ignores Warren's farewell salute. Then, without looking back, he gallops down the muddy road toward Dinwiddie Court House.

Behind him, Warren thoughtfully watches the small figure on the big horse disappear then, aware that his staff is waiting, half-smiles, "Bobby Lee has been known to disappoint a lot of generals in their expectations; I expect he'll do so again."

Sheridan has barely returned to his headquarters at Dinwiddie Court House when Warren's grim prediction begins to come true.

He's dismounting before his tavern-headquarters when he hears faint firing to the north, toward Five Forks.

Devin's brigade of Merritt's cavalry again have run into Colonel Thomas T. Munford's Confederate cavalry. Munford's troopers hold their fire until the leading Federal riders are just too close to miss. Then their bullets empty a dozen Northern saddles and the fight is on.

Devin studies the thin line of enemy cavalry and orders, "Have Gibbs (Brigadier General Alfred Gibbs) send in a couple of his regiments. That should do it."

He watches as Gibbs' Massachusetts and Pennsylvania cavalry regiments canter into line; color bearers unfurl national and regimental colors; officers, sergeants, and troopers draw sabers. Then they charge, thundering across the field as if they'll engulf the smaller number of waiting Southern horsemen.

When Gibbs' galloping regiments have closed to within a hundred yards, however, Munford's cavalrymen suddenly wheel about and gallop into the woods.

Shouting in triumph, Gibbs' men are almost into the woods themselves when, too late to check their charge, from behind a low, stone wall before them, hundreds of rifles wink fire and smoke. Infantrymen, Pickett's, sent to help Munford's cavalry. Dozens of Union soldiers are shot from their saddles. Their charge broken, the survivors retreat across the field.

"Damn!" Devin mutters. "Well, Merritt told us to go 'til we found 'em. Reckon we've found 'em. Infantry. Lots of them. We've done what we can. Bugler, sound 'Recall'."

Merritt's cavalry, Sheridan's effort to turn Lee's right flank, for the moment at least, have been stopped below Five Forks.

Meanwhile, Pickett has taken the rest of Fitz Lee's cavalry and most of his own infantry on a swing southwest then southeast and is nearing Dinwiddie Court House. Sheridan, alerted by a captured Confederate cavalrymen, has moved troops to confront him.

The quiet afternoon is shattered as Pickett's infantrymen attack across a swollen, marshy creek while Fitz Lee's cavalry attack at a lower ford.

Sheridan has blocked both fords with fresh cavalry, and the fighting becomes vicious, confused, with Union and Confederate charges and countercharges across the marshy creek. For nearly an hour the shallow water is churned as one regiment after another try to drive their enemy back.

Custer's friend from West Point days, Confederate Major General Tom Rosser is wounded, but his men finally force Yankee cavalry back from the lower ford.

At almost the same time, at the upper ford Federal cavalry again learn that men on horses can't stop an infantry charge.

Late in the afternoon, Confederate cavalry and infantry are across the stream and linked within a rifle's shot of Dinwiddie Court House. Before them, Sheridan's cavalry, with their Spencer repeating rifles, have slowed the Confederate advance but are only holding on by a thread.

Sheridan, weighing the steadily growing roar of battle, turns to his chief of staff.

"Forsyth, send for Custer, back there corduroying roads. Tell him to get up here in a hurry; pick up ammunition, all he can carry, on the way. Then I want you to round up every cook, orderly, messenger, walking-wounded soldier who can carry a rifle; give them rifles; and form a reserve. In the center, right behind Merritt's lines."

"While you're doing that," he shouts, "get the regimental bands up here. Even the ones carrying stretchers; we can pick up the wounded later. Put them right up there, behind the line. Mounted, so the men can see 'em and hear 'em. Tell the Sergeants Majors to have them play, play as loud as they can, as long as they can. Never mind a few bullet holes in a trombone or drum. Or in a musician either. Play, damn it, until I tell them to stop."

Then, having done all he can to get as many Northern soldiers into the fight as possible, he snatches up his personal battle flag and, waving it so no one can mistake him or his determination, he gallops the entire length of the Union line.

Sheridan's soldiers, hearing his shouts and seeing the fire in the little general's eyes, grip their weapons tighter. There'll be no more falling back. They'd rather face the Johnnies out there than Sheridan behind them.

By five o'clock the setting sun, lighting the western sky for the first time in three days, streaks through clouds to spotlight a scene stranger than anyone could ever imagine. Long lines of Union and Confederate soldiers loading and firing their rifles as fast as they can: the steady rhythm of Enfields, the sharper, faster crack of Spencer repeaters; cannon belching fire and smoke; men falling everywhere, and firing lines constantly shuffling to close the gaps; battle flags waving defiantly; officers and sergeants moving back and forth, cursing, cajoling, shouting orders; pairs of soldiers carrying blankets heaped with cartridges and percussion caps to riflemen on the firing lines; soldiers helping wounded comrades to the rear; and crumpled bodies everywhere.

Sheridan, on his big, black stallion, Rienzi, is in the center of his line. Nearby his orderly, already wounded but insisting on carrying Sheridan's personal flag until the fight is won, struggles to keep up with his fiery commander.

The regimental bands, mounted on matching gray or white, brown, or black horses, are playing for all they're worth: "Hail Columbia," "Lonigan's Ball," "Yankee Doodle," and "The Girl I Left Behind Me."

Then Custer's men arrive to join the fight. Their initial charge, on foot, is broken, and they're pushed back. Custer, however, cursing, shouting, waving his blue sombrero, rallies them to charge again. Their strength makes the difference. Confederate infantry, seeing Custer's numbers and reeling under the added fire of several thousand more repeating rifles, slow their fire then, still howling their defiant Rebel yell, begin to fall back to the woods behind them.

Sheridan's blood is up. He's stopped Pickett. Now he means to destroy him.

"Custer," he shouts, "Mount your brigades. All of them, every saber. And charge. Is that the new guidon Merritt told me about? Well, I want to see it waving in that wood line. Give it to them, General! You hear me? I want you to give it to them!"

That's all Custer needs. Bugles sound and the horsehandlers (every fourth man holds the reins for three other dismounted troopers fighting on foot) hurry forward. Custer's troopers, knowing what is about to happen without being told, cheer, tighten saddle girths, and spring into their saddles.

Regiment after regiment wheel into line as eager cavalrymen urge their excited horses into regimental fronts. A pause then, across the breadth of Custer's division the steel of thousands of blades flash in the late sun as the men draw sabers.

Behind the regiments preparing to charge, a dozen mounted bands have begun to play Custer's favorite fighting song, "Garry Owen."

The stage is set; all that's needed is for the principal actor to set the drama in motion.

It's a moment Custer won't waste. He gallops to the center of his two-brigade line, then fifty yards ahead of it. Then he waves his blue sombrero so no one can mistake him or why he's there. His long blond hair shining in the setting sun, the red neckerchief about his neck mirrored on the necks of thousands of his troopers behind him, there's little chance of anyone, Union or Confederate, not knowing who or what he is; but he wants to be sure, especially if Rosser is over there, watching.

Sheridan nods, and Custer wheels his horse to face his enemy, draws his sword, and shouts.

"Bugler, blow 'Charge!'; Blow 'Charge'! And keep on blowing it until there's none of them left. Orderly, stay with me and hold that flag high. I want 'em to see it; to remember it!"

Confederate infantrymen, recognizing the hopelessness of trying to stop the charge and choosing to fight another day, begin to back away into the dark woods.

Custer won't have it; he just won't have it. They musn't get away. A beautiful charge, his division's charge, and he means to take it all the way to that railroad Sheridan wants so bad. Then they'll know. They'll all know. Custer's division!

"Come on! Come on!" he shouts left and right and leads the way.

Just short of the woods, Custer's galloping horse reaches a long, broad patch of ground, muddy and slick from the heavy rains. The stallion's hooves slip from under him and he tumbles on his side, throwing Custer from the saddle.

Horse and rider slide through the mud, finally coming to a stop beneath a large pine tree.

Close behind him, and unable to stop, his leading regiments, one after the other, also hit the slick ground. Horses slide and tumble; riders are thrown from their saddles. A glorious charge, but even a chagrined Custer has to laugh at its end.

"Well, Boehm," he calls to an aide lying on his back a few yards away, "you got through the Rebs' line with Libby's flag, but I pretty near got you killed here. At least it wasn't the Johnnies that stopped us! Find a bugler and have him sound 'Recall'; this fight's over."

Darkness ends the firing. Billy Yank and Johnny Reb, still less than a mile above Sheridan's headquarters, turn to building breastworks should morning begin it again.

Pickett hasn't done all he'd hoped to do, but he's won the day: he's stopped Sheridan from reaching Five Forks and the South Side Railroad.

Sheridan, however, remains as enthusiastic and positive as ever. When Grant's liaison officer remarks about the danger of remaining where they are, Sheridan spins on his heels, his black eyes sparkling with anger.

"Turn back? Danger? We've had a long day, Colonel Porter (Lieutenant Colonel Horace Porter), but Pickett out there's in far more danger than I am. If I'm cut off from Meade, he's cut off from Lee. Well, we'll settle this matter tomorrow; and I don't propose to let a single one of Pickett's men get back to Lee. Not one. We've driven them back; now we can destroy them. Go back and tell Grant that's the way I feel about it. Tell him to get Wright's VI Corps to me tonight, and I'll give him that damned railroad tomorrow. Tell him that."

As night falls, Sheridan rides among his regiments, from campfire to campfire, checking commanders, encouraging tired men, gauging their strength.

He especially seeks out Custer; Sheridan will always have a special bond with the boy general. Custer, he muses, we're a lot alike.

Rienzi takes him to Custer's headquarters, a small cluster of campfires. He smiles at their flickering flames casting a ghostly light on a stark reminder of the day's violence: a dozen captured Confederate flags, their staffs aligned and driven into the ground. Battle trophies. Centered before the captured flags, hanging limply in the late night air, are a United States' flag, Custer's division's flag, and Custer's personal guidon.

Sheridan dismounts, extends Libby Custer's silk flag with his gloved hand, and smiles, "A half dozen bullet holes in it already and," he studies the bottom corner of the swallow-tailed guidon, "it looks as if a couple of those bullets have cut her initials right out of it. Custer'll see that as a good sign too."

Waving away staff officers who'd join him, Sheridan walks alone through Custer's camp. Exhausted men are sleeping everywhere while staff officers see that food, forage, and ammunition get to the regiments before morning. Near the center, his back resting against his tree-propped saddle, a blanket thrown across his legs by some caring sergeant or staff officer, and sitting erect with a steaming cup of coffee still clasped in a tight fist, is Custer. Sound asleep.

When Sheridan takes the tin cup from Custer's hand, the young general, unaware, continues to sleep. Sheridan smiles, sips the coffee, then hands the cup to the orderly.

"He'll do," he grins, "a couple hours' sleep and he'll do." Then he growls and snorts, "And Warren and his V Corps'll have to do too."

PICKETT

As Sheridan is returning to his headquarters, across the field Fitz Lee and George Pickett warm their hands over a campfire.

"Things are pretty quiet now, George," Fitz Lee reports. "Got my cavalry tied in on your flanks. Rosser's out with that arm of his; and his horses are about played out too. So I've moved Rosser's brigade back a bit. Did you send back word on what's happened?"

"Yes, awhile back. The thing now is to decide what's best for us," Pickett's voice reveals his uncertainty. "I'd feel better back at Five Forks; Anderson can get help to us a lot quicker there."

"Fitz, you say those Yanks you picked up were V Corps?"

"Uh-huh," Fitz Lee nods. "Bartlett's brigade they said. Caught 'em on a farm, back off to the east apiece."

"And we don't know whether there's a brigade or a division or the entire corps with them?"

"No. The ones we caught say that things are pretty confused over there. They were told to get on over to Dinwiddie as quick as possible, but they think that the whole V Corps and maybe some of the II Corps are coming up behind us."

"Blasted rain," Pickett stares at the fire as if its flames could light his way. "Too dark to see your hand in front of your face, and we're trying to find out what we're facing. Sheridan's got all his cavalry in front of us and now maybe a corps or more coming up behind us."

Fitz Lee nods. "By morning we could be in a real fix."

"All right," Pickett decides, "spread the word. We've done what we can here. And now we're pretty far out on the limb. When things get quieter we'll build up our fires, leave some skirmishers, and pull back to Five Forks. Cover us with your cavalry. When we get there, see to our flanks and patrol the gap to Anderson's trenches at the Claiborne Road. I can't cover all that ground with what I have. We'll let the men rest a couple hours before we start."

"You'll notify General Lee?"

"Yes, soon's I can."

At 4 a.m., leaving burning campfires and skirmishers to give the alarm if Sheridan detects their movement, Pickett's infantrymen quietly shoulder their rifles and march for Five Forks. An hour later Fitz Lee's covering cavalry also leave Dinwiddie. Along the way they have several sharp clashes with Custer's cavalry patrols, but don't encounter Warren's V Corps.

THEY FOUGHT FOR THE UNION

President Abraham Lincoln

**Lieutenant General
Ulysses S. Grant, USA**

Major General
William T.
Sherman, USA

Major General
George G.
Meade, USA

Major General
Edward O. C. Ord,
USA

Major General Philip H.
Sheridan, USA

Major General George
A. Custer, USA

Major General
Joshua L.
Chamberlain, USA

Rear Admiral David D. Porter, USN

Major General Charles Griffin, USA

Major General Gouverneur K. Warren, USA

Major General Philip H. Sheridan, USA, with Brigadier General James W. Forsyth, Major General Wesley Merritt, Brigadier General Thomas C. Devin, and Major General George A. Custer

Lieutenant General Ulysses S. Grant with wife, Julia, and son, Jesse, Headquarters, City Point, Virginia, 1865

President Abraham Lincoln with wife, Mary, and sons (Captain) Robert and Tad

THEY FOUGHT FOR THE CONFEDERACY

President Jefferson Davis

Lieutenant General Robert
E. Lee, CSA

General Joseph E.
Johnston, CSA

Lieutenant General
James Longstreet, CSA

**Lieutenant General
Ambrose P. Hill, CSA**

**Lieutenant General
Richard S. Ewell, CSA**

Major General
Fitzhugh Lee, CSA

Major General John
B. Gordon, CSA

Major General George E. Pickett, CSA

General Robert E. Lee with his son, Brigadier General Washington Custis Lee, and aide, Lieutenant Colonel Walter H. Taylor, Richmond, 1865

"Capture of the Forts at Petersburg"

CHAPTER 5

Five Forks   April 1, 1865

CHAMBERLAIN

At midnight Griffin finds Chamberlain hunched over an ammunition box, writing, beside a small campfire a hundred yards above the White Oak Road.

Nearby, his brother, Captain Thomas Chamberlain, sleeps; Sergeant McDermott is piling kindling beside the fire; and several staff officers are quietly talking about getting food and ammunition to the regiments. Chamberlain's soldiers, too tired to pitch their tents, have rolled up in their shelter halves and are sleeping.

"Lawrence, sorry to interrupt your work," Griffin apologizes.

"It's all right, General," Chamberlain looks up from his paper to study his division commander. "Just a letter to Fannie and the children. Got a little behind these last few days."

Then he adds, "Things have quieted down. Anderson's skirmishers are a couple hundred yards ahead of us. I've been up there several times. Heard them talking; they're expecting a big fight in the morning. I expect they're right."

He looks at Griffin for a moment, "You look tired, General. Guess it's been a long day for all of us. Have you eaten?"

"Yes, awhile back," Griffin answers. "Been at Meade's headquarters most of the evening," he shakes his head as if that had not been pleasant. "Sure could use a cup of coffee though. Reckon Sergeant McDermott could find one for me?"

Chamberlain grins, "He hasn't let me down yet. Sergeant Mac, could you rustle up a cup of coffee for the General?"

Sergeant McDemott, knowing that army etiquette requires his general to drink with their division commander, already is carrying two steaming cups toward them. Griffin thanks him, takes his seat on a log beside Chamberlain, and watches the burly sergeant turning to arrange a bed of straw for Chamberlain.

"A good man, Lawrence. How'd you find him?"

"Didn't," Chamberlain grins. "He found me, at Gettysburg. I had the 20th Maine then; wonderful regiment, then and now."

Chamberlain thoughtfully sips his coffee and continues, "Our Colonel was a wonderful old soldier. Adelbert Ames. You remember him: West Point; to the core. Used to get awfully mad at the informality of the 20th. Anyway, the governor appointed me Adelbert Ames' second in command. I told him that I'd had no formal military training but wanted to learn. So he taught me at night the things I'd need to know the next day. Then he picked my orderly himself; one who'd be around when Ames couldn't be."

"The man he picked," Chamberlain continues, "was an old soldier too. Up and down the ranks a half dozen times before I got him. The army was his family, and he knew it real well. Kept me from a lot of mistakes and helped me when I made them. We shared many a canteen on many a march, and he was always near me in a fight. Saved my life three or four times, and I his. He was my orderly, John, but, far more than that, he was my friend. You understand?"

"Yes," Griffin nods. "I know. I had one like that myself, a long time ago in the West. He'd have died for me and, I expect, I'd have died for him. An officer's lucky to find just one man like that in his whole career; sounds as if you've found two."

"Yes," Chamberlain nods and sips his coffee, slowly, thoughtfully, the hot tin cup burning his lips. Then he continues, "I'd just gotten his sergeant's stripes back when we marched to Gettysburg. On Little Round Top, when we fought the 15th Alabama, he was shot, twice. By the time the surgeon could get to him, it was too late. He bled to death. Right there by that stone wall, and I couldn't do a thing to stop it. Wish I could. We buried him there, but I'll never forget him."

"Anyway," the slender Maine General continues. "The next day, you remember Hancock (Major General Winfield Scott Hancock) put us in the center of the line, where Pickett hit. And Sergeant Mac just walked up to me, saluted, said, 'Colonel, Sergeant Thomas McDermott, reportin' for duty as the Colonel's orderly.' I didn't have time then to ask who'd sent him. Found out later he'd just decided that the Colonel needed help, so he'd sent himself. After a couple days he reminded me to let his regiment know that he wouldn't be back. By then there was no way I'd let him go."

"And," Chamberlain grins, "he's been with me ever since. Sometimes too close: fusses with me to ride the horse, eat my supper, let my family know I'm all right. A good man, John. My mother used to say the Lord never closed a door that He didn't open another; I expect that's so."

"Now," he turns to the business at hand, "you look worn down, General. How are things going?"

"Well," Griffin replies, "you probably saved Warren's hide today. Meade's quick to find fault and, when Ayres' and Crawford's brigades broke, he'd have blamed Warren for it. Instead, you took back the ground they'd lost then took White Oak Road too. So Grant was pleased, and that made Meade happy."

"Happy for awhile," he reflects, "then it seemed as if all the wheels came off the cart. I've been at Warren's headquarters most of the evening, saw it for myself. Warren's caught in a commander's worst nightmare. He has two higher headquarters, Grant's and Meade's, giving him conflicting orders; neither one knowing his situation here and neither one trying to find out. Grant's staffs bypassing Meade to give orders direct to Warren or even me; and Meade won't stand up and tell them to stop it. So, instead of being praised for your cutting that road and getting us on Lee's flank, Warren's caught between a rock and a hard place among Grant, Meade, and now Sheridan."

"We've been attached to Sheridan?"

"Not yet; by morning for sure."

"What's happening with Sheridan?"

"Don't know for sure; just that about sunset he had a big fight near Dinwiddie Court House. Seems he stopped the Johnnies, but he's having trouble hanging on where he is, let alone trying to take Five Forks."

"Any word of Bartlett's brigade?"

"Nothing. They disappeared up that path below White Oak Road about sunset. Warren notified Meade, and Meade seemed happy that he'd sent Bartlett to help Sheridan. Then it all seemed to come apart. About 6:30 Meade ordered Warren to catch up with Bartlett and have him swing down to the Boydton Plank Road. Warren and I talked about it; seemed to us that it didn't matter how Bartlett got there so long as he got there. And our marching him south would have cost another hour or so. But, to keep Meade happy, Warren sent a rider to bring Bartlett back; meanwhile sending another brigade down the Plank Road."

"Then," Griffin continues to relate Warren's problems, "about eight o'clock Warren heard direct from Grant that Sheridan had a big fight above Dinwiddie Court House, and Grant wanted us to hold up here above the White Oak Road. A little later, Meade, not knowing that Grant told us to stay put here, got to worrying about Warren's sending off a couple of his brigades to help Sheridan. Ordered him to pull the rest of us back; give up the road. Warren argued with him; didn't want to give up this ground we won today; suggested, 'If they're between us and Sheridan, General, why not let me take the entire V Corps and hit the Rebs from this end?'"

Chamberlain thoughtfully sips his coffee then turns to his commander, "At night, General? Better than two divisions over that cowpath, in the dark, with enough Rebs around to already have stopped Sheridan? Risky."

"I know," Griffin holds up his hand. "Told Warren that. Too late. He'd already suggested it to Meade. Next thing I know, Warren got Meade's answer: 'Send Griffin's division by the Boydton Plank Road; Ayres' and Crawford's by the route Bartlett took.'"

"Griffin's division?" Chamberlain can't believe it. "Give up the White Oak Road? Try to pull out Gregg's and my brigades within 200 yards of Anderson's corps? Everyone milling around in the dark, making enough noise to wake the dead? Then try to pass us through Crawford and Ayres to get to the road? All in the dark?"

"Well, General," Chamberlain sighs, "you didn't bother us so I'd guess you were able to change their minds."

Griffin nods, "Well, not quite. We still have to give up the White Oak Road. But he's sent Ayres down the Boydton Plank Road instead of us, that is if Warren has rebuilt the bridge over Gravelly Run so Ayres can get across. I understand that Ayres was supposed to be at Dinwiddie by midnight, but an hour ago he still was waiting for the bridge to be fixed."

"I expect," he stares into the fire, "that'll cause Sheridan's kettle to boil over."

"And the rest of us?"

"You'll lead; Crawford'll follow. As soon as it's light, follow the path Bartlett took. If we run into Johnnies above Dinwiddie, we're to pitch into them. That's why I want your brigade in front."

"All right," Chamberlain nods. "I'll let my men sleep a bit more. It'll take Crawford awhile to get his regiments untangled. When he's done that, have them step to one side, so we can get by."

"I'm sorry," he reflects, "for Warren. He's a good engineer, good staff man, but he and Sheridan won't get along. I hope we can pull off this move so he can at least start off on the right foot with Sheridan."

"Yes," Griffin nods. "I think that we're going to have a tough fight before this is over. It'll go a lot better if we don't have to fight Sheridan too. Get yourself a couple hours' sleep too. You'll need it."

Then he stands, again thanks Sergeant McDermott for the coffee, and walks from the firelight, back toward White Oak Road.

Long after midnight, when Grant had promised that Warren's entire V Corps would reach Dinwiddie Court House, Ayres' lone division arrives at Sheridan's headquarters to be greeted by a grinning staff officer.

"Sorry, General, but you've come too far. Had a guide out there looking for you, but he must have given up. Sheridan wants you a mile or so back up the road. There's a crossroads there. Can't miss it. Turn your division around and march it back there; then wait for further orders."

Not, Ayres decides, an auspicious beginning.

Chamberlain quietly lets his men sleep as long as possible. Anticipating that they'll all change their minds again a time or two before morning, and not about to move his men in the darkness so near the enemy, he simply waits. Doesn't clear it with anyone; just quietly orders his officers, "Let them sleep, gentlemen. Let them sleep. I'll wake you when it's time."

Then he goes forward again to check the Confederate outposts for himself.

He's there near daylight when Griffin's messenger stumbles forward to tell him that it's time to pull back. Chamberlain's brigade will lead the V Corps' march, down the path Bartlett had taken, to reinforce Sheridan.

In the cold gray dawn, miles down a dark trail just below White Oak Road, Chamberlain's scouts meet Bartlett's travel-worn infantrymen, recalled from their fruitless cross-country night's march.

"Morning, General Bartlett," Chamberlain grins at the mud-streaked, tired face of his fellow brigade commander. "Don't even ask what's happening. Griffin's back aways, and he'll fill you in. He'll want you to leave a guide for me, rest your men here, then fall in behind Gregg's brigade. We're to follow your path and get on the Confederate rear somewhere between here and Dinwiddie."

"Back again? Over this God-forsaken sea of mud? Last night, Lawrence, when it was too dark to see a blasted thing, we started up this path. Finally bivouacked on the Boisseau farm, a couple miles up the way. Figured to join Sheridan at dawn. Then Warren's rider caught up with us and called us back here. Just in time for you to tell me we're to march it a third time? Three times in one night?"

"I know, Joe," Chamberlain grins ruefully. "So does Griffin. Not his fault. Warren's neither, far as I can see. Look, when I heard you were coming I had some fires built. They're a couple hundred yards back. There'll be coffee there. It'll take awhile for Gregory and me to get by, not being used to this walk the way you are. I suggest that you let your men have some coffee and get what rest they can until we've passed. I think we'll need all the rest we can get before this day's over."

Chamberlain's regiments continue, moving carefully down the dirt path until it becomes a not much better road; his scouts ranging far ahead and on both flanks.

The morning sun and the march are warming his brigade when a scout alerts him.

"Cavalry, General. Lots of it. Up the road about a mile, and comin' this way fast. Didn't have time to see whether they're ours or Johnnies."

From a small rise Chamberlain studies the road to his front. Then he sees sunlight reflecting from saber scabbards and brass belts; close and coming on strong.

"Cavalry, Colonel Sniper. Get ready to fight. I'll pass the word."

SHERIDAN

At his Dinwiddie Court House headquarters Sheridan also has spent an anxious night. It's after midnight before he returns from Custer's camp. Then there are reports to be read, messages to be sent. Besides, he's anxious for dawn. At dawn he means to attack: his cavalry on the left, Warren's V Corps on the right.

Grant's not happy, an impatiently pacing Sheridan reflects. After I talked him into going ahead this morning, we got bogged down in this God-forsaken mud. Couldn't take Five Forks; instead Pickett damn near over-ran us. I told Porter that we can do it in the morning, and he'll tell Grant that but, he angrily mutters, "I've got to have Warren's corps. I've got to have his infantry."

Grant had assured him that Warren would reach Dinwiddie by midnight. Long after midnight a scowling Sheridan interrupts his pacing to ask again, "Forsyth, any sign of Warren?"

"No, sir; not yet."

"Damn!" Sheridan mutters. "They're still not up." Striking the palm of his hand with his clenched fist, he growls, "I told Grant I didn't want them; asked for Wright's VI Corps. Not up yet; and we've got to strike early in the morning."

He studies the map once more then turns, "I'm going upstairs; call me when Warren's here."

———————

At 2 a.m. he's told that Merritt's scouts have contacted V Corps' regiments near Boisseau's farm, several miles northeast of Dinwiddie. No sign of Warren himself, but Ayres' division also has just reported in so the rest of the V Corps must be nearby.

"Send Ayres back to that crossroads below Boisseau's farm, General Forsyth. Tell him to hold his division there for orders. And tell Warren to hold the rest of his corps at Boisseau's. I doubt that they need rest, they've taken their sweet time getting here; but tell them to rest until I send for them."

An hour later he's up again to write Warren:

> I'm holding in front of Dinwiddie Court House with Custer's division. The enemy are in his immediate front....I understand that you have a division at Boisseau's; if so, you are in the rear of the enemy's line....they may attack at daylight; if so, attack instantly and in full force. Attack at daylight anyhow.... If the enemy remains, I shall fight at daylight.

———————

Sheridan's couriers find Ayres bivouacked off the Boydton Plank Road, but they can't find Warren or the rest of the V Corps there or near Boisseau's farm. In fact, they can't find any of Warren's men near Boisseau's farm.

"There's lots of tracks up there, General," Forsyth reports. "The road's all cut up from a lot of men, but not a soul there. They've just vanished. Our courier looked around a bit and gave it up."

"Keep looking," Sheridan scowls. "This throws it all off. Custer's ready to go in at dawn; so's Merritt. But we need Warren's infantry. Keep looking. When you find Warren, tell him to attack at first light. Tear up their flank; get on the White Oak Road. When we hear his guns, we'll hit their front."

Sheridan's scouts, returning to Boisseau's farm, again can't find Warren or his phantom infantrymen.

"Nothing near here now, Sarge," one reports. "But a lot of infantry were here awhile back. At least a brigade. See the tracks in that mud trace? They got this far then turned around and headed back. Reckon we oughta follow 'em?"

"Well," the grizzled sergeant spits into the road, ponders the situation, then decides, "reckon we'll let the Lieutenant decide. If he wants someone to follow 'em, I'll take the lead."

He grins, "Either the Lieutenant goes ahead or he's gonna have to go back there and tell Little Phil we can't find 'em and," he spits again, "given my 'druthers, when the Lieutenant tells Sheridan that, I'd 'druther be a couple miles away. Yeah, we'll let the Lieutenant pick his own poison: Johnnies mebbe up there ahead of us or Sheridan back at Dinwiddie."

Near dawn, a foggy, cold, damp, foreboding morning, Sheridan again steps from his tavern headquarters. Rienzi, bridled and ready, neighs a greeting. Sheridan absently pats the black stallion's mane as he thoughtfully looks about.

The woods to his front are quiet now. No sign of the enemy. Following yesterday's fight Pickett's men have withdrawn; Custer's scouts are looking for them. To the north, far off it seems in the heavy air, Sheridan hears an occasional rifle shot but no sustained firing. Around the courthouse his troopers ignore the scattered firing as they boil coffee, check equipment, feed and groom their horses.

"They're all expecting a big fight today," Sheridan mutters to the horse, "and so am I." Then he curses, "But where's Warren? Where's the rest of his infantry?"

When the horse has no answer for him, he smiles grimly, pats Rienzi again, and calls to his escort, "Lead off, Captain. We'll go up to the left, to Custer's headquarters first; then we'll go see Merritt on the right."

CHAMBERLAIN

Several miles northeast of Dinwiddie Court House Chamberlain's regiments have formed battle lines as they watch the approaching cavalry force grow larger and larger. Then Chamberlain recognizes Sheridan's personal flag.

"They're ours, Colonel; that's Sheridan near the front. Get your men back on the road. I'll send for General Griffin."

Sheridan arrives before Griffin. Chamberlain salutes, "General Chamberlain, General, with the head of Griffin's division."

Chamberlain's courtesy is ignored. Sheridan brusquely returns the salute before he snaps, "Where've you been, General? I expected you about eight hours ago! Where's Warren?"

"General Warren's at the rear of our column, General," Chamberlain answers.

"That's about where I expected to find him," Sheridan retorts. "What's he doing back there?"

"General, we fought hard all day yesterday. Up on White Oak Road east of here. We spent last night, until about three o'clock, within 200 yards of Lee's right at the Claiborne Road. Then we were ordered to disengage, pull back, reinforce you. We've marched without rest ever since. General Warren's with the last of our divisions. If the Johnnies saw us pulling out, they'll hit our rear. That's why General Warren's back there."

Glancing back, he adds, "General Griffin's coming up now. Have you any orders for me or will you wait for him?"

Sheridan, taken back by Chamberlain's calm rebuff, has no time to answer. Griffin has arrived and Chamberlain, saluting smartly, withdraws.

Moments later Griffin reins his horse beside Chamberlain's to tell him, "We'll rest here while Sheridan decides what he wants to do with us. Have the men rustle up any food they can, and be sure they have all the ammunition they can carry. There'll be fighting before this day is over, Lawrence; you can bet on that."

"Yes, sir," Chamberlain salutes, "wouldn't be a bit surprised."

When Warren finally arrives, Sheridan has little to say to him. Warren, introspective, sensitive, recognizing the fiesty cavalryman's rebuff, remains nearby but avoids Sheridan; instead he keeps busy seeing that food and ammunition are brought up before the fight Sheridan's determined to bring on this day.

About mid-morning, having met with Warren, Sheridan returns to his headquarters to find Lieutenant Colonel Horace Porter of Grant's staff waiting for him.

"General, General Grant wants me to stay close to you and report your progress. He said that I'm to make sure that you understand that he's counting on you to turn Pickett from Five Forks and to take that railroad. Said that I was to tell you that the whole movement is in your hands."

Sheridan grimly nods, "All right, Colonel. Thank you. Now the enemy's falling back. I don't think they'll make a stand this side of Five Forks. Custer's located a line they've begun along the White Oak Road from just west of Five Forks to about a mile to the east of it. It's a strong line, but I mean to take it. I'll take it just as soon as Warren can get his damned infantry in position."

"You know, Porter," Sheridan adds, "Warren finally got here this morning, his men all worn out, eight hours after Grant promised they'd be here. That's what I have to work with today, Colonel. But we'll do it, sir, we'll do it. Soon's I can get Warren to go in on their left."

Meanwhile, at Grant's headquarters, a staff officer returning from a visit to Warren's former headquarters on the Boydton Plank Road, reports finding several of Warren's staff officers sleeping.

Awakened, neither officer knew where Warren had gone.

"Well," he'd asked, "where's his headquarters now?"

"Beats me, Colonel. Somewhere up that back road with Griffin's and Crawford's divisions. Figured we'd find him later."

Grant listens to the report, nods, thoughtfully puffs his cigar. Then he begins to write in his message pad. When he's done he hands the message to another aide.

"Colonel Babcock, find Sheridan and give him this. I'm telling him that, if he thinks Warren's men would do better under one of their division commanders, he's authorized to relieve Warren and order him to report to me here."

Grant has placed Warren's career in Sheridan's hands. When Babcock relays the message, Sheridan looks surprised then, turning away with a grim smile, answers, "Well, I hope it won't be necessary, but we'll see."

A message of that sort is bound to be repeated, and it soon is gossiped among Warren's generals. Griffin and Chamberlain, sharing coffee and hardtack on a large stone in an old country churchyard, are concerned about it. Watching Chamberlain's soldiers packing their haversacks with three days' rations and an extra twenty rounds of ammunition, and certain there will be a fight before the day ends, they vow to make things go right.

PICKETT

Meanwhile, at Five Forks, Robert E. Lee's courier finds George Pickett with Lee's answer to Pickett's report of the Dinwiddie Court House fight. Even Pickett, known to his fellow commanders as slow to grasp the broadest subtleties, can't miss the disappointment and anger in Lee's reaction to Pickett's withdrawal to Five Forks.

Lee's message: "Hold Five Forks at all hazards. Protect the road to Ford's Depot and prevent Union forces from striking the Southside Railroad. Regret exceedingly your forced withdrawal, and your inability to hold the advantage you had gained."

Lee, always courteous, allowing his subordinates as much latitude as possible, has left Pickett no options at all.

Pickett's tired command: Fitz Lee's cavalry and five infantry brigades, nearly 10,000 men, set to work building log, dirt, and stone entrenchments nearly two miles long. Their left flank, where the gap between them and Anderson's trenches begins, is bent back about 150 yards. Some of Fitz Lee's cavalry will patrol that gap. General Tom Rosser's cavalry, Pickett's only reserve, are camped north of Five Forks where Ford's Road crosses Hatcher's Run.

By noon they've thrown up breastworks and, anticipating no more fighting that day, Pickett allows his tired soldiers to rest.

SHERIDAN

About one o'clock Sheridan sends word for Warren to bring his corps forward to the Gravelly Run Methodist Episcopal Church, a small white-sided structure less than a mile below White Oak Road and, according to Custer's scouts, just below the eastern end of Pickett's battle line.

As Warren's commanders wait for Ayres' and Crawford's divisions to arrive, Sheridan uses his sword to trace in the sand the enemy's position: a strong line of earthworks running from just west of Five Forks to a point due north of the church; there the line bent northward to protect Pickett's left flank.

"Your corps," Sheridan's loud voice carries across the churchyard, "will strike the Confederate line there," he stabs the sand with the point of his saber, "at that angle. Break their line; then swing west toward Five Forks. When Custer and Merritt hear your guns, they'll hit the Rebs' right and center. We're going to catch Pickett between us, gentlemen; squash him like a bug. Then we'll take that damned railroad."

As Sheridan describes the plan, Warren listens but doesn't join the discussion.

To avoid any misunderstanding, however, he drafts written orders for his officers. Crawford's division will be on the right, Ayres' on the left, Griffin's in reserve. When they've taken the earthworks at the angle, they'll pivot and attack west along White Oak Road. Simple enough. A watching Sheridan nods but growls at Warren's finding it necessary to put it all in writing after he's just drawn the plan in the sand of the churchyard.

CHAMBERLAIN

An hour later, while they're still waiting for Ayres' and Crawford's divisions to arrive, Joshua Chamberlain is joined by Colonel Frederick Winthrop, commanding one of Ayres' brigades.

"Lawrence, would you have any food? I've had nothing since last night. My men are drawing rations, but I came ahead for orders."

"Of course," Chamberlain answers. "Sergeant Mac, please rustle up some food for Colonel Winthrop."

McDermott returns from whatever magical place sergeants turn to at such times with beef, hardtack, and coffee.

"Not much, Colonel," McDermott apologizes. "Hard to pry anything from these Pennsylvania Dutchmen. Now, if it was the old 20th Maine..." he leaves it there, content that Winthrop, a friend of Chamberlain's, won't need any more explanation than that.

"Thanks, Sergeant Mac," Winthrop enjoys the food. When he's finished eating, he lights his pipe, puffs a moment, then again turns to Chamberlain.

"Another favor, Lawrence?"

"Of course."

"We're going to have a big fight here today. Sheridan won't have it any other way. And," he pauses then continues, "I've got a feeling that this will be my last one."

Chamberlain doesn't answer, merely nods. Soldiers have premonitions of death. Doesn't make it happen, but the premonitions matter to those who have them. And not much a friend can do except offer a little comfort by understanding.

"We all figure that you'll be around when the rest of us are gone," Winthrop grins and puffs his pipe. "Look, if something happens to me, would you see that the proper things are done? I'd like to be taken home if possible, and I've left personal things with my Adjutant."

"Of course, Fred. Try not to worry about it. Just do what you have to do, and let Providence work it out. At least that's what I try to do."

Winthrop smiles his thanks. That taken care of, he brightens and the two men laugh at the confusion of the night before. Then Winthrop casually salutes and moves off to find his brigade.

SHERIDAN

Three o'clock now. Griffin and Ayres are ready, but Crawford's division, the last of Warren's corps, still hasn't arrived. Sheridan, more angry and frustrated every time he glances at the sinking sun, growls, paces, and smashes his fist into his hand, ignores Warren.

Later, having gone to check his cavalry, Sheridan returns to find Warren sitting under a tree, sketching the church before them.

"Warren," Sheridan makes no attempt to hide his anger, "this battle must be fought before that sun goes down. We can win it, cut that damned railroad, and end this war. But we must do it now; by morning conditions may have changed entirely. Do you understand that? Do you understand, General, that my cavalry are waiting for the sound of your guns?"

Warren, depressed and uncertain, nods then answers that he'll send another messenger to hurry Crawford's division. Then he adds, as if to himself, "Bobbie Lee has a way of getting people into difficulties."

Sheridan, his face dark with rage, weighs Warren's answer for a long moment then snorts, "I'm going back over with Merritt and Custer. They're ready and waiting. The minute they hear your firing, they'll go straight on in. Every minute counts."

———

From Merritt's headquarters, then from Custer's he still does not hear Warren's guns. Beside himself with nervous energy and anxiety, he paces back and forth, periodically sending a new courier to remind Warren again that the sun is setting low in the west and that everything depends on Warren's moving quickly.

Finally, a little after four o'clock, he's told that the V Corps at last has begun to advance on White Oak Road. Reminding Custer and Merritt to strike at Five Forks the moment Warren hits the Confederate flank, he again spurs Rienzi back toward the Gravelly Church Road.

PICKETT

Confederate General Thomas Rosser, young, broad-shouldered, quick-tempered, wounded in yesterday's fighting before Dinwiddie Courthouse, is bivouacked with his cavalry regiments off Ford's Road north of Five Forks.

Before leaving Fitz Lee, earlier in the morning, Rosser had suggested, "Fitz, I netted some shad in the Nottoway two days ago. I'll set up a shad bake for lunch. You come, and I'll invite Pickett too."

Soon after noon Pickett and Fitz Lee, reassured by the line of earthworks they've erected along White Oak Road and having no strong enemy before them, eagerly anticipate Rosser's shad bake.

As they're about to leave for Rosser's camp, Colonel Tom Munford, whose cavalry guard Pickett's left flank, arrives.

"There's a lot of Bluebelly cavalry crossing White Oak Road to the east, General. They're driving Colonel Roberts' (Colonel William Roberts)

North Carolina brigade back. If we don't stop them, they'll cut us off from any reinforcements from Anderson."

Fitz Lee hears the report, canters his horse a hundred yards closer, listens, but hears no firing. Munford, normally not apt to panic, may be overly concerned. Besides, Fitz Lee sees an impatient Pickett already riding up Ford Road toward Rosser's camp.

He turns back to Munford, "Munford, go back and see what's going on over there. If you have to send in your troops, let me know."

Turning, he rides north to overtake Pickett. Already he can taste the broiled shad.

Munford watches the two generals go. Neither he nor any other Confederate officer at Five Forks knows where their two ranking generals are going, when they'll return, or who is in command during their absence. Major General William H. F. "Rooney" Lee, with Fitz Lee's cavalry west of Five Forks, will be the senior Confederate commander in the absence of Pickett and Fitz Lee, but no one thinks to tell him that they've gone.

The fight on the Confederate left is an attack by Brigadier General Ranald Mackenzie's two brigades of Federal cavalry on Roberts' thin brigade covering the road to the east.

By four o'clock Mackenzie has scattered Roberts' troopers and driven beyond White Oak Road. Then Mackenzie sends his scouts west, behind the Confederate line, to near Rosser's camp on Ford's Road above Five Forks.

Rosser's shad bake has been a great success. Rosser is a fine host, and Fitz Lee and Pickett marvel at the table he's set for them. Large, brown, succulent fish drawn from glowing mounds of hot coals, and fine drinks Rosser miraculously found somewhere. It's a nice spring day; the fire is inviting; and the woods to their front peaceful and quiet. The three generals relax around Rosser's fire.

Two couriers appear. "Bluebellies, General," one reports to Rosser. "Thicker'n fleas on a dog. They're pourin' across White Oak Road east of here."

"Infantry or cavalry?" Rosser asks.

"Both, General. Mostly cavalry, but there's heaps of infantry comin' up too. Colonel Munford said there's V Corps' flags in front of him. Said to tell you there won't be any of our folks comin' down that road to help us."

The generals listen but still hear no firing. It's there, but the thick woods muffle it. Deciding the messengers are overexcited, they relax a bit longer.

Finally Pickett asks Rosser for a rider to carry a message to Five Forks. Rosser provides two. If one runs into trouble, the other will swing wide to deliver the message.

The two riders have hardly galloped off when the generals hear a burst of gunfire down Ford's Road. Then they watch as Union cavalrymen seize the lead courier, and the second courier gallops back to report.

"Can't get through, General. Woods full of Yanks. They're behind our boys at Five Forks too."

Pickett, totally alarmed, springs to his saddle and, calling to Fitz Lee for an escort, gallops toward the front.

A few hundred yards down the road he encounters Munford and, not far away, sees Union cavalry.

Reining his horse before Munford's the sweating, panicked Pickett shouts, "What troops are those?"

Then, without waiting for an answer, he calls to Rosser's escort, "I've got to get to Five Forks. For God's sake hold them off while I get by."

Hearing Pickett, Captain James Breckenridge, 3rd Virginia Cavalry, whirls his horse, draws his revolver and, firing rapidly, charges the Federal horsemen.

Hit by the return volley, he tumbles from his horse, bounces once on the sandy road, then rolls into a ditch, dead.

His diversion is enough, however, for Pickett, leaning over the far shoulder of his horse, to vanish down the road toward Five Forks.

Behind him the shadows are lengthening beside the road as Munford and Rosser rally their men to hold open a way for Pickett's men to retreat. Meanwhile, Fitz Lee, unable to follow Pickett, has begun a long ride west then south to try to reach Rooney Lee's cavalry fighting somewhere west of Five Forks.

SHERIDAN

As Pickett gallops toward Five Forks, back at Gravelly Run Church Road, Warren's skirmishers finally near White Oak Road: Crawford on the right, Ayres on the left, and Griffin behind Crawford. About 12,000 men on a thousand-yard front.

Sheridan, anxious that the long-delayed attack be pushed home before darkness must end it, follows Ayres' regiments.

To their east they hear the harsh, violent rattle of carbines and repeating rifles, Mackenzie's troopers pursuing Roberts' North Carolinians. To their front, however, there is only the scattered fire of Confederate skirmishers slowly falling back before the Federal advance.

Based on Sheridan's sketch, Crawford expects to hit the Confederate angle head on. His infantrymen, however, cross White Oak Road without a fight. Then they advance, faster now, north toward Hatcher's Run.

On Crawford's left and out of contact with him, Ayres' regiments also have reached White Oak Road. Before them they see a large, open field, cut by deep ravines and marked at its center by Robert Sydnor's farmhouse. Then they're hit by heavy cannon and rifle fire from their left. Sheridan's sketch had been wrong. The Confederate angle actually is considerably west of where he'd reported it. Crawford had passed to the east of it, but from its earthworks sheets of Confederate fire lash the left side of Ayres' line.

Pivoting his regiments to the left, Ayres attacks. More and more Union infantrymen fall. Their enemies have no intention of giving up their earthworks, and Ayres' riflemen begin to waver.

Meanwhile, Warren, realizing that Crawford is missing the real fight, gallops off to find him. Sheridan, left with Ayres' hard-hit, wavering regiments, sees Warren galloping away, curses, and takes charge.

Taking his personal battle flag from his orderly, and waving it high above his head, Sheridan shouts, "Come on, V Corps; Come on! Don't stop now! Go at 'em! They're about to break! Quickly now or you'll not catch a one of them!"

Then he gallops a dozen or so yards more along their lines, waves his flag again, and calls, "Come on, men! Go at 'em! They're getting ready to run! Don't let them get away from you! Come on, go after them!"

Waving his red and white swallow-tailed guidon and shouting encouragement, he gallops back and forth along the Federal firing line. Several staff officers, trailing behind Rienzi, are shot from their saddles, and rifle fire again and again rips Sheridan's battle flag. Sheridan, unhurt, all the while shaking his fist, yelling, cursing, cajoling, threatening. Can't be missed; can't be ignored; can't be resisted.

Rienzi rears before a soldier. The man, struck by a bullet and knocked to the ground, has staggered to his feet, blood pumping from his throat.

"I'm killed!" the soldier screams and drops to the ground again.

Sheridan, hardly pausing, leans over him to shout, "Killed? Nonsense! Why, you're not hurt a bit! Come on now; pick up your rifle, man, and move on!"

The startled soldier instinctively staggers to his feet, lurches forward then, covered with blood from the severed artery, falls again, dead.

As Ayres' regiments near their breastworks, Confederate artillerymen harness their remaining horses to their cannon and fall back toward the west. Behind them infantrymen fix bayonets and brace themselves. They don't have long to wait. Infantrymen of the 190th and 191st Pennsylvania Infantry Regiments, a few days ago young men in neat, clean blue uniforms but now dirty, tired, hungry, frightened, blooded veterans, clamber over the logs and heaped dirt into the Confederate line. The fight becomes a man-to-man, rifle, bayonet, clubbed musket brawl.

The 24th North Carolina Infantry Regiment is engulfed by a blue flood that simply washes over them. Only a handful of its soldiers escape. One retreating soldier, looking back, sees his commander, Major Thaddeus Love, wrestling with a Union color bearer. Near Love hangs a lone Confederate flag, its staff stuck in the ground by a dying color bearer; shot to pieces, like a bunch of rags tied to a stick.

An officer of the 56th North Carolina Infantry Regiment has wounded soldiers load and pass rifles to him to fire. Calmly making each shot count, he fires into the mass of Union infantry closing in on him. Then he too disappears beneath the flood.

Generals Ayres and Sheridan are among the first Union officers to reach the Confederate breastworks, Rienzi leaping across the log and dirt barrier to land Sheridan in the middle of a group of equally startled Confederates who've already begun dropping their rifles.

"Whar do y'all want us'ns to go?" one calmly asks the red-faced Sheridan.

"Right over there, Johnnies," the now smiling Sheridan jerks his thumb toward White Oak Road. "Right over there. Lay your rifles on the ground; right where they are. You won't be needing them again. Now, are there any more of you? We need you all."

The fight at the Confederate angle has cost Pickett hundreds of dead, more than a thousand prisoners, a dozen captured battle flags. Federal losses, however, have been heavy too. Ayres has lost two of his three brigade commanders, including Colonel Frederick Winthrop, who less than an hour before shared lunch with Joshua Chamberlain, shot through the left lung and carried to the rear.

CHAMBERLAIN

Chamberlain, advancing behind Crawford, hears the heavy fire raking Ayres' line from the west and realizes that they've come in east of the Confederate angle. He sees Ayres' fight developing before the Confederate breastworks and, to the northeast, Warren riding away from the fight in search of the vanished Crawford. Without waiting for orders Chamberlain pivots his brigade to support Ayres.

His regiments push across a muddy little stream, then up a ravine filled with catbriars and blackberry bushes. To his left front, Ayres' brigade is attacking the Confederate angle. Before Chamberlain, across the field, is another line of enemy breastworks.

He waves his skirmishers forward. Rifle and cannon fire rip into them, but they're already within fifty yards of the Confederate line. Then they're into the tangle of branches, dirt, and stone, and again the fighting becomes a confused hand-to-hand melee.

Glancing about, Chamberlain sees a large mass of Confederate infantrymen dropping their weapons, surrendering. The prisoners, some 1,500 of them, outnumber Chamberlain's entire brigade, and his grinning soldiers point them back toward White Oak Road.

As they pass, herding their prisoners to the rear, a worried Maine youth reaches up to tug at Chamberlain's leg then whisper, "General, my rifle's not loaded, and I don't have one more cartridge in my box."

Chamberlain considers that for a moment then whispers back, "Don't tell them, son; just don't tell them."

The young rifleman, relieved at Chamberlain's solution to his problem, returns his general's grin, waves a casual salute, and sternly hustles the long line of prisoners along.

Chamberlain is reorganizing his regiments when he encounters Sheridan, the fiery general still flushed and excited from the fight. Chamberlain's uncomfortable around Sheridan, not sure how the cavalryman will react to him or to any V Corps' officer.

He's already had several confrontations with Sheridan. The first when they'd met at dawn near Boisseau's farm. Then, early in Chamberlain's assault on Ayres' right, a red-faced, angry Sheridan had galloped up to accost him.

"General, Ayres' men over there are firing into my cavalry! My cavalry, sir! Can't you control their fire?"

Chamberlain glanced at the hotly contested wood lot and shook his head.

"No, sir. That's not your cavalry."

"By God, sir," Sheridan exploded, "I know my own men, and you're firing into them."

Chamberlain looked again; then again shook his head.

"Then your cavalry's gotten into the Rebs' line, General. Someone'll have to get out of the way. What do you want me to do?"

Before Sheridan can reply, Ayres arrived, and Sheridan turned on him.

"General Ayres, I've been trying to tell your officer that you're firing into my cavalry. My troops, sir! What are you going to do about it?"

Ayres, an old soldier, studied the woods a moment then calmly answered, "General Sheridan, as I imagine General Chamberlain told you, we are firing at the people who are firing at us. And those aren't Sharps carbines or Spencer repeaters, sir. That's musket fire. Not your men, General. But pretty quick now we'll take those woods and put a stop to it."

So Chamberlain is skittish about another face-to-face meeting with Sheridan. This one, however, goes well. After his second confrontation with the Maine general, Sheridan had watched Chamberlain during the fight and, liking what he saw, now greets him warmly.

"By God, Chamberlain, that's what I want to see! General officers at the front, in the thick of the fight. Where's Warren and Griffin?"

"General Griffin's off to the left, General, with Ayres; General Warren's gone off to the northeast; I think to find Crawford's division."

"Damn!" Sheridan explodes then orders, "General, I want you to gather all the men you can and push west for Five Forks. Custer's hitting them from the west; you hit them from the east. Take all the infantry around here and break this damn...."

Chamberlain, saluting as he turns to obey, again leaves Sheridan in mid-sentence.

Sheridan, half-angry, half-pleased at Chamberlain's response, watches Chamberlain flush out a Union soldier, down on all fours and trying, without much luck, to hide behind a small tree stump.

"Soldier," he hears Chamberlain call, "come on up out of there. There's too much of you for that stump. Besides, if you stay where you are you'll be killed right there in about two minutes. The Rebs' fire's building up ahead of us. Help me push them back, and we'll end it."

"But what can I do, General," the frightened man answers. "I'm just one man. I can't stand up against all this by myself!"

"No," Chamberlain quietly reasons with him. "Of course not. But we'll start with you. Look, I'm forming a new line. I want you for guide center. Come on now; on your feet. See these other men are coming in."

Then he waves, "Come on, men! Come on! Guide center on this brave soldier. We're going to push ahead. A little more and we'll win this battle. Come on! Follow me!"

Watching and hearing, Sheridan grins again.

"We've flanked them, Chamberlain," he yells. "Flanked them gloriously!"

Attracted by Sheridan's bright scarlet and white double-starred guidon and by his shouting and galloping back and forth, Confederate sharpshooters focus like a swarm of deadly bees on the little officer on the big, black stallion. Bullets fly thick and fast around Sheridan.

Chamberlain, realizing what is happening, suggests, "General, we can handle this. Don't you think you can do better elsewhere?"

Sheridan, as if suddenly aware of the sharp, deadly buzzing of bullets whizzing by his ears, grins and answers, "You're right, Chamberlain. You're right. I'll go see what's happening out the White Oak Road."

He wheels Rienzi about and, as Chamberlain watches, gallops up the road, heedless of the Minie balls still trying to catch him.

WARREN

Meanwhile, Warren's pursuit of Crawford's missing division has taken him completely out of the fight.

He finally finds his errant general and his soldiers on Ford's Road, directly north of Five Forks, far to the west of where their assault began. Crawford, finally realizing that he'd drifted too far to the east, and hearing heavy firing to the west, has swung that way.

Near where Ford's Road crosses Hatcher's Run, Crawford's riflemen run up against a Confederate breastwork across the deep creek. Facing the enemy position, a fallen tree offers the only dry crossing within hundreds of yards, and that one-at-a-time.

The enemy breastworks are abandoned now; abandoned except for one South Carolina sergeant whose made his own decision about this war. It's simple: he'll not give up another foot of ground. Didn't consult with anyone else about it, just decided he'd retreated as far as he intended to go. Gathering an armful of rifles left behind by the others, he'd loaded them and waited.

When Crawford's first soldier is halfway across the tree bridge, the South Carolina sergeant fires. One shot breaking the silence of the dense thicket; the blueclad skirmisher falling dead in the water. A second man takes his place. When he nears midstream, he too is shot down. Then a third and a fourth and a fifth until the lone Confederate sergeant has killed seven Union soldiers and, all alone, stopped Crawford's advance at the creek.

A Union sharpshooter, however, has climbed a tall tree and, finally seeing the flash of the Confederate rifle, finds the South Carolina marksman. One shot and now the sergeant also is dead.

Several Maine soldiers cautiously inch out on the fallen tree. This time they don't draw fire. Then they find the dead Confederate lying among his pile of neatly aligned and loaded rifles. He'd planned to use them all.

"Ornery cuss," a Yankee soldier admires the sergeant's courage. "Say, boys, he deserves a decent grave. Let's bury him here. And we'll mark his grave with the cover of that ammunition box."

They take time to do that, even praying over his grave and saying a few words about his bravery. Then they take up their rifles and begin to move forward. Quietness again settles over the little fort. A pebble on a vast beach.

They've gone only a short ways, however, before they're ordered back across the hard-won creek: Warren, now with Crawford, has ordered them to swing south toward Five Forks.

PICKETT

About a mile below them, Pickett has reached Five Forks to find his entire White Oak Road line crumbling. Ayres and Chamberlain have won at the Sydnor farm then swung west toward Five Forks. Meanwhile, Crawford is astride Ford's Road above him; Custer's cavalry is driving hard from the west; and Devin's cavalry is attacking from the southeast.

A guilt-ridden Pickett desperately tries to rally his men.

"Colonel Mayo, Colonel Mayo," he calls. "The enemy are behind us; if we don't drive them out, we're done."

A disgusted Mayo merely nods, "General, that's perfectly apparent to everyone," and goes on trying to rally his men.

Desperately seeking to atone for his absence, Pickett takes charge of a single cannon. Under his direction it fires eight times before it's disabled. All along his front Confederate artillery fire is lessening. His ranks are much thinner now; ammunition is giving out fast; and Federal troops are closing on the still-defiant Confederate soldiers around him.

Then a blue-coated trooper, mounted on a mule, leaps the barrier to land almost beside Pickett.

Revolver in hand, the trooper calls, "Surrender, you Johnnies! Surrender or you're dead men!"

Pickett, however, wheels his horse to gallop away before the man can fire; minutes before the Union ring closes on the last of his still-fighting regiments.

CUSTER

Custer, anxious to be in on the kill, charges the last Confederate barricade. His orderly, bugler, and color bearer are shot down. Custer, however, untouched, swings from his saddle to snatch the fallen Union guidon from the ground and, waving it, leaps the Confederate earthwork. Around him more and more Union troopers join the fight, firing their revolvers and hacking remaining defenders with their sabers.

Custer's 15th New York Cavalry Regiment charges an artillery battery under Confederate Colonel William Johnson ("Willy") Pegram. Enlisted as a private in 1861 and Lee's favorite gunner, Pegram is 22 years old. This morning, worn out from two days' hard fighting before Dinwiddie Court House and wet to the skin, Pegram stole a handful of corn from his horse's ration and parched it for his breakfast. Then he'd fallen asleep beside his guns.

He'd awakened at Custer's bugles and leaped to his horse to see Federal cavalry and infantry closing on his beloved guns. When they're within thirty yards of his cannon, he'd ordered, "Fire your canister low, men!" It's the last order he'll give. Hit by rifle fire, he tumbles from his saddle.

Evacuated from Five Forks, he'll die after an agonizing night.

Neither Pickett, abandoning his remaining men to escape north toward the railroad, nor Pegram being carried that way in an agonizingly bumpy Confederate wagon, sees the last of the fight for Five Forks: thousands of Confederate soldiers killed, wounded, taken prisoner; batteries and entrenchments overrun; a few exhausted but still defiant survivors fighting hand to hand in the gathering darkness. Fewer, fewer, then the Southerners are borne under and the guns at Five Forks fall silent. Thousands of Union soldiers have overrun the last Confederate earthworks and swept into the woods beyond.

SHERIDAN

Near the end, Sheridan still has not seen Warren nor Crawford's missing division.

An elated staff officer arrives to report, "I'm with General Crawford's division, General. We're behind the enemy, and we've taken three of their guns."

Sheridan glares in withering scorn then snaps, "Three guns! Three guns! I don't care a damn for their three guns, sir, or for you either! Why are you here? What I want is the Southside Railroad. Go back to your business, sir. Go back where you belong. Take that railroad!"

Colonel Locke, Warren's adjutant general, arrives to report that all is going very well. Warren has taken the enemy's rear, cut off his retreat, and now is advancing on Five Forks from the north.

With the report Sheridan erupts again.

"By God, sir, you go back and tell General Warren he wasn't in this fight!"

"Sir?" the startled officer exclaims.

"By God," Sheridan repeats, "you tell Warren he wasn't even in this fight."

"General," the officer stammers, "I can't say that to him. May I write it as a message?"

"Take it down, sir! Take it down! Tell him he was not at the front; nowhere near this fight."

As Locke wheels his horse to gallop back to Warren, Sheridan looks about, makes his decision.

"Griffin, take command of the V Corps. I've relieved Warren."

Then he scribbles a message and hands it to an aide, "Here, have General Forsyth word this properly. Then take it to General Warren."

Turning again to the commanders, staff officers, orderlies, and soldiers around him, and standing in his stirrups and waving his hat so none can fail to see him, Sheridan yells: "Before sundown I want you men to make a record that will make Hell tremble!" Pointing north, he snarls, "I want that railroad! Do you understand? I want that railroad!"

His audience scatter, spreading the word. To a man they'd rather face enemy infantry between Five Forks and the railroad than stand before a thoroughly aroused and angry Little Phil Sheridan.

CHAMBERLAIN

North of the crossroads, Major Edwin A. Glenn's 198th Pennsylvania Infantry Regiment encounters a determined band of Confederates holding a patch of woods to their front.

Glenn, a hero in the past week's heavy fighting and a personal friend of Joshua Chamberlain, is forming his men to attack the woods when Chamberlain calls to him, "Major Glenn, that's the last enemy line between us and the railroad. Break it and you'll wear a colonel's eagles."

Glenn grins, wheels his horse and, waving his sword, calls out, "Come on, boys! Follow me!" Cheering, Glenn and his men charge into a deadly hail of rifle fire. The Pennsylvanians' flag goes down three times before a fourth soldier carries it into the enemy line.

Later, riding forward to congratulate Glenn, Chamberlain finds two soldiers carrying a blanket dripping blood. In the makeshift stretcher, Major Edwin A. Glenn who was shot down while trying to capture a Confederate flag. Glenn is dying.

Chamberlain feels as if every ounce of strength is drained from him. Bending close, he calls, "Glenn, it's Chamberlain. I'm so sorry."

All Glenn can manage is a whispered: "General, I carried out your wishes." Then he's gone.

Glenn's words hit Chamberlain harder than the Minie ball that tore through him a year before. He'd ordered the major to his death, offered a prize for his life. Why, he questions as he will question for the rest of his life, why hadn't he simply let Glenn take his own chances without personally singling out his friend for death?

Then, steeling himself to face his responsibilities, he leans over again, "*Colonel*, I won't forget my promise; I won't forget you!"

Chamberlain turns to the fight with renewed fury. The enemy have re-formed. Charging ahead, he leaps Charlemagne over their breastworks. A bullet strikes the stallion as it begins its leap, but over they go with Chamberlain landing almost on top of one of the last, still smoking, Confederate cannon. The sixth time in this war that a horse has been shot from under him but, at that moment, Chamberlain really doesn't care.

To his left and right he sees his infantry closing on the remaining Confederate line; fields and woods plowed through by solid shot, torn by explosive shells, ripped by hot, whistling canister. Federal infantry scrambling over revetments and into the guns themselves. Cannon still belching smoke and red, scorching flames. Pellets of still-burning powder striking soldiers' cheeks as they climb over the last barricades. Angry Union men now face-to-face, hand-to-hand with lean, dirty, gaunt scarecrows determined to hold those guns: pistol to rifle, saber to bayonet, rammer to musket butt. All in a frenzied rush then a final, convulsive struggle.

When it's done, a loud hurrah by Chamberlain's men; then silence. Always, following the final struggle, he thinks, there's that long, deadly silence. A ghastly scene; the shadow of death everywhere.

Then he watches the survivors slowly begin to breathe again, look about for messmates, reload their weapons. Wait for a counterattack or for word to move on; on to the next woodline, the next breastworks.

WARREN

There is one last burst of fighting above Five Forks. Warren is with Crawford's regiments pushing down Ford's Road when their advance is stopped before a broad field.

Taking his V Corps' flag from his orderly, Warren, the engineer who'd always been uneasy with the role of personally leading men in desperate charges, impulsively rides to the center of Crawford's line. Then he turns and slowly begins to ride toward the Confederate breastworks. Seeing him, regimental color bearers, one after another, begin to follow. Soon Crawford's entire line is moving forward. When they're about halfway across the field, Union cavalry also sweep in from the flank, sabers drawn, to join the fight.

Then infantry and cavalry, Warren in the lead, sweep across the field. Confederate defenders rake their lines with volley after volley of rifle fire. Warren's horse is struck and nearby aides, messengers, and color bearers are shot down, but Warren is untouched. He rides back and forth along the Union line until the Confederate resistance ends, the field won. Then he stops, takes a deep breath, looks about as if trying to figure out he'd gotten there. Finally he returns the bullet-torn flag to his orderly.

Nearly dark now, the day's fighting over. Dozens of bugles sound "Recall." Five Forks won. Warren's proud of the way his men have fought, and he's savoring that when a messenger arrives with Sheridan's final message.

Aware that Sheridan had questioned his courage before V Corps' officers, Warren still is not prepared for the paper's contents. Holding it above his head to catch the last bit of light, he reads:

Major General Warren, commanding V Army Corps, is relieved from duty, and will report at once for orders to Lieutenant-General Grant, commanding Armies of the United States. By command of Major-General Sheridan....

Stunned, the single sheet of paper suddenly so heavy he can't hold it above his head, Warren drops his hand to his side. Absolutely still, head down, an immense weight pressing him into the battle-torn ground, he slumps in his saddle. Then, after a long moment, he straightens and rides alone down dark Ford's Road to find Sheridan.

Sheridan's at Five Forks. Glancing up, he studies the lone approaching rider for a moment then goes on dispatching couriers with orders, ignoring him. Warren can wait, as he'd waited for Warren this long day. Finally Sheridan is alone. The generals' conversation is brief.

Completely drained of strength, and with the agony of death on his face, Warren quietly pleads, "General, I have your order relieving me of my command. Won't you reconsider it?"

Sheridan, still angry, won't even offer the comfort of taking time to consider the stricken man's request.

"Reconsider, Hell! I don't reconsider my decisions. Obey the order, General. Obey the order!"

Turning away to end the conversation, Sheridan rides toward a cluster of officers conferring beyond the road.

"Griffin, gather every man you can find and push north for that railroad. Push ahead as long as you can see your hand in front of your face."

Chamberlain leads off, but they've gone less than a mile when the fading light makes it very difficult and dangerous to continue.

His buglers' "Recall" is echoed by Griffin's other divisions.

Among those drawn to Chamberlain's bugles is a lone rider: Warren. All alone in the gathering gloom, as if not sure where he should be.

Chamberlain salutes and begins his report, "Sir, I'm sounding 'Recall' to rally our regiments here."

"Thank you, General Chamberlain. You are doing just right, but I no longer command this corps."

"I've heard that, General, but this has been a very confusing and trying day. At one point General Sheridan told me to take command of all the men I could find. Surely this will all be straightened out by morning."

Warren smiles, "Thank you, General. Perhaps; we shall see."

TOWNSEND

George Alfred Townsend, reporter of the *New York World*, has missed the battle but at dusk, after a twenty-five mile ride, nears the battlefield.

Once he reins his horse to the side of the road to allow a long column of prisoners to pass. Thirty minutes of them. He'd never seen so many Confederate soldiers taken in battle. Farther along White Oak Road he sees several thousand more, loosely guarded by Yankee bayonets, waiting to begin their march to Grant's prison camp at City Point.

He finds the little country church, where Warren's men began their attack, being used by Union surgeons. A tiny white frame building in a pine woods clearing; with broken windows and bullet-pierced siding. Its pews, covered with wounded soldiers, placed in the churchyard when surgeons gutted the church to accommodate operating stations. Holes bored in the floors beneath the surgeons, a technique they'd developed on earlier battlefields. Every foot of that floor covered with wounded. Moaning, crying, screaming, dying. Blood running in little sluggish streams across the floor; blood trampled by stretcher bearers coming and going. Indelible prints. Union and Confederate wounded lying together, waiting their turns with the surgeons.

"Take them as they come, Sergeant. Yanks or Rebs," a tired surgeon directs. "If we can save them. If you've doubts, put them outside for now; keep this area clear."

Their surgery is very primitive, about three minutes to amputate an arm or leg; surgeons wiping their bloody hands on worse-bloodied aprons then turning to the next patient. Hoping their supply of laudanum will hold out; if not, the surgery must be done without merciful sleep.

In the churchyard burial details are hard at work; severed limbs piled in overflowing carts for the burial ground. All as they've done it many times before.

A Union colonel, dead, is stretched on a green shutter from the church, placed to one side of the churchyard for the burial parties already at work.

Townsend, attracted by the eagles on the man's shoulder straps, studies the pale, now peaceful face, can't identify it.

"Who was that?" he asks a nearby sergeant.

"Colonel Winthrop, sir. Colonel Frederick Winthrop, 1st Brigade, Ayres' Division."

Having seen more than he cared to see, Townsend continues down White Oak Road. At Five Forks men cluster around blazing campfires. Custer is there; no mistaking his long, blond hair or his gaudy olive-green corduroy uniform, now torn, muddy, bloodstained. Custer, his back against a pine tree, is sound asleep.

Nearby, Joshua Chamberlain sits composing a letter; the envelope addressed to someone named "Glenn." Townsend interrupts his work, sensing that Chamberlain, perhaps having trouble with the letter, welcomes the interruption.

"News enough today, Townsend," a tired Chamberlain greets him. "Sheridan fought a big battle here this afternoon. Cut up Pickett's division. Hit Fitz Lee's cavalry pretty hard too. Warren's lost his corps and Griffin's taken it."

Rapidly scribbling notes and nodding, Townsend asks, "Where's Sheridan now?"

"Right over there," Chamberlain points. The little cavalryman rests against a saddle on the other side of their fire, red-faced and beaming, absently chewing a piece of cheese.

"I'd like to talk with him, Lawrence," Townsend suggests, "but Sheridan doesn't like reporters, and you've all had a hard day."

"Go ahead. You'll find that he's all right. You know, he gave us a very rough time. Our officers would rather face the Rebs than Phil Sheridan. And his relieving Warren of his command stunned us."

"Don't quote me on that part," he wearily smiles. "I'll share it with you, but only as a friend. The army's our family here; and what happened to Warren is one of those family things I still hope may be straightened out."

"Anyway," Chamberlain continues, "awhile back we were sitting here by the fire when Sheridan suddenly just walked in on us. He knew he might not be welcome here, and he was quiet, almost gentle. Said 'I've come over to see you because I spoke harshly to some of you today, and I wouldn't have it hurt you. We *had* to carry this place today because tomorrow Lee might have been gone. We *had* to do it, and I fretted until it was done. The truth is I think you did very well.'"

"Hard to understand a man like that, Townsend. Harder yet to stay mad at him. He fights differently than we've fought before. Fredericksburg, Chancellorsville, Gettysburg, but this time, for the first time, we went into a fight knowing what everyone was supposed to do. Sheridan had told us. And he saw to it that everyone did what he'd been told. Pretty solid leadership, I'd say."

"And," Chamberlain continues, sorting it all out in his mind, "his tactics are different. We're used to entrenching; this man isn't much for that. He likes to run, slash, attack. Well, it worked for us today. Warren is smart; a great staff man. But sometimes a brilliant man can think too much. So Sheridan's relieved him. I feel sorry for Warren; I like him. But Sheridan's the best field commander I've seen. He deserves this victory."

"Sorry," Chamberlain manages a tired smile, "needed to sort it out. Anyway, when Sheridan finished talking, I said, 'General, have you had supper?' He hadn't so I had Sergeant McDermott fetch some for him. Then he talked with us for a long time. One soldier to another. Went over the day. Then he said again, 'Try to understand. I know that what I ask is hard for everyone; but we must push hard again tomorrow. If we can take that railroad, we'll be a lot closer to ending this war.'"

"Townsend, I understand this impetuous, driven man a lot better now, and I'm glad he was in command today. It really was his battle, and I want you to say that. But keep this business about Warren to yourself until we see if we can straighten it out. Family matter. Now come on over, and I'll introduce you."

Sheridan greets the young, nervous newspaperman warmly.

"General, you've done a great day's work here," Townsend grasps Sheridan's firm hand. "If you'll just give me some idea of what it was like, I'll leave tonight and get it to the New York papers. The country'll be mighty anxious to know about this day."

Sheridan nods, pulls out a battered field map, and for twenty minutes explains the battle. Chamberlain is amazed at Sheridan's ease in naming the commanders of divisions, brigades, regiments; his grasp of the troops involved; and his willingness to share the roles they'd played.

When Sheridan's finished, Townsend thanks him then ventures, "General Sheridan, most commanders wouldn't have shared all this. Instead they'd have lectured me about things that really didn't matter. I'm very grateful. The country needs to hear about what you and your men did today. One more question: I know the size of your cavalry, but can you tell me how many men were in the V Corps?"

"I see that Chamberlain trusts you so I'll tell you for your own information," Sheridan answers. "But don't print it. We're going to force Lee out of his trenches tomorrow, and it's best that he doesn't know how many of us are out there cutting his last supply lines. There were about 10,000."

Townsend makes a few final notes, shakes hands with Sheridan and Chamberlain, and by midnight has galloped off toward City Point.

LINCOLN

Late in the afternoon Grant had sent another reporter, Sylvanus Cadwallader, to City Point with a half-dozen Confederate battle flags already taken near Five Forks. He finds Lincoln anxiously waiting aboard the *Malvern*.

When the President sees the captured flags, he reaches out to touch them and straighten their folds. He can see in their faded, torn cloth the desperate fight in which they'd been taken.

Then he smiles, "These flags, Cadwallader, they're something very real. Very tangible. Something I can see, feel, understand. They mean victory. Praise God, this is victory!"

Again and again he has Cadwallader repeat details of the developing battle. Then as Captain Samuel Beckwith, Grant's telegrapher, brings fresh dispatches, Lincoln updates his worn map. For the long-suffering President, it's a wonderful day he doesn't want to end.

GRANT

Lieutenant Colonel Horace Porter has left Sheridan's camp to return to Grant's headquarters. Along the way he sees the Union army as he's never seen it before. Fires blazing all along White Oak Road as men boil coffee and relive the day. Bursts of cheering, again and again. Morale is sky high, no mistaking that.

———

Porter and his escort can't keep from shouting the good news to men they pass. Near the Boydton Plank Road one staff officer shouts news of the victory to a squad of infantrymen warming themselves by a blazing fire. Most of them are too stunned to reply; they'll have to ponder it for a moment. One, however, responds immediately. Standing to face the passing officers and raising one hand with his thumb to his nose, he yells back, "No, you don't—April Fool yourself!" It's the first time Porter realizes that it really is the first of April.

———

Porter reaches Grant's camp to find that he's beaten couriers he'd sent earlier with news of Sheridan's victory.

Grant is sitting with most of his staff before a fire. He wears an old, blue, army overcoat and chews upon his usual cigar.

Unable to wait, as soon as he's within hailing distance, Porter shouts the good news. In a moment all but Grant are on their feet, yelling, cheering, throwing caps in the air, slapping each other's backs.

When the tumult eases Grant removes his cigar to get right to the heart of it.

"Porter, how many prisoners?"

"Over five thousand, General."

Only then does Grant relax, even smile. Then, by a glowing lantern in his tent, he begins to write field orders. When he's done, he hands them to an aide. Then he returns to tell them, as calmly as if he were commenting on the weather, "I've ordered an immediate assault all along the lines."

It will be hours before the assault can begin, but he's taken the final step to break the long Richmond-Petersburg siege.

CHAPTER 6

Bugler, Sound 'Retreat'!   **April 1–2, 1865**

LEE

At Turnbull House, Lee's headquarters, the day has passed slowly. There are discouraging reports of Anderson's early fighting at the far end of the Confederate trenches but nothing from Pickett. For hours there is nothing from Pickett.

Late in the afternoon, off to the west, they hear the ominous rumble of cannon, sometimes the sharper crack of rifle fire. Hard to say where, but Lee knows by the rhythm and intensity of the fire that hard fighting is going on somewhere beyond their trenches.

By dusk he's had enough reports to guess that Pickett has lost and lost badly. If so, Grant has turned his flank and by morning, if not already, will reach the Southside Railroad, cutting the Confederates' last rail link with Petersburg.

He orders Major General Bushrod Johnson's brigades to Sutherland Station on the Southside Railroad. Johnson's to rally survivors of Pickett's fight and try to hold the vital rail link.

Below Petersburg Confederate Generals A. P. Hill and John Gordon, their skirmishers already "as far apart as telegraph poles," must spread their men even more.

"They're more than ten feet apart in the trenches, Colonel Marshall (Colonel Charles Marshall, one of Lee's aides)," Lee shakes his head. "Very bad, but we're down to that now. I've repeatedly warned Richmond that we cannot stretch any farther."

"Our lines," he speaks quietly, calmly, as if instructing a student, "will break; perhaps tomorrow. Be certain that everyone is alert; we can expect General Grant to attack any time, anywhere along our lines."

He continues dictating orders, "Have General Longstreet send General Field's (Major General Charles W. Field) division by rail to Petersburg. General Longstreet is to come to me ahead of them, if possible."

"That leaves only General Kershaw's (Major General Joseph B. Kershaw) very thin division and General Ewell's Richmond Reserves above the James, but our concern now is not Richmond; it's saving this army. A bad time, Colonel, a bad time."

Having done what he can, Lee reluctantly agrees to stretch out on his camp cot.

"I *am* exhausted, Colonel, and I must try to rest but," he smiles, "I doubt that General Grant will allow it as I'd not allow it to him."

He doesn't tell Marshall, fussing now to place a quilt over his legs, that the rheumatism is particularly bad tonight nor that the shooting pains and the heaviness in his chest that first came at Gettysburg have worsened during the past year.

"Call me, Colonel," he smiles gratefully at Marshall's concern for him, "if there is a problem or when General Longstreet arrives."

At 9:30, when he's just begun to doze, the whole house trembles from the shock of huge explosions. Instantly awake, Lee knows that Grant's artillery is firing across his entire line; knows too that, when the barrage stops, long lines of Northern infantry will be crossing to his trenches.

"Worse than Gettysburg," he weighs the sound with Marshall, who'd come for him at the first explosions. "Didn't think it could be worse than Gettysburg. The Northern papers said they heard the sound of the guns in Pittsburgh that day, 150 miles away. But this is worse, Colonel, worse."

Wrapping a blanket about him, he walks outside to study the terrible storm of fire. Not one gun out there in the darkness, or a battery of guns, or a battalion; every gun Meade, and perhaps Ord, can muster. Gunners firing their Napoleons and Ordnance Rifles and Parrotts three or four times a minute until, even in the cold April morning, their barrels become too hot to touch.

Higher arcing mortar shells, their paths traced by burning fuzes, add to the terrible noise and acrid smoke. The ground beneath Lee, even this far from the forward trenches, shudders and trembles when their big shells hit, and he knows that it must be terrible in the trenches themselves.

The darkness of the night sky is shattered, again and again, by bright streaks of light: burning fuzes; streaks of light that shriek then suddenly end in explosions and jagged flames. Were it not so terrible, a beautiful display of sound and light.

Huge, dense, acrid, gray-black clouds of smoke from the bursting shells, mingling with the night mists already hanging low over his trenches, make it difficult for Lee and Marshall to see far anywhere along his lines.

Confederate batteries angrily answer: fire and sparks and eerily whistling sounds tracing their own reverse paths toward the Union lines.

As the artillery duel intensifies, a constant stream of fire and counterfire develops; shells arcing between the opposing trenches. Gun pit to enemy trench with the ground heaving and shuddering as the shells explode. And in the trenches soldiers hug the damp, cold earth, thankful that the clods of dirt and stone pelting them aren't red-hot shards of iron.

Lee gauges the fire and waits. Reports come in from the trench lines: casualties everywhere, but his lines are holding firm and still no sign of Federal infantry.

For nearly three hours the storm continues. Then, almost as abruptly as it began, it ends. The sudden silence as ominous as had been the first thunder of exploding shells.

Still no sign of attacking infantry. Lee studies the sky: dark now and cloudy, but night sounds are slowly returning.

After a time he turns back to the house. "They're not yet ready, Colonel. Not yet. When they're ready, they'll come. Any word of Longstreet?"

"No, sir. Nothing yet. He's probably with Field's division. They were expected around midnight; it's past that now."

"Thank you. Please see that our staff get whatever rest they can; we'll all need it." He takes a large pocket watch from his vest, thoughtfully winds it, then gently smiles, "we'll all need it in a few hours."

GRANT

Grant has issued his own orders. At first light Sheridan is to attack north to cut the railroad. On Sheridan's right, Ord also will attack north then swing some of his Army of the James east, toward Petersburg, to keep pressure on Lee. Ord, however, must be careful lest Lee attack west along the Southside Railroad to break the line Grant is drawing around Petersburg. Meanwhile, from the James River to Ord's right flank, Parke's IX Corps and Wright's VI Corps, under Meade, will try to break through Lee's trenches below Petersburg.

It takes time for Grant's orders to filter through all the lesser headquarters. Time to reach the riflemen who, having no one else to pass them to, must take up rifle and bayonet and carry them out.

Meade is enthusiastic. "Parke," he tells Grant, "says he'll go into the enemy works as a knife goes into butter; and Wright," Meade's other corps commander, "promises to make the fur fly. Wright," Meade smiles, "says that, if his corps does half as well as he expects, he'll break through the Rebel lines in fifteen minutes."

Grant, pleased with their spirit, smiles around his cigar, "I like the way Wright talks."

Encouraged by Grant's response, Meade suggests, "General, Parke's and Wright's infantry are almost ready now. Why not make an immediate infantry assault, without artillery preparation; catch them by surprise before it gets light?"

Grant shakes his head, "No, I think you'd best fire your artillery and see what happens before you send in the infantry."

This the three hour barrage Lee has witnessed and which ends, on Grant's order, about midnight.

When it ends Grant decides, "Not yet, Meade. Not yet. Wait until four o'clock. Then fire another barrage and send in your infantry."

The revised time passes down the long chain of command to the waiting rifle companies. A temporary reprieve. Officers and sergeants decide that they must say a few more things. Soldiers recheck their weapons and ammunition; fill their canteens with brackish, muddy water from wells behind their bombproofs; pack their pipes with fresh tobacco, and make sure that they can reach a refill or two if they're pinned down out there and have to wait it out.

Finally, when the officers and sergeants have done all they can, they leave the men to themselves. Some pull their overcoats over their heads for a few moments' sleep; others scribble hasty letters or print their names on slips of paper then pin the papers to their blouses in hopes that, if they're otherwise unlucky, at least their graves may be marked. Those with sensitive consciences empty their packs of playing cards, destroy certain engravings, shoot craps to lose any money they've already won gambling. No sense in taking chances. Most are fatalistic, however, shrugging, "If it happens, it happens; nothin' a body can do about it."

Grant, awake at 4 a.m., realizes that the artillery barrage he'd suggested to Meade has not begun.

"What's happening, Rawlins?"

"Not much. Meade sent word that he's decided to hold up on the barrage another half hour. It'll be lighter. Figures his gunners can see better, and our infantry'll have a better chance of taking out obstacles."

At 4:30 Meade fires his second barrage. From a hundred revetments along the Union line, cannon belch smoke and fire, and shells arc across the sky. Miles to the west, Ord's and Sheridan's men hear the explosions; see the sky glowing below Petersburg; trace the path of burning fuzes through the night sky; know what is happening. Know and are glad it's happening back there and not where they are.

Confederate batteries angrily answer the Union barrage but, pounded by Federal shells and running short of ammunition, gradually stop firing.

Meade's cannon continue to fire then, as if suddenly realizing that their enemy has been hammered into silence, they also abruptly stop.

Staff officers gallop to the regiments: "Get your men moving, Colonel. The signal rockets were fired ten minutes ago; no one could see them in this God-awful barrage. The General says to hurry along now."

Sergeants prod men into skirmish lines and, along Wright's and Parke's front, 60,000 Union soldiers begin to walk toward Lee's trenches. In the darkness ahead of them perhaps 25,000 outgunned, outmanned, but still defiant Confederate soldiers wait.

In Wright's VI Corps an officer, startled by the sudden silence when the barrage ends, becomes aware of another, more mysterious sound: one like a strong breeze blowing through a great pine forest. Puzzled, unable to identify it, he steps to the parapet above his trench and listens again.

Then he realizes that it's the sound of the rough-cut boots of thousands of infantrymen tramping forward over the cold, rough ground.

The sound fades; the long Union lines vanishing into the early morning haze. Then Gordon's and Hill's pickets stab at their advancing enemy. Almost immediately the scattered rifle fire of the pickets is replaced by heavy, rolling, rhythmic volleys of musketry from the fighting trenches.

A Union surgeon sees both Union and Confederate lines lit by the flashes of thousands of rifles. Fascinated, he watches, a beautiful panorama in the darkness. Then, knowing what it means, he turns to his assistants.

"Let's get ready. We'll have a lot of wounded coming in any time now."

Parke has picked for his objective a Confederate strongpoint the Southerners call "Fort Mahone" but which Parke's soldiers, who've watched it for months, call "Fort Damnation."

Mahone: a very strong three-sided earthen fort, its front protected by cleared fields of fire; broad, water-filled ditches; ravines to channel attackers into artillery killing grounds; a maze of abatis and chevaux-de-frise; trenches that will allow Gordon to move men quickly to a threatened area.

"Take Mahone," Parke has told his division commanders, "and the batteries on either side of it, and we'll punch our way through their fighting trenches. Then we'll roll up Gordon's lines. We're going to go through them like a dose of salts."

The soldiers, who'll have to get it all done, hear Parke's optimism, repeated in various forms by their regimental and company commanders, and aren't convinced.

A corporal, realizing that the second barrage is beginning to ease and knowing what that means, tells his messmates, "Well, boys, reckon the ball's about to begin."

Another soldier, perhaps more thoughtful, rejoins, "Don't reckon it's gonna be a ball, Bob. It's Sunday morning and, like it or not, we're all going to early Mass."

West of Fort Mahone, Wright's VI Corps will hit the center of A. P. Hill's lines. If they can break through there, they too will try to take the rest of their enemy's lines from the flanks and rear.

Wright's men fare better than Parke's. They're not facing "Damnation," and, unlike Parke, who has done little to reconnoiter the Confederate line to his front, Wright has carefully studied the enemy positions before him. He'll have no water obstacles to cross, but he'll have to breach five lines of abatis. Strong abatis, probably heavily mined. He's noticed, however, a path from the Confederates' picket line to their fighting trenches, a path through the abatis and, Wright guesses, through their mine fields; a path the Confederates have fallen into the habit of marking with bonfires to guide their pickets at night. He means to take advantage of their carelessness.

At first Parke's and Wright's assaults seem to go well. Union observers, gauging the attacks' success by the volume of rifle fire and the flash of muskets in the darkness, watch as a solid mile of Confederate picket posts, marked by the flashes of enemy rifle fire, dissolves into spreading patches of darkness. Union bayonets have snuffed out the Southerners' resistance there and surviving pickets have withdrawn to their fighting trenches.

Darkness, an ebbing in the rifle fire; then the flash and roar of musketry pick up again as Union infantrymen near the Confederates' fighting trenches.

By 5 a.m. streaks of gray are lightening the sky as Wright reports that he's taken twelve guns and many prisoners and is now fighting in Hill's trenches. Parke's initial reports are more guarded, particularly before Fort Mahone where the fighting is particularly hard.

At 7 a.m. Grant wires Lincoln, at City Point:

Both Wright and Parke got through the enemy's line. The battle now rages furiously. Sheridan...is now sweeping down from the west. All now looks highly favorable. Ord is engaged, but I have not yet heard from his front.

He's right to be optimistic about Ord's, Sheridan's, and Wright's attacks, wrong to count too soon on Parke's. And the fight has not been easy anywhere.

WRIGHT'S CORPS

Following John Gordon's aborted attack on the Union's Fort Stedman, a week before, Wright's men counterattacked, seizing their enemy's former picket line; they'll have less than a half mile to cross before reaching Gordon's trenches.

This evening, covered by the darkness, regiment after regiment from Wright's trenches quietly moved toward the weakest point in A. P. Hill's six-mile line, the bonfire-marked safe zone through Confederate obstacles. Wright's staking everything that his massive force striking this one part of the enemy's line will do what they've not been able to do before.

During the lull between the two Union barrages these reinforcements crowd forward. Knowing that they're so close to their enemy, they lie quietly, shoulder to shoulder, on the open ground—thousands of them. When the barrage ends, they'll try to hurry across the field before their enemy can recover.

Wright's veterans don't share his confidence in the plan. They're thankful that so far the cold, dark, foggy night has hidden them, but it still seems a terrible risk.

"Jeb," one whispers, "I can't see a blamed thing, but there's gotta be thousands of us lyin' here. Jammed in so tight your canteen's poked a hole in my back. Just waitin'. I don't mind tellin' you, I'm scared."

"I know," his messmate whispers back. "One bit of light, and they'll see us. And then we're done. They throw one rock, it's gotta take out half the company. Well," he grins in the dark, "you and I'll make it, Bob; reckon I'm gonna miss the rest of the fellas."

"You two hush up," a voice growls from the darkness. "Johnny over there's as scared as you." Sergeants have a way of ending discussions on a positive note.

Quiet, then a nervous laugh and a whispered, "Don't think so, Jeb. There's no way there's a Johnny over there half as scared as I am."

Then the second barrage begins, and bright flashes of light again cast eerie shadows across the field. Curious, many of Wright's infantrymen raise their heads and are startled at a sight they'll never forget: thousands of Union soldiers, as far as they can see in the flickering light, in places so thick that it looks as if they've been piled one on another, hugging the ground. The entire field is covered by a dark, squirming blanket, like a pile of worms after a heavy rain. Frightening.

Then a Confederate shell explodes among them, and another, and another. All along the Union line men, hit by shell fragments, scream. When a high explosive shell bursts among the huddled men, bodies are thrown into the air, torn apart. Soldiers' rifles, canteens, bits of uniforms are thrown in every direction; severed arms, legs, bloody torsoes falling like hail on the infantrymen below. Men hit hard, in terrible pain, sometimes try not to scream lest their enemy hear and know where they are. Others, not caring who hears, cry out.

Hundreds of shells explode on both sides of the torn field with men blown to pieces or suffocated in collapsed trenches. The only blessing is that the second barrage is much shorter than the first. It ends, and in its place a thick cloud of ugly gray-black, acrid smoke sears their lungs, presses them into the ground.

The sudden silence is as if the entire world has come to an end. A few minutes pass; it seems much longer. Then the survivors begin to breathe again, cautiously raise their heads. Amazing: most of their friends have survived; even now they are returning nervous grins.

"All right," sergeants are calling. "B Company, on your feet. Come on. Before Johnny can catch his breath. No shooting till I tell you to. Use your bayonets."

And they've started forward, testing Wright's theory about getting across before their enemy can recover.

Private C. F. Barnes, a young Massachusetts' soldier starting across the torn field, finds that his heart's much too big for his chest; his breath short and hard to come by; and there's an awful tightness in his throat. He can hear the rest of his squad yelling, but he can't manage a whisper himself.

Until, about halfway across, he just blurts out, "Hey! Hey! Hey!"

He's amazed at how quickly the yell clears away all his symptoms. He tries it again: "Hey! Hey! Hey!" Then "Hey!" he yells to his messmates, "it works; it works!"

Later he'll laugh, "After that first whoop I could have tackled the whole Reb Confederacy. And I reckon you boys felt the same way because we all just kept yelling and going, yelling and going, like we'd never stop. Clear across that field!"

Scattered rifle fire stabs at them, rifles winking in the pre-dawn light. Then, long before they expect it, they've piled into the first line of Confederate trenches.

Here and there, along the firing steps or crumpled on the blood-soaked, muddy floor of the trench, are the bodies of dead soldiers in ragged, butternut uniforms.

A young private in Colonel Elisha Hunt Rhodes' 2nd Rhode Island Regiment, holding his bayonet high as he'd been taught but hoping he'll never have to use it, is stunned by his first sight of enemy dead. One, slumped against the back wall of the trench, his face outlined in the light of a bursting shell, is very young, perhaps fifteen years old. The corpse has a thin, pinched, gray face. His dirty jacket is torn open, revealing a terrible, bloody wound, probably a solid shell. He's barefoot with dirty, torn feet. His rifle, no longer needed, lies to one side. The Union private, forcing himself to look again at the face of his fallen enemy, sees a gentle smile on the boy's lips, as if all this just doesn't matter any more.

The Rhode Island soldier, suddenly much older, hears his sergeant call and turns away. Following his sergeant's voice he moves down the trench, holding his bayonet high before him but hoping he'll not have to use it.

Wright's infantrymen have broken through the Confederate's main fighting trench and near Hill's second line. With that they're suddenly aware that they've survived; taken trenches that they'd felt for months were impregnible. Aware too that it's getting much lighter now. Dawn, and they've survived the night.

Squads of Union riflemen have reached the Boydton Plank Road, beyond A. P. Hill's second line of trenches; some of them are within a mile of Lee's headquarters.

Union soldiers, about to cross the Boydton Plank Road, stop dead in their tracks; their attention caught by something they never expected to see this morning.

"It's some people, Sarge," a nervous rifleman on that flank calls out. "Not Johnnies; just plain people. Colored people. A whole lot of 'em. Comin' this way. And they're all dressed up like they're goin' to a prayer meetin'. Now don't that beat all!"

The sergeant hurries over. A dozen black people: men, women, children, are walking down the road. As if they'd neither seen nor heard the terrible battle the soldiers have experienced this early morning. Old men, with snow-white hair and beards, wearing clean but worn suits, boiled shirts and string ties; and carrying their bibles. Walking behind them, old and young women in equally worn and faded dresses and poke bonnets, carrying baskets of food. A half-dozen grinning children, all very young, barefoot, being herded along.

"Well, grandfather," the sergeant addresses their obvious leader, a handsome, smiling, older man, "where in the world are you folks goin' this morning?"

"Why down the road, sir. Our church is just down this way a mile or two. White, frame building. Have you been that way?"

"No, can't say that we have. Reckon we've been renderin' unto Caesar this morning. Didn't you hear all that ruckus over yonder behind us?"

"Yes," the man calmly replies. "Seemed terrible. But it's died down now, and we reckoned to go on to church."

"Well, sir," the sergeant nods, "I appreciate your faith. I surely do. But this matter isn't settled yet so I'd suggest you turn about and take your little flock back home. Don't reckon there'll be any church meeting down this road for awhile. Why don't you just go on home?"

"Thank you kindly," the old gentleman answers. "I expect that would be best. Bless you now, and have a good day yourselves."

With that they turn about and begin to retrace their steps up the dusty road, the little cluster of Yankee soldiers watching them go.

"All right, boys," the Sergeant waves his men north, into the fields beyond the road. "That's one to remember; somethin' to tell your youngsters some day. Brown, you take the scout up there for awhile; let's push on and see if we can find what's happened to the regiment."

PARKE'S CORPS

On Parke's front, when the second barrage ends, Union infantrymen charge through abandoned Confederate picket lines and are near their enemy's fighting trenches before the Confederates suddenly come to life. Then Parke's men run into a hail of fire.

Sergant Miles C. Huyette, a seasoned Pennsylvania squad leader, sees the flash of cannon' primers before him and shouts, "Down! Down!"

Most of his men quickly drop to the ground, below the whir of passing canister; but they hear the sickening thump of iron pellets striking the men caught standing.

Yankee sharpshooters shoot down Confederate gunners while axemen rip away abatis. Before the defenders can reload their cannon, Huyette's men are into them. In the early morning dawn they fire muskets, thrust bayonets, swing musket butts. Union and Confederate soldiers so caught up in the hand-to-hand fight that they're unaware that soldiers of both sides are being cut down by the hail of shell fragments still falling around them.

A hard, half-hour's fight then the fighting trenches have been taken and Confederate infantrymen have fallen back, through the connecting trenches, toward a second line.

"Hold up, boys! Hold up!" Huyette yells to his squad. Badly winded, he leans against the dark, moist earth of the trench's wall, takes several deep breaths, and wipes his eyes. Then he herds his men together, checks to see who is missing, and takes ammunition from those who have it to give to those who don't (mentally noting for later those who've fired their weapons and those who haven't). When he's satisfied that they're ready, he calls again.

"Now stay near me," and leads them toward the next line of trenches.

Captain J. G. Harker, 109th New York Infantry Regiment, seeing a Confederate gunner hurrying to reload a cannon, shouts, "Fire that gun, Johnny, and you're a dead man!"

The Confederate shrugs, "No point in my dyin' now, Yank," and raises his hands. Harker grins and waves him toward other prisoners already being herded back across the field.

Parke's infantry have reached Fort Mahone's walls: high, thick, slanting walls of dirt, red clay, and pine logs.

Those who try to clamber up Mahone's walls are shot down, tumbling into the soft-bottomed moat where they lie dead or may drown before they can be rescued.

From atop the fort's walls Confederate sharpshooters kill Union soldiers huddled at its base while other defenders roll hand grenades, shells, or stones upon their attackers. From below, Union sharpshooters pick off any heads lingering above the wall for more than a few seconds. Nearby revetments and supporting breastworks are being taken, but Union soldiers still have not taken Fort Mahone.

Across Gordon's front Confederate gunners fire canister and grape shot into Union soldiers crowded around Fort Mahone, tinging its moat red with blood. The fight has become very close-range, very personal.

A Union officer, seeing a Confederate gunner about to fire his cannon, shouts, "Pull that lanyard, and we'll shoot you down!"

There's no hesitation in this defiant Southerner's answer, "Shoot and be damned, Bluebelly!" Then he yanks the lanyard to send a double load of canister into the faces of his enemy.

When the smoke clears, the area before his gun is devastated, dead and dying Union soldiers lying in a torn heap. The artilleryman, riddled by rifle fire, lies beside his gun, his lifeless hand still clutching its lanyard.

Northern infantrymen turn captured cannon on their enemies; one soldier calling to his squad, "Hey, one of you give me a match, or a pipe, or your cigar. Something I can use to touch this off."

Confederate infantrymen take advantage of the maze of connecting trenches and traverses, hiding, moving from place to place, popping up to fire through chinks in the logs at unsuspecting Yankees on the other side.

The fight in the connecting trenches is a series of short, vicious encounters between lone soldiers or infantry squads. Then whoever first identifies the other and is quickest with a rifle shot, the thrust of a bayonet, or a vicious butt stroke from an empty musket may survive.

Union soldiers surround Fort Mahone, but its Confederate defenders refuse to surrender. So it remains the center of the continuing fight. All across Parke's front the fight, begun with the advance of thousands of Northern infantrymen in a solid line, has dissolved into a confused series of squad-sized confrontations as one group after another seizes a section of trenches, is rolled back, then attacks again.

By noon, when his attack has bogged down and Gordon is continuing to mount strong counterattacks, Parke, who'd predicted that he'd go through the Confederate trenches "as a knife goes into butter," calls for help, telling Grant, "I'll have to be reinforced if I'm to do this."

A. P. HILL

At dusk the evening before, Confederate Lieutenant General Ambrose Powell Hill ("Little Powell" to friends of the Old Army), 38 years old, West Point-trained, slender and erect, from a knoll overlooking Confederate Fort Gregg, studied his trenches and, less than a mile away, the strong enemy facing him.

All day he'd ridden his lines, saying little but shaking his head again and again.

"Too many unfinished breastworks, Colonel Palmer (Colonel William Palmer, Hill's Adjutant General). Too few men. Must be ten feet apart on the firing steps. No reserves. And the men are tired, sick, disheartened. Can't push them very hard. A bad fix, Colonel; a bad fix."

"Yes, sir. But the men'll fight hard. Always have."

"Yes; I know. And I expect they'll *have* to, pretty soon. Grant won't wait much longer."

Darkness forced him to give up on the day; he'll do what he can about all of it in the morning. Then he'd ridden to the little cottage he and his wife, Kitty, younger sister of legendary Confederate Brigadier General John Hunt Morgan, and their children shared.

Hill too spends a restless night. He's barely dozed off when the cottage is shaken by Meade's heavy early evening artillery bombardment. He walks outside, weighs the storm of fire before him, knows what it is doing in his trenches.

"Has it finally begun?" she's there beside him, squeezing his arm.

"Afraid so, Kitty. Afraid so. We'll see. If I'm called out, have the children up and ready. In the morning I'll send a detail to help move all of you to a safer place."

She nods, squeezes his arm again, murmurs, "You be real careful!"

Filled with concern about being able to hold his six-mile stretch of trenches, A. P. Hill dozes fitfully for several hours. Then, about three o'clock, unable to wait any longer, he walks to his nearby headquarters.

"Colonel Palmer," he addresses his startled staff officer, "haven't you rested? What is happening?"

"I dozed a bit, General; a bit. Thanks. Reckon I'm as restless as you are. Couldn't sleep. It's quiet now. After the bombardment ended, their infantry probed our line, and we've heard noise out there like troops movin' about, but no sign of them yet and no more artillery."

"I couldn't sleep. Please have my horse saddled."

"Shall I go with you, General?"

"No, you're needed here. I'm going to see General Lee; missed him yesterday, and I must talk with him about our situation. If there's another bombardment, Colonel, or if it nears first light, be certain that everyone is up and ready. At dawn strike our tents and have the wagons packed. I expect we'll move today, no matter what our enemy may do."

Hill rides the mile and a half to Lee's headquarters.

He finds Lee, looking as tired and worn as he knows he must seem himself, lying fully dressed on his bed. The two generals are talking about the situation facing Lee's army when Colonel Taylor interrupts.

"General Longstreet's here, sir."

Seeing Longstreet, Lee smiles as if greatly relieved.

"Ah, here's my old war horse! I'm glad you're here, General. I feel better already."

Then, not wishing to slight Hill, he smiles again, "My two war horses. General Hill, you *do* look tired, sir; should you have ended your recuperation leave so early?"

"I'm all right, General," Hill attempts as confident a smile as Lee's. "That is I was all right until I saw our lines. We're in a bad fix, sir."

"Yes, General, I know. And they'll strike us hard today. I've alerted President Davis that he must withdraw very soon. It will be better then. This army always does well when it can take up the march."

Their talk is interrupted by the thunder of Meade's second barrage. The three generals listen, the sound somehow seeming not so heavy as the earlier barrage, and it ends quickly.

Colonel Charles Venable, another of Lee's aides, again interrupts their conference.

"Sir, we have reports that Wright's VI Corps' Yankees have cut the center of General Hill's lines and are in his rear. Heavy fighting on General Gordon's front, but he's hanging on. And there's been lots of wagons passin' by from the west; teamsters hurryin' down Cox Road as fast as they can. It 'pears the Yanks are west of us and to our rear, and I've just seen skirmishers about a mile to the southwest. Can't tell whether they're ours or theirs, but we may have to move our headquarters."

Lee, draping his blanket around his shoulders, follows his generals outside. Venable is right: off to the southwest, as far as he can see, a double line of infantry cautiously advance. They hear scattered rifle fire, but no volleys that would mark an organized defense.

"I can't see, General," Lee turns to Longstreet. "Are they ours or theirs?"

It's lighter now, and it doesn't take Longstreet long to decide. As calmly as if he were discussing the weather, he answers, "Theirs, General. Theirs. Reckon I'd better go fetch Field's division."

"Yes, as quickly as possible."

His mind already racing, Lee adds, "Get him west to Sutherland Station or wherever you can hold a corridor open for General Hill's men to withdraw. Meantime, I'll try again to get couriers through to General Anderson. We must try to hold our lines until evening. I'll notify Richmond."

He turns to instruct A. P. Hill, but his Third Corps' commander already has run to his horse and, calling for his couriers, Sergeants George Tucker and William Jenkins, turned toward the break in his lines.

Lee, alarmed at the frantic anxiety in Hill's move and remembering the younger general's pale, feverish face, recalls hearing that Hill has said that he does not want to survive the fall of Richmond.

"Colonel Venable, go after General Hill. Tell him that I'm concerned about him. He *must* be careful. It will do this army no good to lose him!"

When Venable delivers Lee's admonition, Hill nods impatiently.

"Yes, yes. Thank you. Now please go back and thank General Lee for his concern. Tell him that I am all right, but I must restore my lines."

Venable nods but decides instead to tag along. Hill, concerned about the Union skirmishers nearing their road, seems not to notice that he's joined their little group.

They've not gone far when they capture two Union stragglers from Wright's VI Corps, their regiments probably already beyond the road.

"Jenkins," Tucker orders, "herd these two Bluebellies back to headquarters. I'll stay with the General."

Hill leads them, more cautiously now, through woods and up meandering streams above the road. Again and again they see squads of slow-moving Union infantry or pairs of soldiers, somehow separated from their regiments and not sure what to do next, moving cautiously ahead.

Nearing the now abandoned huts of Confederate Major General William Mahone's division, Hill's little group encounter more and more Yankee soldiers.

"General," Sergeant Tucker, more alarmed at their situation by the moment, asks, "are those troops ours or theirs?"

"The enemy's, Sergeant; the enemy's," Hill answers.

"Then, sir," the sergeant firmly suggests, "maybe we should get the hell out of here."

Hill nods but continues to lead them forward. They see more clumps of soldiers, all wearing blue uniforms, but so far the three Confederates have not been seen.

A bit more and they come to Confederate Lieutenant Colonel William Poague's artillery battalion, somehow overlooked by the waves of Union infantry and now silently waiting beside Cox Road.

"Colonel Venable," Hill suddenly recalls that Lee's staff officer is with them, "go have Colonel Poague fire on these enemy. Sergeant Tucker, we'll continue."

They begin but Tucker, more and more alarmed at the pockets of enemy soldiers all around them, finally asks, "Excuse me, General; but where are we headed?"

Pointing to the southwest, Hill answers, "Sergeant, we must work our way to the right of our lines. We'll go up this branch to those woods. They'll cover us until we reach that field back of General Heth's headquarters. Hopefully, we can return to the road there."

They pass on, Hill still leading the way. Then, as if suddenly realizing the danger all around them, he stops.

"Sergeant Tucker, should anything happen to me, you must hurry back to General Lee and report it."

Then they again ride cautiously ahead, for a time out of sight of Union or Confederate soldiers. Finally, near the edge of some woods bordering the road, they see another large group of Federal infantrymen moving slowly before them.

"They're everywhere, Sergeant Tucker," Hill lowers his field glasses. "Our line has broken."

Tucker nods, "Which way now, General?"

"To the right. Through the woods a bit more. There are open fields that way that may take us to the Boydton Plank Road."

Among the Federal troops ahead of Hill are soldiers of the 138th Pennsylvania Infantry Regiment. Two of them, Corporal John Mauk and

Private Daniel Wolford, separated from their regiment and deciding that they'd best hang back until things become clearer, see a small group of other Union stragglers boiling coffee over a campfire. Deciding to join them, they follow a small, meandering stream.

Then they see two Confederate riders emerge from the woods and ride slowly toward them. Mauk waves Wolford behind one tree while he takes another. Then both men raise their rifles to cover the approaching riders.

Sergeant Tucker is first to see Mauk and Wolford. Hill, his eyes burning feverishly as he draws his heavy Colt revolver from its holster, orders, "We must take them, Sergeant; we must take them."

Tucker sighs then gives his own order.

"You stay here, General. I'll take them." He's been carrying his own revolver, unholstered, the past half hour. Now he raises it and rides to within twenty yards of the crouching Federals.

"You Yanks! Surrender! Our men are behind us and, if you fire, you'll be swept right into Hell. Surrender!"

Suddenly Hill is by his side, his own revolver raised, echoing, "You surrender! Surrender!"

Behind the large oak trees Private Wolford wavers, begins to lower his rifle. Mauk, however, decides, "Can't see it, Wolford. Just can't see it. Shoot 'em!"

As the two men fire, Tucker instinctively ducks in his saddle. Wolford misses, his bullet buzzing angrily past Tucker's ear. Mauk's aim is better.

Not two feet from Tucker, A. P. Hill, who'd instinctively raised his left hand to ward off the bullet, is knocked from his saddle. The .58 caliber lead slug, capable of penetrating a six-inch pine tree at 600 yards, blows off his left thumb, shatters his heart, and leaves a huge, bloody exit hole in his back. He's dead before he reaches the ground.

As Mauk and Wolford hurry to reload, Tucker glances at the fallen general. Nothing can save A. P. Hill. Realizing that, the sergeant grabs the reins of Hill's frightened horse, wheels, and gallops back toward the woods. There he changes to the faster horse and, leading his own, gallops back toward Lee's headquarters. Behind him the two Union soldiers, as frightened by the experience as Tucker, run the other way. Behind them A. P. Hill's body, its gray blouse now covered with blood, lies in the soft mud of the little creek.

LEE

Lee has emerged from Turnbull House and is about to mount Traveller when Tucker gallops into the yard on Hill's sweat-streaked horse. He knows, without Tucker's reporting, what has happened.

Calmly, but holding Traveller's saddle for support, and in a voice that can't hide his despair, Lee nods, "Report, Sergeant Tucker. What has happened?"

He listens, calm but with tears brimming his eyes, nodding as the sergeant describes Hill's death. When Tucker has finished, Lee sighs, "Thank you, Sergeant. I'm sure that you did the best you could. General Hill is now at rest; and we who are left are the ones to suffer."

Turning, he orders, "Colonel Palmer, go break the news to Mrs. Hill; as gently as possible. Then see that she is moved to a safe place above the James. Send some men; if possible, we must recover General Hill's body."

"Now," he mounts Traveller, "we who remain must see to this army. Move our headquarters, Colonel Marshall, and send a courier to General Gordon. Tell him that he must hold his lines. I will join him after I've seen what is happening."

There is no time for more grieving. For the time being, Longstreet will command his own corps and Hill's.

A bit later Lee notifies Richmond: "I see no prospect of doing more than holding our position here till night, and I am not certain that I can do that....I advise that all preparations be made for leaving Richmond tonight."

Lee, wearing a clean gray uniform and his seldom worn sword, is using his field glasses to study the effect of Grant's attack upon his line. Longstreet, with A. P. Hill's survivors, has fallen back to Petersburg's inner lines. Fort Mahone has been abandoned, but John Gordon is holding his own and even counterattacking to recover some of the ground he's lost. To the west, Union infantry have cut the Southside Railroad and swung east toward Petersburg. No word of what has happened to Confederate General Bushrod Johnson's brigades somewhere near Sutherland Station or to Fitz Lee's cavalry or Pickett's infantry above Five Forks. Lee's scouts are trying to penetrate the screen of Yankee cavalry to reach those cut-off units.

Four Northern corps, perhaps 100,000 men, are striking his army, its back to the Appomattox River. His attackers, however, now seem hesitant, uncertain about what to do next. That will help. Lee will use the time to set up new lines and to hold open a corridor into Petersburg for his army. Holding that corridor open depends upon his being able to hold two forts: Whitworth and Gregg, on his inner line. Hold them until darkness can cover his retreat. He must see to that now.

Lee's last view of Turnbull House is of the mansion, battered by Union artillery fire, burning. Smoke and flames are everywhere; its barns and out-buildings also burning. Lee, who'd always tried to avoid using private homes as his headquarters lest the enemy, knowing he is there, shells them, stiffens in his saddle, smiles grimly, and turns away. Only once, when an enemy shell disembowels a nearby horse and Lee hears its screams, does the deeper red flush spreading across his already ruddy face betray his anger.

For a time, forgetting his own earlier warning to A. P. Hill, Lee personally directs the fire of a four-gun battery of Confederate cannon.

A Northern officer, seeing the fine-looking, gray-bearded, older officer commanding the battery, orders an entire infantry regiment to attack it. Lee's cannon, however, rake the Union lines with canister, breaking up their attack. Then fifty riflemen of the 50th Maine Infantry Regiment concentrate their fire on the Confederate battery's remaining horses and on the lone figure on the large gray horse.

With most of its horses lost, the Southern battery finally is overrun. Its guns fall silent. In the smoke and confusion, however, the old, distinguished-looking Confederate officer on the gray horse has withdrawn with its few survivors.

A wounded Union captain, propped against the wheel of a broken artillery limber, asks a captured Confederate: "Lieutenant, what battery is this?"

"Battery A, Poague's North Carolina," the still-defiant Rebel officer answers.

"And who was that grand officer on the big, gray horse?"

The Confederate prisoner smiles, pulls himself erect at his own mention of the name, and answers, "That, sir, was General Robert E. Lee; and he was the last man to leave these guns."

Lee, cheered by his soldiers wherever they recognize him, works to build up a new line of breastworks that will hold open his army's escape route.

At one point he lets down just a bit, sharing with Brigadier General Armistead L. Long, "Well, General Long, it has happened as I warned them it would. This is bad business; but we must make the most of our opportunity to save the army."

Aside from that slight lapse, and a momentary flush of anger when he receives Jefferson Davis' reply to his alert that Richmond must be evacuated that day, Lee remains calm, confident. Davis' message doesn't acknowledge the critical situation Lee's army faces below Petersburg; instead it complains bitterly that a hasty withdrawal will not allow time for the proper packing and removal of property from the city.

Crumbling Davis' message in his hand, Lee flushes and mutters to himself, "I'm sure that I gave him sufficient notice."

GRANT

By mid-morning Grant knows that Sheridan's men have cut the Southside Railroad and swung west toward Burkeville and the Richmond-Danville rail line. East of Sheridan, Ord's men have swept up the Boydton Plank Road and are nearing Sutherland Station. Wright's VI Corps, having broken through A. P. Hill's lines, has linked with Ord's divisions on their left. Only Parke's IX Corps, east of Wright's men, has been stopped. Like Lee, Grant is drawn closer to the fighting there.

As he crosses the battlefield, Grant, mounted on big, black Cincinnati and accompanied by a small cluster of aides and couriers, is cheered by his soldiers.

"They smell victory, Colonel Porter," he mutters to an aide. "They've seen hardscrabble times. Lots of them. Bled white on one field after another. Until Gettysburg not much to show for it, and since then one hard fight after another. But now they're tasting a big win."

A long speech for the broad-shouldered, heavy-bearded, tired commander of all the armies of the United States. And, having said it, he chomps on his dead cigar and has little more to say. He smiles, however, and waves his thanks for his soldiers' cheers.

Near noon, sitting propped against a shell-battered tree before the ruins of an abandoned farmhouse overlooking Confederate-held Forts Gregg and Whitworth, Grant receives dispatches, sends orders, watches the terrible panorama before him.

Then the farmhouse begins to draw heavy artillery fire. Gray gunners have spotted the cluster of Federals near the lone figure beneath the tree. For more than a quarter of an hour Confederate shells explode all around them , tearing the house and the ground with solid balls and hot iron fragments.

Grant, however, seems oblivious to it. When a large shell explodes nearby, as if bothered by a pesky fly, he quietly interrupts his work long enough to brush dirt from his message pad but ignores that gathering on his uniform.

If he seems unaware of the danger, however, his staff isn't. Several times they suggest that he find another place to work. Grant, however, remains by the shell-torn tree. Unable to find a safer place for themselves until their general decides to leave, staff officers are doubly anxious. Grant, however, works on, ignoring the enemy fire and their hints that he move.

After he's finished his dispatches, however, he stands, stretches, and for the first time notices the anxious faces about him. Smiling sheepishly around his cigar, he surrenders, "Well, they do seem to have the range on us," and moves to another part of the line.

FORT GREGG

The key, he's seen, are the two Confederate forts: Whitworth and Gregg. They must be taken. Grant assigns the job to Major General John Gibbon's XXIV Corps. Gibbon will commit three infantry brigades, perhaps 5,000 men, to getting it done.

Fort Gregg is a large, ominous mass of dirt and stone and wood crouching over the muddy, flat, shell-torn fields around it like a lion waiting for its prey. Its earth walls, eight feet thick and topped with heavy pine logs, are further protected by a flooded ditch fourteen feet wide and six feet deep. Inside there are embrasures for cannon and firing steps for riflemen. Solid shot, explosive shell, and canister rounds are stacked beside the fort's cannon.

Fort Whitworth, near enough so the two forts can support each other by fire, is somewhat smaller.

Gregg holds more than 200 Confederate soldiers, most of them from the 12th and 16th Mississippi Infantry Regiments; 200 more Southerners are behind nearby Whitworth's walls.

As Grant watches Confederate soldiers burning abandoned huts to clear fields of fire before the forts, a handful of North Carolinians from Brigadier General James Lane's brigade join the force already inside Fort Gregg.

Confederate Major General Cadmus M. Wilcox appears at Gregg's lone entrance to call, "Who's the commanding officer here?"

"Colonel James Duncan I believe, General. It's all sort of mixed up."

"Well, send for him."

Before Duncan can arrive, however, a nervous Wilcox, seeing the enormous mass of Union infantry gathering across the field, yells out his message to the few who can hear it.

"Men, the salvation of the army's in your hands. You must not give up this fort. If you can hold it for two hours, Longstreet'll be up."

Crashing shells, the first of hundreds about to pound Gregg, drown out any answer. Then someone inside yells, "Tell 'em we'll not surrender."

Wilcox doesn't hear him. He's gone to join Lane, huddled against the log wall behind the fort.

Pointing toward Petersburg, Lane suggests, "General, some of my men are in Gregg, but most of them are over there building that new line. I figure that I can do more good back there. You know what's going to happen here and, when they break through, I'll be there to dam the gap."

Wilcox nods, "All right, Jim; go back and get ready. They'll come soon."

Before leaving, Lane sends an aide to count his North Carolinians inside the fort. The officer, however, quickly returns.

"Can't do it, General. They're all mixed up in there. Must be a half-dozen regiments. Can't tell one regiment from another and can't count the men. And, if I call them out here, they're going to come under heavy fire."

Already Union shells have begun to straddle Gregg; hot iron shards and splinters from shattered logs stabbing at the men huddled behind its walls.

Lane, giving up trying to account for his men in the fort, starts back across the field to the breastworks most of his men are manning. He begins at a walk, but, as Federal shells tear the ground around him, he sprints the last hundred yards.

Inside Fort Gregg Confederate infantrymen know that they've been left to face their enemy. For about half an hour (it seems much, much longer) they're pounded by Union cannon. Many of the defenders are killed or wounded; all but one of their cannon disabled.

After the cannonading stops, there is a brief, ominous silence. Then dazed Confederate soldiers, cautiously peering over Gregg's battered walls, see more massed Federal infantry than they've ever seen before. Double and triple lines of it, stretching as far as they can see. Bayoneted rifles carried high and ready. Coming for them.

When the lines get within 200 yards of the fort, the defenders open fire. Volley fire: low, solid, rhythmic. Each volley taking its toll. They can't miss; not at that range and with that many enemy before them.

Federal flags fall then are snatched up again. Union lines constantly close to fill the huge gaps where soldiers have fallen. The survivors lean into the storm of fire and begin to run toward the fort. Soldiers on both sides add to the confusion, shouting to each other and to their enemies.

When Union infantrymen get within thirty yards of Gregg's walls they pass below the Confederates' view. A momentary refuge but, unable to go forward or back, they're stalled there until the next wave can reach them.

Fort Gregg, almost surrounded now, is getting no help from Fort Whitworth, under its own attack. Thousands of Union infantrymen are closing on both battered forts.

Confederate Surgeon George Richards, the only doctor in Gregg, squats before Captain W. S. Chew and suggests, "Let it go, Captain. Tell Colonel Duncan to surrender this place. The army's had enough time to get in line, and the next wave'll get in on us."

Chew grimly shakes his head. "Let it go as it will, Doctor; we'll not give up."

Gregg's commander, Colonel James Duncan, watching the second wave of endless Union lines coming closer, has his riflemen reload then wait.

"Pull your heads down, boys," he quietly, firmly orders. "It'll make you a mite nervous to see them out there. But when I give you the word, get up on these steps and make every shot count."

Finally he alerts them, "All right, boys. Get ready now. Hold your fire until I tell you. Steady now. Hold your fire."

Gregg's defenders, huddled below its parapet, can't *see* but, despite the heavy firing, can *hear* thousands of heavy-booted Yankee soldiers getting nearer, nearer. The waiting is very hard.

Then Duncan yells, "Fire!" and they spring up, and a sheet of flame erupts from the fort. When Duncan's first line have fired their weapons, another line take their places. Then they too jump down to allow a third line of riflemen to fire into their enemy. Some Confederate riflemen refuse to step down, instead using rifles passed to them. When a soldier tumbles from a firing step, another man jumps up to take his place.

A third Union wave reaches the survivors of the earlier assaults, huddled below Gregg's earth walls. Clambering up its sloping walls, some reach its parapet only to be shot down or spitted on Confederate bayonets. Then they tumble into the muddy ditch below, a steady stream of dead and wounded joining those already there.

Inside the fort, the dead and wounded have been dragged to the center of Gregg's earth floor. So many are there on the bloody floor that it's hard to move around without stepping on someone. Firing steps become slippery with blood. The noise inside the fort is deafening; the smoke is suffocating. Still it goes on.

Then two Federal soldiers follow an unfinished connecting trench to leap into Fort Gregg. They are immediately bayoneted. More follow, however, and now within the fort Union and Confederate infantrymen fight with bayonets, musket butts, fists, whatever they have.

Ignoring the vicious fight that has erupted on the floor behind them, Mississippi soldiers on Gregg's parapet continue to roll solid shot and explosive shells among their attackers. When the shot and shells are gone they turn to bricks taken from bombproofs' chimneys; when the bricks are gone, they shake their fists and curse their enemies.

A soldier of Company D, 37th North Carolina Regiment, stands on a firing step to the very end, carefully firing the rifles passed to him. More than eighty times his rifles spit fire before he falls, his jugular vein cut by a Union bullet. Beside him lies a dead Union color bearer, his flag draped over the fort's parapet.

So many Union battle flags now circle the fort that to observers across the field they resemble bolts of draped bunting.

More and more Yankee infantrymen have breached Gregg's walls to join the hand-to-hand fight inside. The uproar inside the fort is earsplitting, frightening, horrible; the curses and cheers and grunts and screams of the men sound like animals.

Many Southern soldiers are shot down or bayoneted before they can surrender. Others fight to the very end. Even when Union and Confederate officers shout orders to stop the slaughter, it will take twenty minutes to persuade both sides to stop.

When it's finally over, a dazed Confederate prisoner stares at the pile of dead and wounded and recalls the Federal dead he saw before Marye's Heights at Fredericksburg and the Bloody Angle at Spotsylvania and reckons that this is even worse.

Like so many cords of wood, the Union dead will be loaded into carts for the long trip back to City Point; Confederate dead will be buried in shallow, partially covered mass graves, pretty much where they fell.

Confederate prisoners being herded toward the Federal rear feel sad, but they're also grateful. They've survived, and for *that* some feel guilty.

LONGSTREET

Longstreet, watching from the Confederate's final line, sees a friend from the Old Army, Union General John Gibbon. Instinctively he raises his hat but Gibbon, directing the fall of nearby Fort Whitworth, doesn't see Longstreet's gesture.

Farther off, "Old Pete" also recognizes Sam Grant, whose wedding he'd shared a long time ago. Grant's busy too, weighing whether to continue the attack.

"He's had enough," Longstreet mutters to himself. "He'll hold up where he is; reorganize before coming on again. They've taken an awful beating too, and that sun's pretty low. I think he'll wait till morning; I hope he'll wait till morning. That might give us just enough time to save this army, or what's left of it."

He watches as Federal signalmen wigwag Grant's instructions; couriers gallop from regiment to regiment.

Across the torn field more Union troops form ranks and begin to march toward the Confederate lines.

"So many of them, so damned many of them," an anxious Longstreet mutters. Then, seeing the blue mass begin to turn, he sighs in relief, "They're not coming this way; thank you, God, they're swinging west."

Brigade after brigade of Federal infantry, in clear view of Longstreet's breastworks, have turned, drawn toward the dull thump of artillery they hear off to the west. Artillery that marks where some of Lee's army still fights.

"Why've they stopped, General?" an anxious young aide asks. "They must know they could finish us off."

Longstreet shakes his head, "Grant knows that we mean to pull out of here tonight, Lieutenant. No need to lose more men assaulting these breastworks when he can catch us on the road and end it there. Well, I reckon that we'll have somethin' to say about that; at least we've got us a chance to say somethin' about it."

Until darkness closes around them, the two badly mauled armies lick their wounds, cautiously eye each other. The stubborn fight for the two forts has won Lee a few hours' time. Perhaps enough to save the rest of his army.

SUTHERLAND STATION

The rumble of artillery Longstreet hears to the southwest has been Ord's men fighting four shrunken Confederate brigades before Sutherland Station on the Southside Railroad; about 4,000 Confederate soldiers facing a Federal line that curls around their flanks like a huge blue snake trying to envelop them. Lee's veterans, however, have no intention of making it an easy fight.

Twice Ord's infantry charge; twice they're driven back. Each time fewer defenders remain, however, and more Union soldiers join the fight.

Brigadier General Samuel McGowan's South Carolinians are there. Following the Federals' second attack, one of his officers sees a wounded Northern soldier lying in front of their lines, his thigh shattered by a musket ball, and sends men to get the fallen Yankee infantryman out of their line of fire.

The wounded man, however, won't be taken prisoner. As Confederate soldiers near him he yells, "God damn you, Johnnies! God damn you! Get away from me. I'll not be taken!"

In agonizing pain, he begs them to shoot him and end his misery. They won't. Then he screams again and, as they draw closer, slashes his throat with a pocketknife.

Soon after the lone Union soldier has taken his own life, a third Union assault overruns McGowan's thin line.

Several Confederate soldiers who escape at the last moment glance back to see the last of their regiments finally enveloped by a living cloud of blue uniforms.

Weary, demoralized, hammered-into-the-ground Confederate soldiers, many throwing down their weapons and running, melt into the fields or hide in the willows and thickets along the Appomattox. Others try to swim the broad river. Its waters are black, deep, spring-cold, and they are very tired. Many of them don't make it, sinking unnoticed below the water.

Those who escape will try to make their way west, hoping to join Pickett's survivors, somewhere, they reckon, along the river.

GRANT

Meade urges Grant to continue the fight, to take Petersburg that night. Grant, however, shakes his head.

"More slaughter, General; and the city destroyed and civilians killed. No; they'll pull out tonight. Let's let them get out in the open. Sheridan'll cut them off to the west; we'll take them from this end. We'll end this thing with as little bloodshed as possible."

LEE

He's right about Lee's plans. Already Lee's orders for the retreat of his army have begun reaching his commands:

General Longstreet's Corps and General Hill's Corps will cross the pontoon bridge at Battersea Factory and take the river road on the north side of the Appomattox....General Gordon's Corps will cross at the Pocahontas and Railroad bridges....General Ewell's command will cross the James River at and below Richmond, taking the road...to Amelia Courthouse....

Amelia Courthouse, forty miles away. He'll assemble his army there. Meanwhile, there's much to be done if he's to hold Richmond and Petersburg long enough for his army to escape. Much to be done if he's to destroy the supplies he'll not be able to carry. Like Longstreet, Lee wonders how much time Grant will allow him. Darkness in two more hours; the retreat to begin as soon as darkness can cover it. Time will tell.

JEFFERSON DAVIS

Two dozen miles north of Lee's embattled lines this Communion Sunday, St. Paul's Church on the corner of Grace and 9th streets, Richmond, is filled with worshipers, the crowd suggesting the state of the city itself, swollen now to more than 100,000 inhabitants.

As Lee's emaciated regiments battle four Union corps below Petersburg, the first President of the Confederate States of America, Mississippi-born Jefferson Davis, not yet aware of the final struggle already begun to save his capital, alone, hurries up the church's wide stone steps to enter the large sanctuary with its gray walls and white pews.

He's late, last minute meetings and his reading the latest dispatches delaying him but, late or not, he feels it's better to make his usual appearance at the Sunday worship service. He finds that the pastor, the Rev. Charles Minnigerode, perhaps reading his mind, has delayed beginning the service until Davis' arrival.

William Irving, the elderly, stout sexton of St. Paul's, is very aware of the importance of his task of escorting the President to his reserved pew. Irving's bearing is impressive; so is his dress: a worn but formal blue suit with polished brass buttons and ruffled shirt. When he closes the door to Davis' pew, the low buzz of conversation among the restive congregation ends. Davis, knowing that many eyes are on him, searching his presence for some comfort from the nearly constant rumble of artillery below the city, takes his seat without a word or glance at nearby worshipers.

He's a slender, West Point-erect man. His hair is trimmed, his boots polished, his clothing (a Prince Albert coat and a vest and trousers of Confederate gray) cleaned and pressed.

For all that, and his attempt to present a confident appearance, Davis' high cheekbones, hollow cheeks, thin lips, and deep-set eyes (one, stone-gray, is blind) cause him to appear haggard, careworn, exhausted. He can't recall when he last slept well, and to ease that problem he's been trying a daily regimen of chloroform, inhaled and rubbed on his temples; inhaled vapors of rosemary leaves; and a mixture of two grains of opium, five grains of quinine, a teaspoonful of calchocum wine, and castor oil.

The remedy hasn't worked, but Davis continues to use it. He's 56 years old but seems much older. Neither Jefferson Davis nor his wife, Varina, has been happy for a long time.

Varina, his second wife, is eighteen years younger. Dark-eyed, beautiful, patrician, once called the "Mississippi Rose," Varina Davis has never been well received by a Richmond society which at times has described her as fat, cross, and ill-tempered. Her husband, faring little better, has been labeled reserved, fanatic, distant, proud or, as Sam Houston put it, "One drop of Jeff Davis' blood would freeze a frog."

Davis is aware of all these things but for months has gone about the business of being President of the Confederacy as if, amid the important problems of state he faces every day, public opinion is the least of his worries.

This morning, despite the cannon fire and the last-minute, disheartening reports he'd just read from General Lee and from General Joe Johnston in North Carolina, his mind is very much on Varina and their children.

For months he's been selling their personal property at quiet, private auctions: horses, furniture, silk gowns, laces, gloves, china, silver, paintings. Trying to set something by for when they might have to flee Richmond. Several days before he'd suddenly realized that Robert E. Lee's warnings that he must move his government and his family to a safer place have become far more insistent. Davis won't be sorry to leave Richmond; he's never liked the city, especially since their second son, Little Joe, died from a fall from the porch of the Confederate White House. Good to put Richmond and all the concerns he's known there behind them. Still, any move must be made discreetly, carefully lest it weaken public confidence.

He'd begun that weeks before, moving certain government offices, their papers, and their clerks to Danville; meanwhile preparing Varina and their children to go too. She'd been difficult to persuade. Sitting on the uncomfortably thin, patched pew cushion, waiting for Revered Minnigerode to begin the service, he recalls the arguments he'd used.

"I must take the field, Vinnie...you and the children would only grieve and embarrass me there.... I know that you want to help me....You can best do that by taking care of the babies...in a safe place.... If I live, you can come to me when it's over, but I don't expect to survive...."

She'd finally accepted his decision. Then he'd had her sew a small heap of gold coins into her dress, an emergency fund. He'd held back a check for $28,400 Confederate, about $450 hard money, payment for auctioned goods. When he can find a bank that will accept it, she'll have that too.

Then he'd handed her a small pistol. At first she'd shrunk from it: cold, hard, deadly, so impersonal, the end to all their dreams now lying in his hands. He'd made her take it, however, and using terms he'd learned at West Point years before, he taught her how to load it, twirl its chambers then, holding it firmly with both hands, to aim at the belt buckle of her enemy and squeeze its trigger.

"If you fall into the wrong hands, Vinnie," he'd explained, "you can at least force them to kill you."

Two nights before, afraid to wait longer, he'd placed her, their four children, Varina's sister, and their escort on the Danville train. The parting was hard; Varina accepted it stoically, but the children clung to him until he lifted them to Burton Harrison, Davis' personal secretary, on the train's platform. Then he'd stood, feeling terribly alone, for a long time watching the wretched, ancient train slowly limp out of the station and out of sight.

Doctor Minnigerode's deep voice beginning the morning prayer jerks him back to reality. Must be careful he reminds himself. Because he knows that frightened citizens constantly watch him for a sign, he disciplines himself to seem calm, focusing on the service. Particularly during its silences when everyone in the church can hear the dull rumble of artillery somewhere off toward Petersburg.

Halfway through the service Sexton Irving quietly hands Davis a folded message from his Secretary of War, John Breckenridge: "General Lee telegraphs that he can hold his line no longer. Come to the office immediately."

Davis scans the message twice, pale but calm, knowing that others are watching his every expression. Then, nodding his apologies to his pastor, he stands and strides from the church.

Behind him, other government officials also are being summoned. So many of them that Minnigerode ends the service as quickly as possible.

After he's read Lee's last telegram, advising that he will try to hold his lines until nightfall but that Richmond must be evacuated that day, Davis summons his cabinet to his office. They must have their departments' most valuable remaining records delivered to the Richmond and Danville Railroad Station that afternoon. Peter Helms Mayo, at twenty-nine a veteran railroad man, has arranged for a special train to carry the President, his cabinet, their effects, and their horses to Danville that evening.

As his cabinet scatter to carry out their duties, Davis lingers at his office. About three o'clock, when another message from Lee insists that the city must be evacuated that night, he signs the last papers before him, cleans out his desk, and prepares to return to his home.

As a final duty he approves the Treasury Department's boxing some $528,000 in double-eagle gold pieces, Mexican silver coins, and gold and silver bricks and ingots, the last of the Confederate treasury, for shipment to Danville. A guard of sixty midshipmen from the training vessel *Patrick Henry*, long docked on the James, will escort the treasure. When the young cadets have come ashore, the *Patrick Henry*, as well as Admiral Semmes' James River fleet of gunboats, will be scuttled to prevent their falling into Union hands.

On Richmond's streets Davis sees citizens hurrying to and fro. Some government clerks burn papers while others load wagons with documents to be spared. Messengers gallop from office to office. Military units, their soldiers seeming very old or very young, quietly pass, bound to perform some duty. Other Confederate soldiers, alone or in pairs, most seeming dirty, hungry, unshaven, and uncertain about where they are going, also appear: deserters, stragglers, or those who've simply lost their regiments.

A few citizens turn to Davis for reassurance, news of what is happening. Most, however, hurry about their own personal concerns, pausing now and then to gauge the nearness of the artillery still rumbling somewhere below the city. He notes that many of them seem unusually considerate of one another this afternoon, already resigned to something they'd never expected to happen: the arrival of the hated Yankee army, perhaps as soon as tomorrow.

Davis knows that at that moment Lieutenant General Richard Ewell, commanding all the Confederate troops north of the James, is planning the destruction of government stores in the city and how to enforce order until the last soldier has gone to join Lee's retreating army. When the last man has crossed the James, Ewell will blow its bridges to delay the Federals. After that, Richmond will be on its own.

When Davis returns to the Confederate White House he finds that several of his slaves have fled and that others who remain are drunk, ill-tempered, frightened. His temper, always a problem, flares at their attitudes, but he controls it; best to save what he can, any way he can. He scolds his slave housekeeper, Mrs. Omelia, several times and reminds her that he wants the furniture carefully dusted so that his home will be presentable the next morning.

Then, the fate of Lee's army unknown but his own government crumbling around him, Davis divides the late afternoon between attending to messengers from various departments and to worrying over personal items he'd like to save: bedding; his favorite war painting, "The Heroes of the Valley"; a favorite saddle; the family cow; an inkstand; the marble bust of himself which he'll not see fall into Yankee hands. He directs this to be hidden here, that there. A trusted slave, John Davis, will take the marble bust to a friend who'll bury it in his yard where the hated Yankees aren't apt to find it.

He hands the personal check he'd saved from Varina's small treasury to an aide.

"Take it to the Bank of Richmond, Mr. Hendera. Perhaps they will cash it."

A bit later, Hendera returns to report, "Sorry, sir. They say that the bank no longer can cash checks for such large sums of Confederate currency."

"Very well," Davis sighs. "Take it along. Perhaps we can cash it in Danville or along the way."

When railroad officials refuse to put Davis' carriage aboard the special presidential train, he sends word, "All right; put it on the next train." Railroad officials, knowing well that there probably will be no more trains, solemnly assure him that it will be done.

When he's done all he can, he walks the mansion a final time, his mind flocked with memories. Once more he reminds Miss Omelia, "Be certain that everything is dusted and put back in its proper place after I've gone."

Shortly after eight o'clock he's told that the special train is ready. Riding his horse "Kentucky," and accompanied by two aides, he sets out for the station.

Along the half-mile ride he sees much that disturbs him: government warehouses, opened to distribute whatever remains on a first-come, first-get basis, are being mobbed. Convicts, their heads shaven and wearing prison garb but deserted by their guards, are looting stores. Worse yet, patients of Richmond's mental institutions, now turned loose, are leaping, yelling, cavorting on unfamiliar streets. He sees signs of increasing hysteria. Davis is horrified but rides straight ahead, seeming not to notice the bedlam around him. Better to ignore what he cannot correct; and easier to ignore what he does not see.

At the station they find that the train, a leaking, rusty, shabby, flea-bitten antique that looks as if it will not move at all, still is not ready. Most of his cabinet, however, are there waiting.

Judah P. Benjamin, his swarthy, stout, deep-voiced Secretary of State, lightheartedly puffs his usual huge Havana cigar and twirls his goldtopped cane. Benjamin's busy greeting everyone around him, as if they were all going for a pleasant spring outing. Attorney General George Davis, the burly North Carolinian Davis' close personal friend and advisor; Postmaster General Judge John H. Reagan; and Secretary of the Navy Stephen B. Mallory are talking among themselves. Mallory, hurrying from a last conference with Admiral Semmes about the destruction of the James River gunboats and the last of the navy's ammunition, seems confident, unruffled. George A. Trenholm, Davis' Secretary of the Treasury, is there too. Trenholm, once the very wealthy owner of steamship lines, railroads, and hotels, now is nearly bankrupt in the cause of the Confederacy. Trenholm, so ill that Davis has permitted Trenholm's wife, the only woman in the party, to accompany them. She's brought along a demijohn of peach brandy to comfort her ailing husband, but before the long night ends they'll all put it to good use.

Secretary of War Breckenridge, Davis notes, and Vice President Alexander H. Stephens, who'd flat-out told Davis that he planned to go home to Georgia and stay there, are not with the party. Davis hopes that they and other government officials may yet join them in Danville.

Finally they board the presidential train only to be told that there will be more delay until the treasure train, with its naval cadet escort, clears the Danville tracks.

Finally, about 11 p.m., as Robert E. Lee is standing at a bridge of the Appomattox River watching scattered elements of his army begin their march to Amelia Courthouse, Davis' train slowly puffs from its Richmond station. Unevenly worn wheels clack on worn tracks, the ancient engine barely reaching ten miles per hour. Near Manchester, a western suburb where they have a last view of burning Richmond, neither Davis nor his cabinet have a word to say. They simply stare into the darkness, hearing the thunder of explosions in the city and watching the flames spread. Then their tired train, gathering itself for one final trip, rattles out of sight.

LINCOLN

Back at City Point, Lincoln has haunted Grant's headquarters' telegraph office. Grateful for the periodic dispatches Grant sends him, he plots troop locations on his own war map.

During the day he pecks at the light snacks they bring and, from time to time, he lifts the kittens they've placed near his rocker to his lap. He absently strokes their fur and smiles at their antics, but his mind is focused on Grant and Sheridan and all the others somewhere to the west where artillery still rumbles like a spring storm.

A little before sunset Grant wires that he's closed the ring around Petersburg and that, if the President wishes, it should be safe for Lincoln to meet him in the captured city the next day.

Lincoln quickly answers: "Allow me to tender you and all with you the nation's grateful thanks for the additional and magnificent successes. At your kind suggestion, I think I will meet you tomorrow."

About 8:40 in the evening, having received Grant's report of the fight at Sutherland Station and his assurance that all goes well, Lincoln leaves the telegraph office to return to the *Malvern*. From its deck he and Admiral Porter still hear occasional artillery fire and other, heavier, explosions. Even at this distance the glow of burning Richmond lights the dark waters of the James.

Despite Porter's suggestion that he rest, the anxious President refuses to let the day go, insisting on watching and listening. Finally, beside himself with nervous energy, he turns to the Admiral.

"Porter, can't the Navy also do something to make history this evening?"

"We're doing our best, sir. Our job's to block the four ironclads they have between us and Richmond. If they decide to come down river, they can cause a lot of grief. They almost did it once before."

"Well then," Lincoln nods, "can't we at least make some noise?"

"Yes, sir," Porter smiles, "and, if you wish, I'll order it."

Lincoln doesn't answer, only nods enthusiastically and turns to watch.

It takes time for the guns of every Federal gunboat above them to be loaded with high explosive shells, but at last they're ready.

About 11 p.m., at Porter's signal, the heavy naval barrage begins. It will continue, growing louder by the moment, for nearly an hour; a deafening crescendo of explosions, the dark sky arced again and again by the burning tails of fuzes searching for remaining Confederate shore batteries, ammunition dumps, gunboats.

Halfway into the barrage the heaviest explosion of the day rocks the *Malvern*. Lincoln, alarmed, turns again to Porter, "Admiral, I hope to heaven that one of our own vessels hasn't blown up."

"No," Porter reassures him. "Too far upstream. I'd guess, sir, that the Rebels are scuttling their ironclads. If so, we'll hear several more like that one."

He's right; several more very heavy explosions follow. Finally Porter smiles, "That's it, Mr. President. The last of their gunboats is gone. And I expect that the last of their batteries along the river are gone too. Perhaps tomorrow we can go up to Richmond."

The last echoes of cannon fire finally die away and, although the angry red glow in the sky continues, the acrid smell of burnt gunpowder begins to lift.

Lincoln, at last about to enter his cabin, pauses at a new sound: man, having done all he can with this day, frogs in the nearby marshes have begun their earnest night conversation about all of it.

The tall, gaunt, one-time prairie lawyer turned President smiles. It's been a long, long time, but surely the end must be in sight. He'll see Petersburg with Grant tomorrow then, he chuckles to himself, "By golly, reckon I'll just take Porter up on his invitation. We'll go on up to Richmond. Stanton," he continues laughing aloud, "will have kittens when he hears about it and, knowing that, will make it twice as pleasant a day for me."

CHAPTER 7

A Tale of Two Cities   April 2–3, 1865

GORDON

Lee's courier finds General John Gordon organizing yet another counterattack to recover the ground his Second Confederate Corps lost earlier in the day.

"General Gordon," he reports, "General Lee says you're to hold up where you are and keep those Yanks back 'til nightfall. He's fixin' to pull out the army soon's it gets dark, but you've got to hold 'til everyone else clears out. Longstreet'll be ahead of you through the city and, once we're on the march, you'll take up the rear guard. You'll get written orders soon's Colonel Marshall can get 'em out."

"Thank you, Colonel," Gordon's hawk-like eyes still glitter from the day's fighting. "Any word of General Hill's corps or Anderson's?"

"Not good, sir. You know the General was killed this morning. And his corps' all cut up and scattered all over creation. Longstreet's taken what's left of it for now. Bushrod Johnson's four brigades were pretty much lost at Sutherland Station this afternoon. General Anderson's trying to rally everyone he can find at that end of our line. Far's we know Pickett and Fitz Lee are somewhere's off to the west. Anderson's probably hooked up with them; reckon they'll make for the Bevil's Bridge crossing. We'll all be heading for Amelia Courthouse soon's we can get across the river. Ewell should join us along the way."

"Richmond abandoned too?"

"Yes, sir. No choice. General Lee sent them word hours ago that he'd have to give up the city."

"My wife's there," Gordon lets down his guard for a moment. "Our son was born this morning so she'll have to stay and take her chances. She won't care for that."

"No, sir," the colonel smiles. "Don't reckon I'll recognize this army without Mrs. Gordon's buggy taggin' along, givin' General Ewell fits." Then he adds, "She'll be all right, General; that lady's a good soldier."

"Yes," Gordon appreciates the kindness, "she is. Tell General Lee that we'll hold. He can bet on that."

"Knows that already, General, and he's counting on it," the staff officer waves a casual salute and gallops back toward Petersburg.

When he's gone, Gordon turns to his staff.

"Pass the word, gentlemen. We'll hold where we are. The army'll pull out of these God-forsaken trenches tonight, and we've got to keep those Yanks off their backs 'til all of us can get across the river."

"Captain," Gordon calls to one, "remember the prayer meeting we had in that little cabin right after the Stedman fight? When General Heth stepped outside to invite one of his commanders to join us?"

"Sure do, General," the younger officer chuckles. "He thought that General Heth was invitin' him to breakfast. Waved and answered, 'No thank you, General; no more at present. I've had plenty.'"

"That's the time," Gordon smiles. "Gentlemen, no time for a prayer meeting now, but remind our commanders to say a prayer or two to themselves; and tell them to stay real close to their men. Let our officers know what's going on, but see that they don't lose heart. Once we're out of these trenches we'll be all right. General Lee'll see to it."

He needn't remind them that a retreating army's apt to become very demoralized, particularly units like his own that must face the enemy alone while the others withdraw.

LEE

Lee, thankful for every moment Grant allows him without renewing his attack, issues orders to his army and tries to keep Richmond abreast of his situation. Meanwhile, he's trying to contact units cut off by Sheridan's and Ord's attacks to the west and hoping to hold Petersburg until his army can withdraw.

A delegation from the Petersburg town council arrive to ask when they can surrender the town to avoid further destruction. Lee, busy saving his army and in no mood to discuss the surrender of anything, is uncharacteristically brusque.

"Glance out that window, gentlemen. Their infantry are just across that field. I hope they'll not try to come farther tonight. If they do, General Longstreet and General Gordon will try to stop them. It's all we can do. By nightfall their intent should be clear, and I will be in touch with you. I'm afraid that's all I can do for you."

At ten o'clock, as promised, he sends an officer with word that the Confederate army will withdraw that night. Once his soldiers clear

Petersburg, the council must do as they feel best. Petersburg's mayor, W. W. Townes, and his council members decide that at dawn they'll set out in two-man teams on the major roads. Whoever first meets Federal troops will surrender the city.

Lee finds time for another personal commitment. Months before the Banister family lent him a big, deep chair with an extended table on its right arm. He'd found it more comfortable than a desk for writing orders for his army. Now, as the army prepares to retreat, his soldiers return the chair with Lee's thanks for its use.

There's another diversion. At dusk his aide, Colonel Walter Taylor, approaches him.

"General, if you can spare me tonight, I want to go into Richmond. I can rejoin you by morning."

"Into Richmond? Why Richmond, tonight, Colonel?"

"My mother and sister are there, sir; and my fiancée, Miss Saunders. You've met her. We want to be married, tonight; while we still have time."

"Married, tonight?" Lee smiles. "You know what is happening here. Are you certain?"

"Yes, sir. She's alone in Richmond. Once we've established our new line, she can join us there."

Lee, not prone to surrendering, does in this instance. Smiling, he nods, "Go ahead. Catch up with us in the morning."

About midnight the Reverend Minnigerode will marry the young couple. Their honeymoon will be brief; by 3 a.m. Taylor's galloping back across Mayo's Bridge to rejoin Lee, somewhere west of the city.

DOCTOR JOHN CLAIBORNE

Colonel Henry Peyton notifies Doctor John H. Claiborne, the surgeon in charge of several Confederate army hospitals in Petersburg, of the impending retreat.

"We're pulling out this evening, Doctor. We'll need all the surgeons and orderlies you can spare, but we'll be leaving our worst wounded here so you must provide for them. Soon's you can get going, cross the river at Campbell's Bridge. Then go west along Chesterfield Courthouse Road. There'll be guides there."

"All right; thank you. I'm not surprised." Claiborne smiles, "One of my officers came in from the Fair Grounds hospital an hour ago. Said I have surgeons out there hiding behind trees and dodging artillery fire."

Then he chuckles, "He also said that when some shells landed near the wards a lot of our wounded, to quote the Scriptures, 'took up their beds and walked.' Except, as I got it, they did more running than walking. Seems they weren't as bad off as my doctors thought."

By sunset Claiborne has given orders for the army's Petersburg hospitals. He, four other surgeons, several hospital orderlies, one ambulance driver, one buggy, four colored servants, and his own scarred, yellow terrier, "Jack," will go with Lee's army. Jack, a twelve-year veteran of many Petersburg canine adventures and, as Claiborne solemnly attests, "an irritable, selfish, self-asserting, tail-wagging, frail of virtue but full of faith in his master, that is up to a point, dog." Jack: a survivor.

Also in Claiborne's little hospital train will be a fat Confederate chaplain and a pretty seventeen-year-old girl who will care for her wounded captain-brother in Claiborne's medicine wagon.

One other civilian is "assigned" at the last minute when one of Claiborne's slaves presents her muscular, gap-toothed, grinning, sixteen-year-old son, Romulus, with the admonition, "Now, boy, don't you dares come back. You follows Doctor Claiborne here to the ends of the earth." Claiborne, faced with that charge, waves the youth to his buggy.

As Claiborne is about to leave, wagons arrive with more wounded. He's helping his surgeons decide which of them can be helped when a sergeant begs him to examine a wounded officer, his company commander.

"Please, Doctor," the sergeant pulls at Claiborne's arm, "can you help my Captain? He's a fine officer. Best man I ever knew. Did the best he could for us. And now I'm afraid he's dying. Can you help him?"

Claiborne kneels to examine the unconscious officer. His examination brief; the story quickly told. The captain's arm has been blown off at the shoulder. His uniform is soaked in blood, the dirty bandages only slowing the flow, and the terrible wound is covered with dirt and powder burns. Not a chance; but Claiborne takes an extra moment to give the sergeant the comfort of knowing he's tried.

Then he recognizes the wounded officer. He's an old friend, a man Claiborne's known since childhood. The doctor sighs, straightens, pats the sergeant's arm.

"I'm sorry, Sergeant. I also know your captain; known him for years. And he *is* a good man. But I can't save him; no one can. Leave him with me. I'll do everything I can for him, and I'll see that all the proper things are done. You've done all you can; leave him with me while you go find your unit."

He's hardly straightened when a soldier's wife, who'd accompanied the wagons bearing the wounded, begs him to examine her husband.

"Over here, Doctor, right over here," she grips his arm.

Claiborne's examination again brief. The man, an older Petersburg militiaman, has much of his skull blown away, the gray mass of his brain visible.

He straightens, shakes his head, tries to soften the sentence, "I'm sorry ma'am; right sorry, but I can't help him. The wound is mortal." He'll always remember her screams.

GORDON

Darkness ends the heavy fighting. Across the battlefield Union campfires wink to life.

"They're boiling their coffee and eating their rations; settling down for the night," General John Gordon tells his staff. "Pay no mind to their artillery. It's spaced out to keep us worried and awake, but I don't think they'll attack again until morning. Let the men get whatever rest they can, but tell our officers to stay alert; just in case. We're supposed to pull out some time after midnight; whenever Longstreet clears the bridge."

Soon after dark Confederate regimental commanders relieve their pickets with fresh riflemen. One, a young Georgian, is posted by a nervous, young lieutenant who whispers instructions as if Union pickets a hundred yards away can hear him.

"Stay here, Bradwell. Just stay put until we relieve you. There's nothing to worry about; you've got other fellows on your left and right. One of us'll be back for you about midnight."

Bradwell is young, but he's a veteran, aged fast in the Confederate army. He watches his regiment march toward Petersburg and doesn't expect to see the officer or anyone else in a gray uniform at midnight. Then he's all alone.

Despite the artillery fire, random shells fired into the darkness every two minutes, and an occasional nervous Yankee skirmisher's rifle shot off to a flank, the field seems as empty as a vast desert. Even the wounded, out there in the dark, have stopped calling out; Bradwell's grateful for that.

As the moon rises he can see no one to his left or right, before or behind him. And no sound, except the rhythmic cannon fire. Surely midnight has come and gone, and, as he expected, there's no relief in sight. Anxious and frightened he finally stumbles a long, long way to his left until he finds another Confederate picket.

"You seen an officer with orders for us to pull out?"

"Damnation," the equally young and nervous Confederate soldier snaps back, "I ain't seen no one 'cept you since they left me out here. And I don't reckon to see anyone, lest it's a Yank. Our boys done skedaddled."

They talk it over, as American soldiers do when left on their own; then they decide to check farther. Another hundred yards to their left they find a third sentinel. He's seen no one either.

"Let's leave," Bradwell suggests. "There ain't a soul on this whole line 'cept us and, if the Bluebellies come, a fat chance we'll have to do anything about it."

The vote is unanimous. They half-walk, half-run, stumble and fall then pick themselves up, back across the field, through the now deserted Confederate trenches, and into Petersburg itself. No sign of their regiments; no sign of the whole blamed army. The sun will be high over his shoulders the next day before Private Bradwell finally catches up with his regiment, catches up just in time for the sergeant major to scold.

"Bradwell, where in tarnation you been? Boy, we done give you up for lost or skedaddled. Fall in there and see you don't wander off agin."

Bradwell, the veteran, figuring there's no use fighting it, shrugs his shoulders and turns to find his messmates. Maybe, if any of them are left, they'll have some feeling for what he's been through.

PETERSBURG

During the early morning hours Gordon's men, the last of Lee's army to pass through Petersburg's nearly deserted streets, march silently, gloomily. They're not worried about noise because Federal artillery fire, continuing through the night on Grant's orders, masks the sound of Lee's retreat. No matter; Gordon's tired men have little to say anyway.

Seeing a wounded Confederate soldier lost from his regiment, two of Gordon's riflemen nod to each other, take up the wounded man, then half-carry, half-walk him into their column.

"Wait, wait," the man protests. "Don't forget Sue."

"Sue?"

"My rifle. Had her with me near four years now, and I may have to use her again. Don't leave her behind."

A third Georgian understands, nods, and returns with the weapon. He glances at it then chuckles with admiration, "Look at that, boys. Loaded and ready; cap and ball. All he's missin's the bayonet. Reckon if we hadn't picked him up he'd have given some Bluebelly a fight, that hole in his shoulder notwithstandin'."

Farther they see a Confederate soldier lying in a drunken heap beside a building. The man is dirty, unshaven, without a weapon. Gordon's men glance at him and one decides, "Leave him for the Yanks. He's trash; ain't worth totin' along." And so they do.

Several times women, some with children, appear at windows or come to porches to call out.

"God bless you," one touches a ragged Gray sleeve.

"Boys," another sobs, "are you going to leave us?"

A third laughs, "Goodbye, Rebels. Goodbye. We don't expect to see you again!" And beside her, another taunts, "Yanks'll be here in the mornin', boys. Reckon if we're nice to 'em we'll have coffee and cream for breakfast. What'll you be eating about then?"

As they march, Union shells burst above the city; and the long, bright-colored tails of signal rockets add their own flickering light to the dark sky. Many Petersburg buildings are burning, and the streets tremble as Union shells explode or Confederate engineers destroy munitions the retreating army can't carry.

Near the Woodpecker Road Railroad Station, Lieutenant Joseph Packard waits with forty-four heavily loaded ammunition wagons. Packard's men have taken all the munitions they can carry from nearby ammunition storage sheds, but many more shells and much powder remain.

At last a messenger arrives, "Colonel says you're to keep what you can carry on the wagons, Lieutenant, and blow the rest of it to Hell."

Packard and his men spend nearly two hours rolling mortar shells into nearby Swift Creek. Then, realizing that they can't get rid of all of it that way, he orders the ammunition sheds set afire.

His heavily loaded wagons haven't gone far when the ground rocks with a tremendous explosion behind them, and angry red flames brighten the sky as if it were day. Packard feels the heat on the back of his neck. The first blast quickly followed by several more. Then thousands of mortar and artillery shells arc into the sky to detonate over their heads. Packard doesn't even look back.

When his sergeant with the demolition detail returns to report, Packard waves to him, "No need to report, Jim. Heard it and felt it from here. Good job. Join the column."

The sergeant, however, lingers. There's something he needs to share with the young officer.

"There's more, Joe. While we were settin' the charges at the far end a whole bunch of women and kids got into the buildings on this side. Reckon they were looking for food, or blankets, or anything they could use. We yelled, tried to scare 'em off, but no use. Minute we'd turned our backs they'd be back in there again. Well, all the buildings and those boxcars went up before we could make 'em go away. There's a lot of dead women and kids back there, Joe; scattered all over. Couldn't even bury 'em. Don't reckon I'll ever forget it."

Packard, suddenly a lot older than his rank would warrant, just stares at him. Then he takes a deep breath and nods, "All right. There's nothing you could do about it and nothing we can do about it now. Got to keep going. Find a place in the line; we'll talk in the morning."

Off to the northeast they see the angry glow of Richmond burning, the arc of burning fuzes and rockets above the stricken city; hear a series of rumbles then several huge explosions. Admiral Semmes destroying Confederate gunboats on the James.

Burning tobacco and cotton warehouses tell them that they're nearing the Appomattox. At the Pocahontas Bridge, an ancient watchman stands, waving his lantern to hurry them along.

"Come on, boys; come on! I'm going to touch her off now."

Then John Gordon appears behind him.

"Not yet, sir," he reaches from the dark to touch the old man's shoulder, "not yet. When my last man has crossed. Be patient. He'll be along soon."

Among the last of Gordon's units, Sergeant Will Barbee, the color sergeant of Company G, 44th North Carolina Infantry Regiment, reaches the bridge.

As Barbee starts across the Appomattox he pulls his regimental flag from its staff, considers it a moment, then carefully, tenderly wraps it around a stone. It's an almost brand new flag, issued when their old one became so torn from enemy fire that it wasn't much more than a rag. And already several Yankee bullets have torn it. When the bridge crests at the center of the Appomattox, the sergeant moves to the rail, stares at the dark river a final moment, then hurls the weighted flag into the stream. A momentary flash then it's gone. Behind him the Petersburg sky is lit by lurid flames and the earth continues to tremble. None of them even looks back.

When Gordon's soldiers reach Hickory Road, above the Appomattox, they see Robert E. Lee quietly standing beside Traveller, the big gray horse's bridle in Lee's gauntleted hand. He's chosen this spot that he might gauge them and they him.

As regiment after regiment passes, Lee's busy receiving messages, dispatching couriers; calm, composed, alert. Each Confederate regiment, as it nears the junction and recognizes first the horse then the man, erupts in a spontaneous cheer. Lee smiles in return, doffs his hat, then quietly waves them west toward Amelia Courthouse.

At last seeing Gordon, and knowing that he will be the last man from Petersburg, Lee raises his hat to the Georgia general. Then he mounts Traveller and slowly picks his way toward the head of the long column of men and horses, cannon and caissons, and wagons.

Behind him Gordon finally nods to the ancient bridge tender, and resin-soaked buckets begin to burn along the wooden span. Slowly at first, then much faster, the entire span is outlined in the flames, groans, then, like the color sergeant's battle flag, drops into the Appomattox.

Below Petersburg soldiers of the 60th Ohio Infantry Regiment have cautiously crossed the field so torn in the bitter fight for Fort Gregg. This time they draw no enemy fire. Not even when they enter Gordon's breastworks. The Confederate line is empty, and a Union sergeant says it all, "Come on, boys; the Johnnies are gone."

All along Gordon's former line Union riflemen cautiously pick their way forward. Soldiers of the 51st Pennsylvania Infantry Regiment and the 38th Wisconsin Infantry Regiment push through Colquitt's Salient and into the outskirts of eastern Petersburg. South of the city, the 200th Pennsylvania Infantry Regiment also enters the town. Men of the 121st New York Infantry Regiment, however, are ahead of them and hurry to hoist a Union flag on the first public building they reach.

About 4 a.m. Petersburg's Mayor, W. W. Townes, and Councilman Charles Collier, dressed in their best suits and waving a white flag from a stick, are nearing an abandoned breastwork near Old Town Creek, west of Petersburg, when a squad of Union riflemen appears before them. Townes and Collier try to surrender the city, but the Yankee sergeant and his soldiers just don't seem to have time for them. It's the town that matters, they tell him, not ceremonies.

Frustrated, Mayor Townes protests, "But we want to surrender the city of Petersburg."

Finally the sergeant takes them to his company commander, who seems to understand the delegates' problem but also isn't ready to accept their surrender.

"Come on," he finally decides. "Come along with us. We mean to be first into the city; don't have time for anything else right now, but you come along. We'll take your surrrender there."

The captain will be disappointed as the 1st Michigan Infantry Regiment will always claim to be the first Union troops to reach the heart of Petersburg. Led by Color Sergeant William T. Wixay, a squad of Wolverines race up the steps of its courthouse steeple to hang the Star-Spangled Banner from the town clock. It's nearly dawn, April 3 and, as if everyone knows what they've done, the distant rumble of artillery fire to the west suddenly seems to pause. Union soldiers, from one end of Meade's line to the other, cheer. Petersburg has fallen.

RICHMOND
MAJOR ROBERT STILES

Southeast of Richmond, along the James River, Major Robert Stiles commands a Confederate artillery battalion. Except he doesn't have much left in the way of men or guns and not many horses to pull his remaining cannon.

If they have to pull out, he's to drive rattail spikes into the vents of the guns, get out as many men as he can, and be prepared to fight them as infantrymen. Bad enough to have to give up their guns; worse yet to fight as infantry!

Stiles is worried about his men, even more than usual. Many of them had been so badly wounded earlier in the war that the surgeons have said that they're not capable of fighting again except in a static situation. Others, pink-cheeked or gray-haired militiamen or home guardsmen, wear uniforms but have never seen combat. They know only garrison life on the banks of the James. Put to marching thirty or more miles a day, let alone to facing their enemies with rifles and bayonets, they'll have a very rough time. Stiles knows that; worries about it.

A veteran of many battles, Stiles sleeps lightly, and the first thunderous volleys of cannon fire below the river wakens him early. All day long he listens to it, knows that Grant's finally begun the all-out attack they've expected for months. Shifted most of his army toward our right, Stiles reasons, but he'll have left enough here to finish us off whenever he wants to do it.

Well, while we're waiting, he decides, we'll go ahead with the services. Lee's army periodically is swept by deep, far-reaching religious revivals. The current one has focused on a real Christian soldier's resisting temptations of the flesh: adultery, gambling, drinking, profanity. Stiles, as concerned for his men's spiritual health as for their physical needs, has arranged for one of Ewell's chaplains to hold a religious service in his battalion this evening. When the chaplain sends word, however, that he'll not be able to come, Stiles decides to hold the service himself. Perhaps he can say something that will help in the ordeal he's sure they'll face.

At dusk, using a flickering pine torch for light, he reads from the 91st Psalm. Stiles calls it "The Soldiers' Psalm."

Thou shalt not be afraid for the terror by night, nor for the arrow that flieth by day.

Nor for the pestilence that walketh in darkness, nor for the destruction that wasteth at noonday.

A thousand shall fall at thy side, and ten thousand at thy right hand; but it shall not come nigh thee.

His words, slowly, thoughtfully read, are punctuated by the dull thump of artillery fire below the river; the sudden flaring of a large fire and the arc

of signal rockets toward Petersburg; and, even at this distance, the rumble of heavier explosives.

Pausing in his reading, Stiles sees that one of his soldiers, a youth named Blount, open-mouthed, is watching with tear-filled eyes. The major gropes for words that somehow will comfort the boy, strengthen him; let them all know that, whatever happens to them, God will be there, and Major Robert Stiles will be there too.

Then his adjutant appears with a message, and Stiles quietly nods, "Just a moment. I know what it says; been expecting it."

Turning back to his men, he quietly ends the service, "Let's pray."

He's right about the message. At midnight he's to lead his gunners turned infantrymen through the city then west to join Lee's army.

Despite his warnings, and the efforts of his sergeants, when they begin their march Stiles sees that many of his garrison soldiers are burdened with swollen packs piled high with blankets, overcoats, and other things that they feel they just can't give up.

"Shall I have 'em throw it all out, sir?" his Sergeant Major asks.

"No," Stiles answers. "Let it go. They'll learn for themselves. A few miles down the road and they'll figure it out."

He's right. By mid-morning the dusty, horse- and wagon-churned road behind them is littered with discarded clothing, blankets, pots and pans, armored vests, playing cards, so much more that no longer seems worth carrying.

EWELL

Earlier this Sunday Lieutenant General Richard S. Ewell is at Longstreet's headquarters when a messenger calls him back to Richmond. The city must be evacuated; Ewell is needed.

Ewell: 48 years old, sometimes called "Baldy" for the obvious reason; other times "Old Woodcock" because he has a habit of munching on bird seed and turning his thin, wizened head from side to side, much like a bird, as he speaks.

Badly crippled, Ewell has given his leg to the Confederate cause. Since then, wooden leg and all, he's ridden into battle in a buggy or strapped to the saddle of his nondescript gray horse, "Rifle"; usually accompanied by an Apache youth Ewell acquired during his days in the West with the Old Army.

He's also more than a little absent-minded. While recovering from the amputation, Ewell, a long-time bachelor, married his widowed cousin, a Mrs. Brown. Sometimes he'll forget and introduce her as "Mrs. Brown," something she doesn't appreciate but has learned to live with.

Ewell: nervous, excitable; responsible for the defense of Richmond and, when the army withdraws, for the destruction of all government property in it.

He finds Richmond's mayor, Joseph Mayo, resplendent in white cravat, ruffles, spotless vest, and blue, brass-buttoned coat, waiting for him. Mayo insists that Ewell not burn the tobacco or cotton warehouses. Ewell doesn't offer much comfort, shaking his head in that odd, nervous way, and telling him flat out, "All of it must go, Mr. Mayor. Warehouses, remaining stocks of military material and ammunition, the bridges behind us. No exceptions, sir; it all must go. Fortunes of war."

He spends most of the afternoon seeing that it will be done. At midnight Major General Joseph Kershaw will withdraw his division. Brigadier General Martin Gary's South Carolinians will stay behind to hold back the Yankees long enough for Ewell to complete the demolition he's ordered. As for the city, his soldiers will keep order as long as they can, but once they've crossed the James and burned the bridges behind them the town must look out for itself.

MAJOR EDWARD M. BOYKIN

With the withdrawal of Kershaw's division the last regular troops Ewell will have before Richmond are General Martin Gary's small cavalry brigade east of the city along the Charles City Road.

Gary, a hard-fighting veteran, has in his brigade the 7th South Carolina Cavalry Regiment and a handful of the 7th Georgia Cavalry Regiment, most of whom have no horses.

With the 7th South Carolina is Major Edward M. Boykin, 44 years old. Boykin was educated to be a physician but has fought with the 7th South Carolina for nearly four years. Last year, near Cold Harbor, he'd been in the fight with Custer's cavalry where the regiment had 21 of its 26 officers killed or wounded. Among the casualties was Boykin's son, Sergeant Thomas L. Boykin. Boykin, like the rest of the 7th South Carolina, is cold, hungry, tired; but he still has a lot of fight in him.

This Sunday he's been scouting the woods and fields charged to his regiment and culling its ranks of all men without horses; they're to report to the 24th Virginia Cavalry Regiment for duty as infantrymen.

At dusk his men build fires to confuse their enemy, somewhere out there in the dark. Then they pull back to now-abandoned breastworks at the edge of the city to wait for their rear guard to catch up. Most of Boykin's men use the delay to roll up in their overcoats and try to sleep.

Two o'clock passes before their rear guard, cavalrymen forced to unaccustomed marching, finally join them. Then Boykin's troops withdraw through the city, a trip they'll not soon forget.

They're on the bluffs above the James River when a huge explosion startles their horses and knocks several half-asleep men from their saddles: Semmes' crews blowing their gunboats sky-high. Boykin's cavalrymen feel the intense heat, smell the sharp-biting smoke, see livid red flames light the night sky. Light that continues until the gunboats burn to their waterlines.

Near daylight Boykin's column enters Richmond itself. As they pass, groups of hard-looking men, and even harder looking women, cluster on sidewalks and porches to study them.

One citizen, a large, noisy woman, scornfully watches them ride by, so close that Boykin could touch her with his boot and later wishes he had, taunting in her shanty-Irish way, "Yas, and after fightin' 'em for four years y're runnin' like dawgs!"

It's even worse in the heart of the city. Bareheaded women, their arms filled with loot from warehouses and shops; their hair disheveled; some wearing a half-dozen layers of stolen clothing, rushing to deposit their plunder then return for more.

When the 7th South Carolina passes between burning buildings, horses and men shy in fright at the heat, the roaring sound, the crackling flames. The flour mills of Haxall and Gallego, ten stories high and reputedly the largest in the world, burn fiercely; flames leaping from its windows and its walls collapsing.

At 14th and Cary Streets, the Confederate army's largest commissary depot lies abandoned, its huge warehouse invaded by a large crowd of men, women, and children. Some clamor at its large, wooden door for their turn at the goods inside while others struggle to escape with their plunder. Outside are wagons already loaded with barrels of flour, ham, bacon, sugar, and whiskey.

Only flickering pine torches light the cavernous building, and many of its floors have collapsed. Looters tumble down in the darkness. Some die; others, badly hurt, scream for help; louder yet when they realize that the building has caught fire. Few of the mob hear their cries; fewer yet answer.

Ewell's militiamen have carried barrels of whiskey outside, filled their own canteens, then emptied the casks in the gutter. More and more casks until a steady steam of whiskey races around the cobblestones. Looters use cups, pots and pans, whatever they have to gather it up. If they have no containers, they get down on all fours and, cupping their hands, lap the whiskey from the gutters until they can handle no more. They're still at it as the 7th South Carolina passes, many of the drunken mob staggering, leaping, yelling, howling like animals. Then they turn to looting nearby warehouses and shops.

Gary's officers spread the word: "No looting. Any man caught looting will answer to General Gary, real close and personal like."

At least one officer, however, dares risk the general's wrath. A colonel of the 7th South Carolina spots Lieutenant David Walker with a new pair of shoes slung across the neck of his horse. Walker, however, has a ready explanation.

"A miracle, Colonel. A damned miracle! I was ridin' by, mindin' my own business like the General says we're to do, and these here shoes flew right out a warehouse window and landed right there," he lifts a leg to show the remains of a worn-out boot tied with string around his foot.

The Colonel smiles and waves him on.

At Mayo's Bridge, Boykin sees a dirty, ugly white man tussling with a woman over a stolen barrel of flour she's struggling to roll across the James. The major's about to settle the argument with his saber when a large, muscular black man steps from the refugees to grasp the bully's arm.

"You let her go, suh," the black man suggests. "You let her go and get out of here lest I throws you off this bridge."

The white man hesitates, perhaps thinking that no one will help the woman's rescuer; then he sees Boykin with his saber half-drawn and, turning away, melts into the crowd.

Gary is waiting when Boykin's men, among the last to cross the river, reach its western bank. As the 7th South Carolina clears the bridge, he sees a troop of adventurous Union cavalrymen near its Richmond side. The crowd of refugees prevent Gary's troopers' firing at the Union soldiers. Instead, Gary waves his hat and commands, "All over, Lieutenant. Blow her to Hell."

When his engineers set off their demolitions, Gary doesn't even bother looking back.

Soon after Gary's regiments have crossed the river, fire reaches the main Confederate ammunition magazine behind them. Thousands of shells and tons of gunpowder suddenly go up. With the explosion Richmond is shaken end to end. Huge, bright red, angry tongues of flames snap, hiss, leap into the sky and from building to building. High explosive shells, their fuzes burning then exploding above the city, rain iron fragments on anything below. Rockets cross and crisscross, cutting stripes in the dense, acrid clouds of smoke.

From Manchester's heights Boykin and his Carolina cavalrymen stop to look back at the city. Richmond's ammunition magazine still burns; so do the remains of four gunboats, the training ship *Patrick Henry*, and the navy yard. Warehouses, churches, and buildings of every description are burning; more than twenty square blocks on fire. Heavy smoke billows over the city; and from it still come the roar of flames and huge explosions, one after another.

Ahead of Boykin's battalion is a long, winding column of men and horses and the equipment of a battered army. Already there are signs of its disintegration: exhausted horses left by the roadside; abandoned limbers and caissons; soldiers sitting beside the road, debating whether to continue or to give up.

Also beside the road are hundreds of civilians fleeing the dreaded Federal army. Lost souls sitting disconsolately beside broken wagons piled high with goods their horses have no hope of drawing.

Boykin tries not to see them; just looks straight ahead, down the long road toward Amelia Courthouse.

DRUMMER JOHN L. G. WOODS

John L. G. Woods, drummer boy of Company B, 53rd Georgia Infantry Regiment, one of the last Confederate regiments to leave Richmond, somehow is overlooked. He shouldn't have been. Johnny has been with the regiment longer than most of the other veterans. Through all the hard fighting: the Peninsula, Antietam, Chancellorsville, and Gettysburg. When he isn't playing his drum he's mighty handy cooking, fetching water or firewood, helping care for wounded soldiers. The men like him.

But Johnny Woods isn't very big, especially in the dark. Not much bigger than his drum, they say. In the confusion he'd simply not been missed. Normal times they'd have missed him right away because his drum paced their march. Not this night when they had to quietly slip away from the Yankees.

The pre-dawn cold wakes Johnny and, still sleepy, he looks about. Instantly awake; he can't find a single friend. Only a few scattered, deserted campfires. Aside from the debris left behind by soldiers not caring to carry some things any farther, there's no sign that his comrades had even been there. For the first time in a long time, Johnny Woods is frightened; feeling as if he's the only soul on earth.

Despite his size and his years, however, he's a veteran. Quickly he slings his blanket roll over his shoulder, straps his drum across his back, and hangs the empty oyster tin he uses as a skillet beside his canteen.

In Richmond there are no officers or sergeants to direct his march so he joins the mob looting the government commissary. He's just finished filling his haversack there when someone yells, "Fire!"

His size helps him wiggle through the crush at the door. Then he runs until he's across Mayo's Bridge. Just in time; behind him Gary's engineers have dropped its spans into the James.

It will be hours before Johnny Woods catches up with Lee's army; two days before he finds Kershaw's division; and another before he finds Company B, 53rd Georgia.

PHOEBE YATES PEMBER

Perched on a broad hill east of Richmond is the hospital-city of Chimborazo: 150 one-story, white-washed, wooden hospital wards grouped into five hospitals which have served 75,000 wounded Confederate soldiers. It also boasts five icehouses; five soup kitchens; a bathhouse; a bakery that turns out thousands of loaves of bread a day; a brewery; and herds of cattle, hogs, and chickens.

Chimborazo, one of six military hospitals in the Richmond area in the spring of 1865, is one of the largest hospital complexes in the world.

This Sunday afternoon, however, its wards are nearly empty of patients, its support buildings deserted, its staff almost entirely gone.

About 1 p.m. Ewell's messenger had arrived.

"Doctor McCaw, suh, General Ewell says you're to turn out all the lightly wounded. If a man can walk and carry a rifle, we need him. Reckon you'd better gather up what's left. The army's pullin' out tonight; expect the Yanks'll come in tomorrow."

A little later, a pretty nurse, Phoebe Yates Pember, walks to the quiet place she'd found months before at the edge of Chimborazo's grounds, high above the river.

Pember, a 41-year-old young South Carolina widow, has served as chief matron (nurse) at Chimborazo's Hospital Number 2 for three years. And now she's been told that her duties there are nearly over.

She feels exhausted, frightened, lonely. Lonelier than she can recall feeling since the death of her husband nearly four years before. Except for three weeks the previous October when the surgeon, seeing her exhausted, had ordered her away, she's not missed a day at Chimborazo. And now the hospital she's come to know as home already seems a ghost town.

As she sits on the small bench several soldier-patients, knowing her need for her own refuge from time to time, had fashioned for her, she hears the rumble of artillery below the river and the first of many explosions she'll soon hear along the James and in Richmond. Closing her eyes, she thinks of the months she's spent at Chimborazo.

The first female on the hospital staff, she'd never been more than reluctantly accepted by the surgeons, one of whom had announced her arrival in a tone of ill-concealed disgust, "Well, one of them has come!"

The next day she'd made her first trip to meet a hospital train with wounded at the Richmond Railroad Station; a scene she'd never forget. Black servants lighting the pavement around the depot with flickering pine torches. Hundreds of stretchers bearing wounded soldiers, some with light blankets against the cold; others left on bare bricks with no blankets at all. Hideous wounds wrapped with dirty, bloodied strips of coarse, unbleached, galling bandages of homespun cotton. Dirty, ulcerated, open wounds. Surgeons moving back and forth, deciding at a glance, "He won't live; put him over there with the others. Put this one with the group for immediate surgery. That one can wait a bit until this God-awful mess is clear."

Women volunteers, ranging from working women to aristocratic belles of Richmond's society, carrying food and water, moistening fever-blistered lips, bathing dirty faces, holding dying hands.

Men crying out in pain or despair, and Pember feeling she can offer little help or consolation.

And it never got easier. Each train of wounded somehow worse than the ones she'd met before. Still, in three years she'd never missed one of them.

Fisher. Private Henry Fisher. Strange that she'd think of him now. Yet not so strange; he was the first one she'd lost. Her first, and perhaps her hardest death though she'd never grown numb to any of them. Fisher, a young, handsome soldier everyone liked, slowly recovering from a hip wound. Seemingly doing well. One day, after ten months at Chimborazo, able to walk from one end of the ward to the other. She'd been so happy to see it. Then, that very night, Fisher crying out in pain and she, finding blood spurting from his wound, had pressed her finger to seal the artery then screamed for help. The surgeon's examination brief: a splintered bone has cut an artery. It can't be repaired; the soldier will die.

Told that he can't be helped, the young soldier asked, "How long, doctor, can I live?"

"Only so long as Mrs. Pember keeps her finger on that artery."

A moment's thought then he'd calmly told her, "It's all right, ma'am. You can let it go. You can let it go."

But, even now her eyes fill and her breath catches short as she recalls that moment, she'd not been able to take her finger away. Not if her own life depended upon it. She remembers the hot tears scalding her cheeks, the surging sound in her ears, the numbness in her lips, then the pain of obeying him spared her: for the first and last time in her years at Chimborazo, Phoebe Yates Pember had fainted dead away.

There were others. So many others. After the battle at Fredericksburg, the mortally wounded boy who'd turned aside the food, drink, fresh pillow, anything she offered to comfort him.

Finally, as if to ease her pain as much as his own, he'd simply said, "Ma'am, I want Perry."

Quick investigation revealed that his friend, "Perry," had been lightly wounded and was at Jackson Hospital. She'd hurried in Doctor McCaw's buggy to bring him to Chimborazo; then she'd watched as Perry sat beside the dying youth. The boy opened his eyes, smiled in recognition, then with a quiet, satisfied, "Perry, Perry," died in his friend's arms.

The courtesy, gentleness, love the wounded men showed to each other, and to her. She'd never forget that.

Like the time she'd tried, for the first time in her life, to make chicken soup for a soldier who'd refused everything else. She'd turned the hospital upside down to find a chicken, then cut it up (a hateful task), and prepared the soup. Then she'd found there was no parsley; she'd not done much cooking, but chicken soup without parsley was unthinkable. Finally, Jim, the ward boy, had found a sprig. Then she'd carried a bowl of her very first chicken soup, duly salted, peppered, and parsleyed to her patient.

He'd tried; he'd surely tried. One long, painful gulp, then a judgmental shake of his head and the bowl passed back to her.

"I'm might sorry, ma'am; but my mammy's soup was not like that," he'd said. Then he'd considered a moment and added, "I 'spect I might worry a little of it down though, if it warn't for them weeds a-floatin' 'round in it."

If they didn't care for her chicken soup, they still liked her. So many compliments, from rough-sided, combat-hardened veterans to boys in soldier's uniforms.

Like the upcountry Georgia boy who'd tried to dictate a letter for her to write.

He began, "My dear Mammy," but then wandered meaninglessly until she'd simply talked it out of him and then composed the letter herself. When she read it back to him, he looked at her in astonishment.

"Did you write all that?"

"Yes."

"Did I say all that?"

"I think you did."

A long pause of admiration then, in a quiet voice, "Ma'am, are you married?"

"No, I'm not. I'm a widow."

"Well," he considers and, pointing a bony finger at her, concludes, "you just wait!"

Or the rough Kentuckian who'd warned her, "Ma'am, you'll wear them little feet away, runnin' 'round so much. They ain't much to boast of anyway."

Or the equally rough-looking Texan who'd slowly walked around and around her desk as she worked, studying her, until, feeling uncomfortable, she'd snapped.

"What in the world is the matter with you? Have you never seen a woman before?"

"Jerusalem!" he whistled, not for a moment retreating, "Jerusalem! Dogged if I ever did see such a nice one. Why you's as pretty as a pair of red shoes with green strings!"

In her quiet place, drawing some comfort from her memories this long, anxious afternoon, the explosions, louder now, pull Phoebe Yates Pember back to the present.

Drawing a deep breath, she stands to straighten her hair and adjust her skirt. Then she returns to find papers, records, clothing, and other debris of a hastily evacuated hospital scattered everywhere; all but a handful of her patients already gone.

Sighing, she calls to her ward boy, "Come, Jim, let's clean up this mess. I'll not have a Yankee doctor criticizing us."

The night is short, and she doesn't sleep well, interrupted again and again by huge explosions that shake her small room. Through the window the sky to the west is a fiery red, and she hears many bells constantly ringing. Church bells, fire bells; everywhere. Richmond burning. It seemed to begin with the blowing up of the *Patrick Henry* docked below the hospital. Other explosions quickly follow; everywhere. Warehouses and tobacco factories burning, their flames spreading to houses and shops. As she watches entire blocks of Main Steet are burning. Then the flames reach the armory and thousands of shells are hurled into the air to explode above the city. Thousands of tons of gunpowder also going up in explosions that cause the floor beneath her to tremble. Richmond hammered from every direction.

At daylight Phoebe Yates Pember returns to the bluff; looks out over the wreckage. The fire still burns; as far as she can see.

Below the hospital two carriages carry Richmond's mayor and several councilmen toward the Federal lines. A white flag flies from each carriage.

A little later she sees her first Yankee soldier, a single blue-clad infantryman with rifle and bayonet, rising where the road from the east crests the hill then stopping, transfixed with astonishment at the view before him: Richmond, its heart burned out and still burning; the remains of ships, down to their waterlines on the James; a heavy cloud of black smoke hugging the city.

Then another Federal soldier, and another, and another seem to spring up, as if from the earth, until they've formed a solid line across the hill. A line that slowly advances toward the city.

RICHMOND

About seven o'clock a small, compact body of Federal cavalrymen ride past the hospital. Splendid horses, soldiers well accoutered and well fed. Major General Godfrey Weitzel's advance guard. Then come the infantry. Company after company; regiment after regiment; brigade after brigade. Federal bands, swinging along, playing "Yankee Doodle" and "Rally Round the Flag" for all their worth.

Federal troops entering Richmond see handkerchiefs and strips of white cotton cloth pinned to doors and windows; women and children begging for food. Negroes, hundreds of them, celebrating in the streets as they call out to Weitzel's soldiers: "All gone, masters. They's all gone."

Confederate stragglers come out to surrender. One calls, "Hey, Yank. What y'all payin' now when we-uns come in with our rifles and such?"

"Nothin', Johnny. That market dried up this morning. Just go on over there and join the others."

"Well," the Gray soldier shrugs his thin shoulders, "I reckoned the Confederacy was about played out at last."

Northern soldiers march past Libby Prison, now emptied of its Union prisoners. At the Capitol Building, a squad of infantrymen from the 4th Massachusetts Infantry Regiment runs inside, and about 8:15 the Stars and Stripes, for the first time in four years, again flies over Richmond. A military band plays "The Star-Spangled Banner"; they'll play it a lot in the next few days.

Federal General Weitzel is there, looking out over a Richmond still rocked by explosions; more than twenty square blocks burned out; and the fire still uncontrolled.

"Colonel Ripley," he orders, "set the men to work. Post security near the bridges that are left, but I don't think we have to fear a counterattack. Restore order; put out the fires; see what we can do to help these people. I want no criticism of our troops; not one."

His men *do* behave well. More than that, they seem to understand the despair Richmond's citizens must feel; and most of them try to help their beaten enemy.

Like the tall Yankee soldier assigned to guard the home of Amelia Gorgas, wife of Confederate Brigadier General Josiah Gorgas, who endears himself to the Gorgas children by setting his rifle aside to play with them and when he's relieved of his duties, as if to ease their fears, promises, "Next time I come, I'll be a nice Confederate and not a bad Yankee."

APRIL 3, 1865

Petersburg fallen; Richmond fallen. The Confederate government, confined now to a single rickety railroad train, fleeing to the temporary safety of Danville, Virginia where its President, Jefferson Davis, hopes to rally the Southern states to continue to fight.

Lee's Confederate army also in full retreat, above the Appomattox River. Hoping to rally at Amelia Courthouse then to march to join General Joseph Johnston's army 150 miles below Richmond. Grant's Federal army pausing to regroup, preparing to push west below the Appomattox to sever the Confederates' last rail link with Lee's badly mauled army and to intercept its march. The war, for the moment, a foot race between the Blue and Gray armies.

The end of the long war is not yet in sight but surely is near at hand. And a jubilant, thankful Abraham Lincoln prays that might come without another bloody fight.

This story of American soldiers and civilians caught up in the last weeks of our Civil War, begun in this volume, is not complete. The last of it concerns the retreat-pursuit of Lee's army; it begins where this story ends and ends at Appomattox, Virginia.

I'm grateful for your interest and invite you to share the rest of my story in the companion volume, APPOMATTOX.

Selected Bibliography

Bearss, Edward, and Christopher Calkins. *The Battle of Five Forks.* Lynchburg, Va.: H. E. Howard, Inc., 1985.

Bernard, George S., Ed. *War Talks of Confederate Veterans.* Petersburg, Va.: Fenn and Owen, Publishers, 1892.

Boykin, Edward M. *The Falling Flag.* New York: E. J. Hale and Son, 1874.

Calkins, Christopher. *From Petersburg to Appomattox, April 2–9, 1865.* Farmville, Va.: The Farmville Herald, 1990.

———. *The Battles of Appomattox Station and Appomattox Court House: April 8–9, 1865.* Lynchburg, Va.: H. E. Howard, Inc., 1987.

———. *The Final Bivouac: The Surrender Parade at Appomattox and the Disbanding of the Armies; April 10–May 20, 1865.* Lynchburg, Va.: H. E. Howard, Inc., 1988.

———. *From Petersburg to Appomattox.* Farmville, Va.: The Farmville Herald, 1990.

———. *Thirty-Six Hours Before Appomattox: The Battles of Sayler's Creek, High Bridge, Farmville and Cumberland Church.* Farmville, Va.: The Farmville Herald, 1980.

Chamberlain, Joshua Lawrence. *The Passing of the Armies.* Dayton, Ohio: Morningside Press, 1991.

Claiborne, Dr. John H. *Seventy-Five Years in Old Virginia.* New York: Neale Publishing Company, 1904.

Davis, Burke. *To Appomattox; Nine April Days.* New York: Rinehart and Company, 1959.

———. *The Long Surrender.* New York: Random House, 1985.

Freeman, Douglas Southall. *Lee's Lieutenants.* New York: Charles Scribner's Sons, 1944.

Gerrish, Theodore. *Army Life: A Private's Reminiscences of the Civil War.* Portland, Me.: Hoyt, Fogg and Donham, 1882.

Gordon, John B. *Reminiscences of the Civil War*. New York: Charles Scribner's Sons, 1903.

Grant, Ulysses S. *The Personal Memoirs of U. S. Grant*. Vol. 2. New York: Charles L. Webster and Company, 1886.

Johnson, Robert U., and Clarence C. Buel, Eds. *Battles and Leaders of the Civil War*. Vol. 4. New York: Thomas Yoseloff, Inc., 1956.

Longstreet, James. *From Manassas to Appomattox: Memoirs of the Civil War*. Philadelphia: J. B. Lippincott Co., 1896.

Merington, Marguerite, Ed. *The Custer Story*. New York: Devin-Adair Company, 1950.

Pember, Phoebe Yates. *A Southern Woman's Story*. New York: G. W. Carleton and Company, 1879.

Porter, Horace. *Campaigning with Grant*. New York: The Century Company, 1897.

Pullen, John J. *The 20th Maine*. Dayton, Ohio: Morningside Press, 1984.

Rodick, Burleigh Cushing. *Appomattox: The Last Campaign*. Gaithersburg, Md.: Olde Soldier Books, Reprinted 1987.

Schaff, Morris. *The Sunset of the Confederacy*. Boston: John W. Luce and Company, 1912.

Sheridan, Philip H. *Personal Memoirs of P. H. Sheridan*. Vol. 2. New York: Charles L. Webster and Company, 1888.

Stern, Philip Van Doren. *An End to Valor*. Boston: Houghton Mifflin, 1958.

Stiles, Robert. *Four Years Under Marse Robert*. Washington, 1903.

Taylor, Walter H. *Four Years with General Lee*. New York: Reprinted by Bonanza Books, 1962.

Trudeau, Noah A. *The Last Citadel: Petersburg, Virginia, June 1864–April 1865*. Boston: Little, Brown and Company, 1994.

———. *Out of the Storm: The End of the Civil War, April–June 1865*. New York: Little, Brown and Company, 1994.

Trulock, Alice Rains. *In the Hands of Providence: Joshua L. Chamberlain and the American Civil War*. Chapel Hill, N.C.: University of North Carolina Press, 1992.

Urwin, Gregory J. *Custer Victorious*. Nebraska: University of Nebraska Press, 1983.

Wheeler, Richard. *Witness to Appomattox*. New York: Harper and Row, 1989.

Woods, John L. G. Article in *Confederate Veteran* (1919).

Woodward, C. Vann, Ed. *Mary Chesnut's Civil War*. New Haven: Yale University Press, 1981.